Girl on the Ferris Wheel

Girl on the Ferris Wheel

Julie Halpern and Len Vlahos

FEIWEL AND FRIENDS

NEW YORK

A Feiwel and Friends Book
An imprint of Macmillan Publishing Group, LLC
120 Broadway, New York, NY 10271

Our books may be purchased in bulk for promotional, educational, or business use.
Please contact your local bookseller or the Macmillan Corporate and Premium Sales
Department at (800) 221-7945 ext. 5442 or by email at
MacmillanSpecialMarkets@macmillan.com.
Library of Congress Control Number: 2020911020
ISBN 978-1-250-16939-6 (hardcover) / ISBN 978-1-250-16938-9 (ebook)
Book design by Mallory Grigg
Feiwel and Friends logo designed by Filomena Tuosto

First edition, 2021

10   9   8   7   6   5   4   3   2   1
fiercereads.com

To Romy, my rock star
—Julie

For all of my Greek family and friends . . .
Σας ευχαριστώ.
—Len

Fall

Eliana

I don't think I'll ever get over the fact that my guidance counselor's name is Mr. Person. Is that his real name? Would someone who chose the field of guidance counseling give himself an alias? What if he had to? What if Mr. Person is not merely a guidance counselor? By day, he sits in his five-foot-by-five-foot, poorly lit office, weaving his schedule-balancing magic. By night? He squeezes his desk-trapped gut into figure-flattering spandex and flies around the city of Minneapolis, valiantly moving people's cars out of unexpected snow tow zones.

"What brings you here today, Eliana?" Mr. Person knows my name without looking into my file. Mr. Person keeps my file in a special place on his desktop for easy access. This is not my first visit to Mr. Person's rodeo. (Maybe he's a rodeo clown?)

"I want to drop out of physics," I tell him. This sounds as pathetic to me as I feel. "Dropping out" is such an extreme expression, like first it's physics, and then high school, and then I'm competing with Girl Scouts outside the local Walgreens for spare change. But I don't have any cookies to sell because I also dropped out of Girl Scouts!

"You don't like Ms. Keeter?" he assumes. I have left three classes since my freshman year based solely on negative teacher vibe. Not this time. "No, she was fine. She seemed to know what she was doing."

"Glad to hear that." Mr. Person barely contains his sarcasm. Let it out, I say. The more the merrier.

"I got a C on a test," I admit.

He waits for more. I have no more. "So I want to drop out," I say, hoping that he understands.

"Eliana, a C on a test is hardly reason to drop out of a class. Have you never received a C before?" Mr. Person clicks on his keyboard. A piece of me is bummed he doesn't have my grades memorized.

"I'm sure I have. At some point." I pretend I don't remember the exact test and date (seventh grade, algebra, I had a 103 degree fever that day and argued for a retest).

"A C is average, Eliana, and it's just one test. I'm sure you will do even better on the next one. Why don't you give it another couple of weeks—"

I cut him off. "Mr. Person, it will be midterms in a couple of weeks. I don't want to do better. I want out. I don't like physics. I don't get physics. I won't use physics. Just get me out of the class." He looks down at me scoldingly until I add, "Please?"

"You need at least one more science class before you graduate to fulfill your requirements." He does his keyboard-clicking thing again. I am nearly certain he is not looking at my file but playing Words with Friends.

"I'm only a sophomore. I can take earth science next year. That will be more practical. I live on Earth. For now." My head takes me to that sweet place where Doctor Who arrives in the TARDIS just outside Mr. Person's office to whisk me to a far-off planet where I won't need a guidance counselor to reschedule my day into a slightly more bearable state than it is currently in.

Mr. Person rudely interrupts. "I have another appointment in three minutes, Eliana. Do you really need to leave physics?" *Click. Click. Clickety click click.*

"Would I be wasting your time, Mr. Person, if I didn't really need something?" I realize I'm potentially setting myself up for a roasting, but Mr. Person knows this is a battle he will not win. Not without his spandex suit, anyway.

He puffs out a deflated sigh, does his clicking magic, and presents me with this option. "If we don't want to rearrange your entire schedule, and I really do not want to do that, we need to fill your third period."

I'm about to spew a truly inappropriate joke about maxi pads when Mr. Person saves me. "Looks like your only two choices are study hall or the Art and Craft of Cinema."

"I thought that class was filled! I tried to get into that last year."

"I recall that appointment." Mr. Person nods, and I flash back to how I completely lost myself and both cried uncontrollably and called Mr. Person a dicktag when he couldn't make that happen. I guess he would remember that.

"Is there really an opening?"

"Looks like someone dropped out last week. Maybe they got a C."

I ignore the guidance counselor sass and relish the rare good fortune. "Can you put me in? Please?" I smile my brightest fake smile at him, which makes no sense because this moment is totally deserving of a real smile, but sometimes my face just can't make the leap.

Click click and *click.* "Done. You are now a physics-class dropout and a film student. Your future's looking bright, Eliana."

I sneer at him in that charming way I have and say, "Thank you, Mr. Person. Your guidance counseling skills are once again top-notch."

"I'll put that on my tombstone," he retorts.

I leave the tiny office with a reprinted schedule in hand and a spring in my step. Stuff like this never happens to me. I'm out of physics and in film class? That's luck. That's kismet. That's actually good news.

I stop my bouncy walk.

What terrible crap is going to happen to balance it out?

Dmitri

School days after gig nights are the worst, especially if the gig was on a Sunday. As if Mondays need any new reasons to suck.

My mother's already yelled up the stairs three times—the first two in English, the last one in Greek—for me to get out of bed. It's not until Yia Yia, my grandmother, pokes her head into the room that I finally stir. She's wearing the same plain gray dress she always wears. One of these days I'm going to sneak into her closet to see how many of these dresses she owns. She either has like fifteen, or she wears the same one over and over again. Inquiring minds want to know.

"Dmitri-moo." Her accent is thick, but her voice is sweet. "Don't make you mother work so hard. Nico ees downstairs already, you go too, ναι?" I like it that Yia Yia speaks to me in English. I know more than enough Greek to converse with her, but she works hard at trying to fit in, to be more American, and I appreciate it. She definitely works harder than my parents.

"Dmitri!" My mother's voice rattles the window. "Ελα εδώ τώρα!" *Come here, now!*

"He coming!" my grandmother shouts. "Give boy a chance!"

"Thanks, Yia Yia," I say through a yawn. She turns, winks at me, and leaves the room.

I reach for my phone and scroll through the texts from last night. "Great gig!" "You guys killed it!" "The drums never sounded better!" I flop my head back on the pillow and smile.

When I hit the kitchen dressed and ready to go, my brother, Nico, two years younger, is already at the table reading a book. Nicky always has his face buried in a book. I swear it's why he needs glasses. This one is something called *The Last True Love Story*.

"How was the gig?" he asks, looking up.

"Great," I answer. "There were a ton of kids there. What are you reading?"

Nicky kind of smirks. He does that like he's in on a joke and no one else knows the punch line. "You'd like it. It's got a punk rock theme with a kick-ass girl bass player."

"Yeah?" I ask, intrigued.

"Language!" my mother barks at my brother's use of the word "ass." She's emptying the dishwasher.

"When did you learn curse words, Mitera?" Nicky taunts.

"Enough. Read you book and eat you breakfast. What you want, Dmitri? What I cook for you?"

"You don't have to make me breakfast, Ma. I can handle it myself." I open the cupboard and reach for the cereal.

"I like to help!"

"Let the boy get his own breakfast." I didn't hear my father come in. He's dressed in a suit, the same gray suit he wears every day. I wonder if he and Yia Yia shop at some secret gray clothing store just for Greeks. "You out too late again last night."

"Sorry, Dad, but the gig went long. And then, you know, we had to pack up and stuff."

"Gig." He spits the word like an olive pit. "You concentrate on schoolwork. In two years you apply to colleges. You need scholarship money."

I pour some Cap'N Crunch in a bowl but don't answer. How can I tell my dad I have no intention of going to college? What good will college do if all I want is to play music? He's either gonna have a heart attack or ground me for life when he finds out. Probably both.

Nicky looks up from his book and glances at me. He knows my post–high school plans but has been sworn to secrecy. We make eye contact, he shrugs his shoulders and goes back to his punk-rock love story.

"Hurry," my mom says to my father, "you going to be late for work."

"I never late for work!" my father answers with pride. It's actually true. My father has never been late for anything in his entire life. It's weird, like he's some kind of time lord. We can leave our house at four thirty to go someplace an hour away, and somehow we still arrive by five. Just. Weird.

I take the drumsticks out of my back pocket—I always carry sticks in my back pocket, because, well, you never know—put them on the table, and sit down. I prop my phone against a small vase of flowers my mother likes to keep fresh, and plug in the earbuds.

"What is this?" my father asks, an annoyed look on his face.

"I'm going to watch a movie."

"A movie?" he bellows. "Our people did not invent physiki, mathematics, and drama for you to watch movies at the breakfast."

"It's 'at breakfast' or 'at *the* breakfast table,'" I correct him. "And actually, Dad, they kind of did. Streaming content on a phone is the perfect blend of science and art, don't you think? Aristotle would be proud." I'm not sure if my dad understands that I'm tweaking him. His sense of humor is more slapstick than subtle. He laughs himself stupid at old Mel Brooks movies. I have to admit, I kind of do, too. "It's okay," I assure him. "This is for school."

"You watch movies . . . for school?" His annoyance blends with confusion.

"Yeah, for my film studies class. We're getting grounded in classics before we start to learn how to make our own movies."

"Movies in school," he half says, half mutters. "How this country become superpower is mystery to me."

"Hurry," my mother admonishes again, "you going to be late!" Mom creates a constant aura of free-floating energy that attempts to consume all in its path, like something from a science-fiction story.

"Baaaah," my father grumbles, as if the mere thought of being late is ridiculous.

"What movie?" Nicky asks.

"*North by Northwest*. It's kind of long, but Mr. Tannis says the way Hitchcock framed certain shots to create tension was groundbreaking." I shove a spoonful of the Cap'N in my mouth and add, "I'm liking it."

Yia Yia enters the kitchen, takes her favorite teacup—fake porcelain, blue with a noticeable chip—and pours a small serving of thick black coffee. Yia Yia drinks more coffee than a cop. "When you boys get girlfriends?"

Nicky and I groan in unison.

"What? They not have Greek girls at you school?"

Nicky just shakes his head and goes back to his book.

"Yia Yia," I answer, "between my band and school, I don't have time for girlfriends."

Yia Yia smiles, this time like *she's* in on a joke no one else understands. At least now I see where Nicky gets it. "Time and love are like river. Sometimes they take you where you do not know you need to go."

Great. My Greek grandmother is now writing copy for cookies.

The truth is, I've never had a girlfriend. I did have one date in the eighth grade: Jessica—long hair, straight bangs, and a really nice laugh. We went ice-skating, which meant that she did twirls in the middle of the rink while I hugged the wall. I might be the only boy in Minnesota who doesn't know how to skate, let alone play hockey.

Anyway, when we got hot chocolate and hot pretzels after, she talked about books and current events like she was a college student or something. I was intimidated. I'm not dumb, but I didn't think I was smart enough for her.

It was really soon after that I got into the band.

It's not that I haven't noticed girls since then, but really, it's easier to just focus on the band. There's less drama this way. Well, mostly.

Eliana

$\mathcal{I}$ take my time walking the one-point-two miles home from school. No matter how painful the heft of my backpack, the pinching cold of the weather, or the size of the hole worn into the bottom of my ratty and beloved Chucks, I always take my time walking home from school. School equals nearly two thousand people bumping into me in the hallway, gagging me with body spray in the locker room after gym class, and answering every inane question in English Lit with "Is that going to be on the test?" I shuffle up so many stairs behind groups of people who find it necessary to walk with their friends in a spread-out line, as if they're playing Red Rover and Eliana can't come over, making me late for class. I buy Nutty Buddies for lunch out of a vending machine in order to gain myself solo time in a desolate corner of the library, only to find a jock couple making out. I cannot find any space in which to be alone. Anywhere. Ever. It's no wonder I can't manage to keep my depression at bay.

When I arrive home, shoulders aching from the weight of the books in my bag, I unlock the front door in slow motion. The instant I click and open the door, I am bombarded. "Hey! Ellie's home!" It's my dad, who is also home. All the time. Like, every second of every day and night. He used to run his own business, previously a video store when videotapes were a thing, which, out of necessity, morphed into a DVD store, which then, also out of necessity, closed when people stopped renting DVDs. I hate all of the people who stopped renting DVDs, because now not only do we have a basement filled with old DVDs that my dad constantly watches and fails to sell over the internet, but my dad has nowhere to go. In the three years since his store closed, he hasn't found another job that holds his interest enough. Hence, the Dad-is-always-home situation. He is a fine dad and tries to be helpful when Mom is at work (high school science teacher and traveling basketball team referee), which is most of the time. But since I'm the eldest of five, it feels like the moment I get home he wants me to be Second Mommy. I have no plans to have any children of my own after witnessing four home births, so is it really my responsibility to take care of my siblings?

I know. I'm an asshole. I'm a horrible person for not wanting to help my bumbling dad and my hardworking mom and my four poor, defenseless brothers and sisters. I hate me, too.

Before I can make it up the stairs and into my tiny bedroom sanctuary, there is family to attend to.

"Hey, guys," I say, depositing my backpack next to the front door. My shoulders thank me.

The littlest ones, Ava and Asher, always greet me first. "Ellie!" they scream, and ram me with hugs. Asher, the youngest at five, is a professional cuddler, but Ava always manages to jab me with a sharp part of her body—an elbow, a knee, and in this case a chin straight to my gut. I resist the natural urge to vomit into her curly rat's nest of hair. "We made weather predictors in school today." Ava extracts her chin from my abdomen and thrusts into my face a paper plate dotted with scribbly images of four weather conditions: sunny, rainy, snowy, and cloudy. She uses the arrow mounted with a brad in the center to mark "sunny." "See? Now you always know what the weather is."

I stop myself from commenting on how it would be just as easy to look out the window for the same effect. Because the project is sweet, and so is Ava, which is why it is all the more painful that I can't muster up the energy to care. Will she recognize my forced smile? "That's great, Ava. Put it on the fridge so you can set it every morning before we get dressed." She scuttles over to the refrigerator and fails at all attempts to hang the paper plate with a weak Wall Drug magnet. Asher regales me with a story about a kid throwing up at recess into the twisty slide, and I nod enthusiastically while a part of me dies inside at the prospect of another round of the stomach flu going through the house.

My ten-year-old brother, Isaac, and thirteen-year-old sister, Samara, sit at one end of the dining room table doing their homework. The other end of the table is strewn with jigsaw pieces and half of a completed puzzle exhibiting a pyramid of old tin cans, a family project meant to keep idle hands busy. I used to have a passion for the puzzles, but these days I only manage to build the border before I tire of the physical and social exertion that comes with putting together a puzzle with four brothers and sisters and a dad with no life.

"Hey," I say. "Need anything?" I ask this out of habit, out of guilty obligation for my mom and pity for my dad.

"Nah." Isaac shrugs. Samara doesn't even bother with words,

just a lazy dismissive wave. My cue to grab my backpack and escape to my room.

The original parental plan was to give me, the eldest and wisest of the spawn, the basement when I turned into a "woman" post bat mitzvah. Thanks to my dad's career choice and the world moving on without him, the basement was handed over to 4,723 inanimate objects. The only option to claim any space of my own in our three-bedroom house was to move into the meager walk-in closet attached to the Sisters Room (what we call the girls' bedroom in the house, even though it has a somewhat terrifying polygamist-sounding title). I fit in a single futon mattress plus a compact IKEA bookshelf. Lucky for me there is a small, octagonal window in the closet, so I can tell what time of day it is as well as estimate the weather without a paper plate.

It's not as bad as I'm making it sound. Except on those days when I just want to be alone. Which is pretty much most days. I feel like my medication should take care of that more than it does.

I struggle past my sisters' bunk bed with my backpack and heave it onto my futon mattress, pulling my door closed. Solitude. I click on the overhead bulb and the string of Jack Skellington lights I bought at Walgreens for ambience. The small and high window provides little actual light. I have often imagined whether I could escape through the eight-sided hole if there were ever a fire or a home intruder.

I position the futon so it becomes a makeshift couch and breeze through my homework. With physics out of the way, school should be relatively easy this year. At least the classes will be. Living through each day in that building, surrounded by people who either remember who I was or have no idea I exist, is another matter. My close friends all but abandoned me while I languished in a mental hospital last year, and the rest of the student body didn't even know I was gone.

This is one of those moments my therapist says I should call a friend or journal to escape my dark thoughts. Dark thoughts, however, pretty much smother all motivation to do anything but watch movies.

I pull out my laptop and stuff on my headphones, click on *Harry Potter and the Goblet of Fire*, and settle into my usual position until someone forces me to go downstairs for dinner. This is my favorite Harry Potter movie because, aside from (or because of?) the death, it is kind of romantic. Everyone is preparing for the Yule Ball, and you can practically smell the hormones wafting off the screen. Plus I really like all the shaggy hair. When I watch movies, I am able to leave my head for a spell. Go somewhere instead of here. Be someone instead of me. But sometimes a crappy thought can still sneak in. Would I be the depressed weirdo at Hogwarts, too?

Dmitri

*A*rt and Craft of Cinema is third period, and I'm already in a pretty good mood.

First, Tuesdays are exponentially better than Mondays. This is a scientifically proven fact. Second, I was kind of bummed yesterday that not one person in school mentioned the Unexpected Turbulence show from over the weekend. We definitely killed, and I'll admit, I had walked into school—okay, strutted into school—thinking I would be the happy recipient of praise and adoration.

Nada.

This is partly because I'm a drummer. We're kind of invisible, shrouded and shielded by our drum kits. Singers and guitar players get way more attention. I'm sure Chad basked in the warm glow of his fans yesterday. I can picture his self-satisfied swagger and it makes me sick.

I'll put it out there right now: I don't like Chad. He is a pretty good singer and a solid front man for UT, but I've been in the band since I was thirteen and Chad has never taken me seriously. The one time I tried to introduce a song to our set, I got this "you're a drummer, Dimmi; drummers don't write songs" crap. Chad can be a douche when he wants to. ("Hey, Dmitri, what happened when the bass player locked his keys in the car? It took him half an hour to get the drummer out." Ha. Ha. Chad.) It doesn't help that the other guys in the band are all seniors and I'm a sophomore. They never really let me forget that.

So today, when Jimmy Roach (yes, that's his real name) gave me a high five and raved about the gig, well, I felt redeemed. It was a solid gig, and it's good to be acknowledged for it.

Mr. Tannis, our film teacher, wears his hair long and has a thick black moustache. He looks like something out of a movie from the 1970s or 1980s. I guess that makes sense. He was probably a film student back then. He smiles at me as I take my seat and open my notebook. We don't have a textbook for this course; Mr. Tannis told us on the first day that our learning would all be done on screen. I love this class.

When we're settled into our seats and Mr. Tannis has started writing on the board, the door opens just wide enough for a new girl to slink in. And I mean slink. Her shoulders are hunched and her eyes are down. She kind of shuffles to Mr. Tannis and hands him a slip of paper. He reads it, looks up, and smiles. "Welcome to the class"—he looks down again—"Eliana. Find yourself a seat."

Eliana stops and scans the room like she really wants a desk up front, but the only empty seat is next to me, in the back. She shrinks into herself a little more—I'm not sure how that's possible—and makes her way toward camp Dmitri.

She's about five three, has a nose that turns up at the end, hazel eyes, and straight and shiny brown hair that hangs down over half her face. She's wearing all dark clothes and this pair of Chucks that look like they're being held together by sheer force of will. For some reason, when she takes her seat, I notice that she smells good. Like, really good. I can't tell if it's perfume or shampoo or just her, but it's distracting the hell out of me.

"So how many of you watched *North by Northwest*?" Mr. Tannis asks.

I raise my hand, trying to keep my gaze on the new girl. I think I've seen her around but can't be sure. She didn't go to my middle school or elementary school, and with more than four hundred kids in my grade alone, it's hard to know everyone. Her eyes are forward, but I can tell she knows I'm staring at her and she doesn't like it. I figure I should break the ice.

"Hi," I whisper.

She doesn't even flinch. She's still looking at Mr. Tannis. "Who wants to share," he's saying, "some impressions of the movie?" Margaret's hand shoots up. She's in the front row and her hand is always the first one up. In every single class. "Margaret?" Mr. Tannis asks, a note of exasperation or resignation or some other-ation in his voice.

Margaret starts a soliloquy about the crop duster scene—um, yeah, pretty obvious, Margaret—but I'm not really listening. I kind of feel like the new girl has thrown down a gauntlet, daring me to break through her tough exterior. Challenge accepted.

"Hi," I whisper again. "I'm Dmitri."

She side-eyes me, and I'm pretty sure I see a tiny smirk before her eyes dart back to the front of the class.

"I'm the drummer for Unexpected Turbulence."

She places her index finger against her lips.

"What's your na—"

"Shhh!" Her smackdown is loud enough that Margaret stops talking and everyone else cranes their necks to look in our direction.

"Everything okay back there?" Mr. Tannis asks.

Neither one of us say anything, but we both nod.

Margaret doesn't miss a beat, launching once again into her description of the plane chasing Cary Grant through the cornfield. It's like a play-by-play of the action in the movie, but misses what I think must be the larger point about how Hitchcock used the absence of dialogue, sound editing, and unusual camera angles to build tension.

Eliana—I think that's what Mr. Tannis called her—tucks her hair behind her ear, and for some reason my heart beats a little faster. "Have you seen the movie?" I whisper.

I detect the slightest nod.

Honestly, I don't know why I'm so transfixed by this girl. Maybe it is just the challenge of trying to get her to pay attention to me, maybe it's a bit of ego from playing in a band, or maybe it's Yia Yia's voice in my head, talking about girlfriends and love.

My phone vibrates, jolting me back to the moment. I sneak a peek—something totally forbidden during class, but something every kid with a phone (so every kid) does. It's from Chad.

CHAD: Rehearsal today after school.

Another Chadism—everything's a demand, nothing's a question. Whatever.

ME: K. See you then.

Eliana's shoulders have relaxed a little now that my attention is off her, and I decide it's best to leave her alone.

For now.

Eliana

*M*r. Tannis (how I am not going to constantly refer to him as "Mr. Tennis," I do not know) looks like the cover of one of my dad's seventies videotapes. I don't think I'll ever find a moustache an acceptable form of facial hair. Really, I find most forms of facial hair off-putting: Goatees are clearly cover-ups for problem chin areas, sideburns are never symmetrical and are, therefore, meant to distract from some other sinister personality flaw, and topping it off are moustaches, which repulse me to my core. Why would anyone want to grow several layers of hair above their lip? How can that feel good? Do they really think it looks attractive? It's like standard poodles, which I find terribly disturbing. As my mom says, "There's nothing standard about them."

How am I supposed to learn anything in a class run by a man with a moustache?

And, frankly, how is anyone supposed to teach me anything about films when my dad has been schooling me on them since before I could talk? I want to say something about *North by Northwest* being too obvious a choice of Hitchcock films. Why not go with something more obscure, like *Marnie*? Who wouldn't want to talk about a movie where a woman can't handle seeing the colors red and white together? That's a brilliantly random plot point there. I consider raising my hand to bring this up, but Mr. Tennis Moustache is already engaged in a conversation-for-one with a girl in the front row. Plus, this guy sitting next to me is trying to talk to me.

I caught a glimpse of him before I sat down: dark hair, dark eyes, straight teeth. I am fascinated by braces-straightened teeth. My parents gave me the choice in middle school: braces or Disney World. I was somewhat of a late bloomer when it came to caring about my appearance, so of course I chose Disney World. I do not regret the decision, but it does mean that my teeth aren't Hollywood-worthy. They're not horrible or snaggly or even that noticeable unless I smile. Even then, there's nothing wrong with them. They're just not perfect. Forgive me, world, for not being perfect.

I look ahead, trying to listen to the moustachioed man, but I can feel the eyes of this guy next to me searing into my skull. What does he want? Does he need a pencil? A cough drop? The Heimlich?

My bangs are not sufficiently covering my view of Staring Boy, as much as I try. He keeps whispering something to me, but I can't hear him over the music from the girl's poorly hidden earbuds on my other side. Is he really trying to get my name? Why would he want that? He's far too cute to want it for any good reason.

I can't take it anymore, so I full-on librarian "Shhh" him. I know it's a cliché to say that librarians shush people, but it's one I quite like. I dream of the day I'm in a powerful enough position in life to officially tell people to be quiet.

He continues talking, undeterred by my shushery. Maybe he hasn't heard of the patented librarian shush. Maybe he doesn't speak English. Does one need to speak English to understand a *shhh*?

By the grace of modern technology, the guy's cell phone buzzes and he loses interest in whatever it was he was interested in. Was he interested in me? Nah. I probably have a giant booger hanging from my nose, and he was trying to give me a boog report. I casually nudge my nose with my knuckle, but it feels clean.

Three minutes later, the bell rings and I scuttle out of the classroom before I have to engage with anyone. My best friend (and pretty much my only friend at this point), Janina, waits for me at my locker, long, dark hair effortlessly coiffed in a messy bun. She towers over me, obscuring the fluorescent hallway light. Ironically, Janina has been the only light for me in these hallways for the last year or so. Friends are hard to keep around when you aren't pleasant and easygoing. Never mind the fact that I have zero control over the chemical imbalance altering my brain. My dad tried to feed me the "real friends stay with you through thick and thin" BS. My mom, with her standard-poodle-loathing wisdom, put it better: "People can be assholes. You don't want those people." Still, it would be nice to have more than one person to eat lunch with. Sucky for me, that one person isn't even in my lunch period.

"How was the film class? Do you just sit around and watch movies?" Janina is in the career program at our school, so she goes to regular high school in the morning and buses to a different campus for cosmetology classes in the afternoons. If not for

Janina, I would still have the crooked bob I cut myself in junior high. *I* thought it looked edgy. Janina thought it made me look "like Vanessa Hudgens playing a runaway teen."

"Too early to tell. I spent most of the class not talking to a guy next to me who very possibly wanted to learn my name. It was confusing. I just want an A after my grade crash last year." I slam my locker and spin the dial. This year my locker dial is particularly fluid, which I appreciate much more than last year's sticky spinner. It is far more satisfying to watch the numbers fly by than to have them stop shy of my combination

"That sounds promising. Was he cute?" Janina, having blossomed as she has, is light years ahead of me in the boy department. While she goes out and does sexy things with actual people, I find I'm more comfortable having fake dates in my head with Bill Weasley.

"Maybe? I barely got a look at him. I mostly heard his voice. His appealingly deep voice."

"I prefer talkers to the silent types. We're supposed to think there's something mysterious when a guy doesn't talk, but I think it just means he's a dumbass."

"I'll keep that in mind." I file this away in the "Things I Will Never Need to Know Because I Will Never Be Asked on a Date Anyway" drawer. "I better get going," I tell Janina. "I can't be late for gym again this week. I tried to get Mr. Person to let me drop it, but he gave me some statewide mandate bullshit."

"Catch you later." Janina floats off, and I hit the gym locker room precisely as the bell rings. "I'm here!" I scream to Ms. Conway, my beleaguered gym teacher.

"You're lucky!" Ms. Conway replies from her office.

I quickly shrug off my clothes and dress in my gym uniform: rough green shorts and a worn green t-shirt. Inside my locker is a travel-sized deodorant stick, and I rub on an extra layer. Today is running day, my favorite gym day of the week, because all I have to do is shuffle my way around the track while the conglomerate of gym teachers blasts "motivational" running music. It beats the volleyball unit, where Megan Thickpenny's main goal is to hit me in the head with her serve just because I did that to her one time. And it's not like I meant to (on a conscious level).

Before I start my run on the track, I lean against the cinder-block wall and stretch my calves. If I were a serious runner, I would probably change into shoes without tape holding parts of them together. But in my opinion, serious running isn't something one should aspire to in PE.

Ridiculously loud bass pumps through ancient, crackling speakers while the gym teachers ignore their students and pretend they are in da club. I wouldn't be surprised if that wasn't Gatorade in their sports bottles.

I keep to the slow lane, jogging behind two speed walkers.

And then I notice him. It's that guy from my film class. At least I think it's him. Sometimes it's hard to recognize people in this sea of green polyester. He's one lane over, the lane that says, "I'm not trying, but I'm kind of fit," jogging with a friend. I slow down so as not to pass him, which I shouldn't be doing anyway by lane protocol. He speeds away, and I breathe a sigh of relief. I'm still wary about why he would even want to know my name. I find my jogging groove, and as I run I pretend I'm on the Hogwarts track, prepping for my role in the Triwizard Tournament. (In this scenario, I am the Hufflepuff representative, and I do not die.) I'm feeling good, endorphins kicking in, fantasy in full effect, when I see the guy from film class pass me in the next lane. He turns around to look at me, and I'm certain it's him. That's when he trips over his friend and slams into the track. So much for my Triwizard Cup.

Dmitri

When I was eleven, my parents took Nicky and me to the Valleyfair theme park in Shakopee. They've got roller coasters and log flumes and these pretty cool animatronic dinosaurs. Nicky hated roller coasters back then—actually, he still hates them—so my parents left me alone on the line at the Excalibur, an old-style wooden coaster, while they took him to some tamer rides. The real thrill of the Excalibur wasn't the twists and turns, it was not knowing if the whole thing's imminent collapse was going to happen while you were on it.

When the ride finished (still intact), I didn't see my parents anywhere. So, on my mother's very strict instructions, which were more or less yelled at me—"We not here, you go straight from roller coaster to bumpy car ride. No talking strangers!"—I walked to the "bumpy" cars. On the way, I couldn't help but notice this gaggle of girls about my age sitting on benches and looking at their phones.

This was sixth grade, which meant that all of a sudden there were girls in the world. I mean, I noticed there were girls before the sixth grade, but not *noticed* noticed. (Girls had started noticing boys in the second grade. Go figure.)

Anyway, there was this gaggle of girls in short shorts and bikini tops—a lot of Valleyfair is a water park—and one of them looked up from her phone and stared at me. I'm not the best-looking boy, but I'm not the worst, either. This girl and I held each other's gaze, and, not knowing what else to do, I gave a small wave of my hand. Only I hadn't stopped moving while this was going on, and I walked directly into a light post.

It was a full-on, face-first collision—me and the light post—and it knocked me back on my ass. Hard.

The entire gaggle erupted into laughter, like doubled-over, crying laughter. There was nothing for me to do but get up, smile, and bow, as if I had planned the whole thing. (I hadn't.) Then I turned and continued to the bumper cars, my cheeks red, my dignity left in tatters at the base of that pole. It was the most embarrassing thing that had ever happened to me.

Until today.

For the most part, I don't like gym class. Let's face it, most rockers are drawn to music because we're not good at sports. Running day in PE is the only one I sort of like. You run. That's it. No rope climbing, no volleyball serves, no having to catch things.

Karl Bloomfield and I started a light jog to warm up, and after a lap we both hit the gas, kind of egging each other on. We've been friends since the fourth grade, when Karl moved here from Arizona. The dude still hasn't gotten used to the cold weather. While the rest of us wore shorts and t-shirts, Karl opted for the school's green sweats and hoodie. And we're indoors.

It felt good to run. The strain of my leg muscles and the rhythm and meter of my normally uncoordinated body working together remind me a lot of drumming. It makes me think I should try out for the track team. (Not really.)

I'd just started my third lap when I saw her. Eliana. The girl who wouldn't talk to me in film class.

Anyway, it didn't register that it was really her until I ran past her—she was in the jogging lane—so I turned around to make sure it *was* her, and just as her eyes were going wide when she saw me staring . . .

WHAM!

Karl and I were hitting the turn when I looked back over my shoulder. With my attention behind me, I kept going straight; I veered off my path and ran right into Karl.

I go down. Karl goes down. The kid behind us—I don't know his name, but I think he actually *is* on the track team— goes down. The three people behind them have to stop so short that one of them loses her balance . . . and she goes down. It's like a snowstorm-induced, twenty-car pileup on I-35. There are groans, cuss words (mostly at me), and at least one knee scraped badly enough to be bleeding.

The gym teachers, who were off in a corner talking about whatever gym teachers talk about—I'll go out on a limb here and guess sports, or, I don't know, maybe sadomasochism—don't notice at first. When they do, they come running like a herd of buffalo.

I look up just in time to see Eliana's butt disappear into the door that leads to the girls' locker room. Getting blown off in film class was kind of hard, but knowing she witnessed this cluster, and probably knowing my looking at her was the reason, is a whole new level of embarrassment. Worst of all, I couldn't help but notice that the butt retreating through the door was kind of cute.

Why am I thinking about this girl so much?

Curse you, Yia Yia!!!

Eliana

I am such a turd. Like, the world's largest, stinkiest turd that comes at the worst time, when you're in a school bathroom and you think you're by yourself, but then a group of girls comes in and you're the only one behind closed doors, so when you flush and exit the stall, they know it was you that stunk up the place.

That's the kind of turd I am.

The boy from my film class fell on his butt, and I didn't even stop to see how he was. I ran and left him in a pile of jocks and gym clothes. What could I have done, though? It wasn't my fault he fell. Who am I, *Carrie*? Oh my god. What if I have telekinesis?

If only.

He was probably just noticing I forgot to shave my legs. Or what a clompy runner I am. I hope he wasn't checking out the lack of support this bra gives me during gym class. But who wants to change their bra for gym class? That would require actually getting naked in a room full of other people. I'm still grateful the school phased out showering after gym class to allow for more time in the day for actual education.

He couldn't have been looking at me because he likes me. I mean, he doesn't even know me. What could he see in me? Aside from how hot I look in green polyester. Even if he did like me, which I highly doubt, I'm sure he thinks I'm a complete fart-blossom for running and then, you know, running.

I'm not a girl who makes people trip and fall. Most people tend not to know I exist, which is generally how I like it. I am, however, a girl who can't help but notice pairs of other teenagers grinding against each other in the hallways. I try not to stare, but I doubt they'd notice if I did. How is it a person can be so intimate with another person in front of everyone? How is it that they have so much confidence that they not only find their ways into relationships but put themselves on display? And how is it that they have any freaking idea what to do in those situations?

I watch movies. Lots of movies. I have seen people kiss. I have seen people get naked. I have seen people do . . . other things. But when it comes to real sexy stuff . . . not so much. I have kissed a boy. One time. It was at this girl Mara Sidell's bat mitzvah, during the snowball dance. This is the dance for which I both shivered in anticipation and sweated profusely with dread. At the start of the song, kids paired off with a partner and glided around the floor until the DJ called, "Snowball!" That was when you were supposed to kiss your partner. My partner at the time was Adam Schulman, a boy who stood one inch shorter than my already not-very-tall height. He had braces, and our kiss was more like a scraping of metal against enamel. After the kiss, the goal was to switch partners until the DJ called "Snowball" again, and the magic continued. Somehow, there wasn't a spare partner for me after the initial snowball, although admittedly I didn't search that hard. Envision the awkwardness of scanning a dance floor for your next lip-crushing victim. Instead, I bolted back to my designated table and played a game on my phone. That is until Adam approached me several songs later and asked if I wanted to see the sculpture in the banquet hall foyer. He pronounced it "foy-yay," which I thought was wrong at the time but didn't say anything. It didn't occur to me that this "foy-yay" visit was a ruse for him to bump his braces into me again. We made out in a corner of the golf club's lobby until I was sufficiently grossed out and excused myself to pee. I believe my exact exit words were "I have to pee." I was never attracted to Adam Schulman, and I have no idea why he was the boy who I kissed in the foyer. I suppose because he was the one who asked me. End scene.

I change out of my gym clothes and stuff them back into my gym locker, the ripeness of the fabric a reminder that I haven't brought the ensemble home since school started. It would be a shame to stink if, say, a definitely cute boy from one of my classes possibly was looking at me for good reasons rather than the innumerable bad ones I can concoct in my saboteur brain. But that's a ridiculous thought. Clearly.

The bell rings, and I check myself in the mirror before my next class. I finger-comb my bangs over my left eye and smooth some cherry-flavored lip balm over my lips. I consider what a foyer make-out session with the boy from film class would be like. Then I realize I'm standing in a gym locker room and berate myself for thinking such thoughts in a public locale.

Ten feet out the door of the locker room, I run back inside, slam open my gym locker, and grab my gym clothes. Might as well take them home and wash them tonight. Just in case.

Dmitri

"Your politics
Make me sick,
So I'm gonna kick
The shit out of you!"

Okay, maybe not the best lyrics Chad ever wrote, but he's singing it well.

More than that, the tune sticks in your head.

More than *that*, the groove, if it doesn't sound too egotistical to say, is crazy good. Drew uses a pick to play bass, which gives it a clicky, trebly vibe, and his lines are so full of melody they sound like they're intended for a six-string guitar. Because of that, or maybe in spite of it, the bass complements my drumbeat unlike anything I've heard before. Kyle's guitar—distorted, but not so much as to be muddy—fuses with the rhythm section to create this wave of sound that crashes over you again and again.

In short, it's a really, really good song.

At one of our gigs a few months ago, some older guy in a denim jacket—he was like maybe thirty-five or forty, so too old to be wearing a denim jacket—told me we sounded like Hüsker Dü.

Truth is, I had no idea who that was, which kind of blew the old dude's mind.

"You've never heard of Hüsker Dü? Kid, they were Minnesota punk rock royalty!" Chad was eavesdropping on the conversation and jumped in, heaping praise on Hüsker Dü and doing his best to make me feel stupid. When I got home that night I went straight to iTunes and downloaded this album called *Candy Apple Grey*. I really wanted to hate it—mostly because Chad liked it, but partly because the old dude was a bit sanctimonious (thank you, PSAT prep, for the vocab word)—but holy crap! Those guys were awesome! And while our sound is different, I did get where Old Denim Dude was coming from.

"My generation
Has no admiration
Or veneration
For your worldview."

Chad likes to think he's political, but really he's full of hot air. Plus, I'll bet Chad has never used "veneration" in a sentence in his life. I think he wrote this song entirely with a thesaurus.

Anyway, Drew, Kyle, and I come to a screeching and simultaneous halt, with me bringing the full force of my stick down on the crash cymbal and then deadening it immediately with my hand. The effect is a musical exclamation point . . . on steroids. I normally love this trick, but I scraped my palm during the seven-person collision in gym class and it still hurts.

After a three-beat pause we slam back into the song in unison and Chad starts belting out the chorus.

Besides the cut on my hand, I have a bruise on my ass that is making drumming harder than usual today. Not to mention the bruise on my ego. Apparently the whole school heard about the PE pileup.

"How's it going, Trippy McTripperson?" was Drew's greeting when I arrived at rehearsal, which cracked Chad up.

Kyle, who is the nicest of my three bandmates, tried to suppress a smile but didn't do a very good job. "What happened?" he asked.

I'm the only guy in Unexpected Turbulence without a girlfriend, something about which I'm frequently teased. How these guys have time for relationships, I just don't understand. Anyway, I can't tell them the reason I tripped the entire gym class was because I was ogling a girl. First, they'll demand to know who she is, and second, they'll never let me hear the end of it.

I make up a lie for Kyle about my shoelace being untied. I know. Lame. But I figure it's such a cliché no one would use it unless it was true.

While I don't say a word about Eliana, I haven't been able to shake the image of her since I took my seat behind the drum kit an hour ago. I think it's her eyes that get me the most. It's not that they're Disney-character big or anything, but they have this incredible depth, like there's a whole other person hiding behind them. Yeah, it's definitely her eyes. Or maybe it's her—

"Dmitri!" Chad's voice cuts through my snare drum. It's only now that I notice the rest of the band has stopped playing and they're all staring at me.

"What?"

"What do you mean 'what'? You played right through the change, dumbass."

Oh my god, Chad's right. I never do that. *Never.* The look on Kyle's face can only be described as shock. "Dimmi, you okay?"

I nod. I'd rather have them think I got a concussion in PE than know the truth. "I'm fine," I say, "maybe just a bit dizzy."

"You wanna take a break?" Kyle asks.

"No breaks." Chad would be the kind of officer to get shot by his own troops in Syria or Afghanistan or wherever we're at war this week.

"Shut up, Chad." I love that Kyle doesn't put up with Chad's crap.

"Up yours, Kyle. The gig is in two weeks. We need to be perfect."

The gig Chad's talking about is our first-ever show at the First Avenue and Seventh Street Entry. It's the coolest club not only in Minnesota, but really the whole Midwest. Prince made it famous, but bands like the Replacements and U2 played there. (And yes, so did Hüsker Dü. I looked it up.) Chad has been at DEFCON 1 over this gig since he booked it a month ago. The truth is, I agree with him. This gig is, as my Spanish teacher would say, muy importante.

"No, I'm good. Chad's right; we need to nail this. Let's just play."

Chad gives Kyle a "told you so" look, which makes me mad at

myself for giving Chad an opening to be right about anything. Kyle shrugs and starts the guitar riff to our next song.

I try to put Eliana out of my mind and focus on drumming. It only partly works. I don't screw up again at rehearsal, but images of Eliana's butt—her eyes, I mean her eyes—dance across my mind.

I either need to give up on this girl, or I need to find a way to get her to notice me. No, that's not right. She's definitely noticed me. In fact, that's the problem. Now I need to get her to *want* to notice me.

There's only one person who can help. I have to talk to Reggie.

Eliana

My walk home is particularly slow today. I need time to think. Or maybe I need less time to think. Thinking often brings my mood levels way down, so I attempt a detour. As I walk, I listen to music on my phone to create a sort of soundtrack to my life. If I can get my brain to stop thinking about *me* things, I can sometimes deter the inevitable drop into bummerville. Sometimes, when I'm overthinking things or just hating on myself even too much for, well, *myself*, I turn up the volume on my music really loud in hopes of jarring the thoughts right out of my brain. I don't know if that's why it works, or if it's just the shock to my eardrums, but it usually helps me switch brain tracks for a little bit.

Today I'm surprisingly not thinking in a downward spiral, even though I know it will be Groundhog Day at home (one of my dad's favorite Bill Murray movie references, where the same day repeats over and over again). I waffle between mortification that I may have caused the PE Accident of the Century and blushing at the potential that I, Eliana Hoffman, may have caused the PE Accident of the Century.

The other day I reread my seventh-grade diary to see if I always felt so crappy. In it I talk about this boy, Arlo Eggers, from my science class who, every single day, would ask me about my gym shoes. This was way back with my first pair of Chucks, black high-tops that have disintegrated since then. I liked to draw on them with a white paint pen, mostly nerd symbols from TV shows and movies I hoped nobody would understand (but secretly hoped they would so they'd know how cool I was). A direct diary excerpt:

> *Arlo asked me about my shoes today. Again. He asks me almost every day about them. Today he pointed at the* **Supernatural** *anti-possession symbol and asked, "Are you a Satanist?" I looked at him with a total eye roll. "What do you think?" He smiled so cute, and I almost died but tried to look like I thought he was an idiot. I wish I could make a face that says, "I like how you keep asking me about my shoes. Ask me about them again while we're naked in the Caribbean."*

Man, I was a weird middle schooler. Why would I want to be naked with Arlo Eggers in the Caribbean, of all places? Also, what did I think we would be doing while we were naked? Like, just sitting there, getting a tan? I was in seventh freakin' grade! What a doof. And yet, when I look back at that journal entry (I really should burn it before I die or someone else finds it), I think that maybe he kind of liked me. Yes, he danced with someone else at the mixer (classiest name for a middle school dance ever), and all I did was stand in the corner with Janina and make fun of people. But if I had been a different sort of person, say, one who actually knew how to read the social cues of boys, I would perhaps have played the whole shoe-admiring thing differently.

And then what?

Would we have dated in seventh grade? Fallen in love? Gotten married? Ended up naked together in the Caribbean? (Seriously, what the hell was that?)

My point in taking this death-defying walk down memory lane is that I now realize that maybe boys have liked me in the past. (Does the snowball kiss count? Or was it just par for the bat mitzvah course?) And maybe that means a boy could like me again. Like a particular boy who I totally made face-plant into the gym floor.

God, I'm an idiot.

I decide to survey the members of my household. Isaac and Samara, my two oldest younger siblings, are dutifully doing their homework at the puzzle table. I think their schoolwork ethic has been drilled into them by our mother, the teacher, but even more so by watching our dad spiral into a jobless, basement-dwelling, online DVD seller. Ava and Asher wrestle on the kitchen floor. Dad is holed up in the basement, per usual.

The sibs barely acknowledge me as I sit down and deftly fill in two barren sections of the tin-can puzzle. I get right to it. "Let's say you're in a new class, and the guy next to you won't shut up. What do you do?"

Isaac answers with his obvious "Raise my hand and tell the teacher."

"It's not that kind of talking, Isaac. It's more like he's talking to you, and he won't stop even when you act like you care what the teacher is saying."

"So, like, he's flirting with you?" Samara, all dramatic black hair, black eyes, and black soul, asks incredulously. If she weren't my sister, I might be afraid of her. I might be a little anyway.

"If that's what it sounds like. I'm just trying to get a feel for what a normal person would think if this were happening to them," I agree pathetically.

"Meaning, not you." Samara fills in the gap.

"I set you up for that one, I realize, but yes."

"He could like you. It depends on what words he says, too. Was he just asking to borrow a pencil?"

"Noooo," I draw out defensively. "I don't actually remember what he was saying. It wasn't really anything. I was trying too hard not to listen, frankly. I didn't really realize until I made him fall on top of a bunch of people in gym class that maybe he was talking to me for *reasons*, and by then he was too busy hating me for making him fall, for him to probably even consider liking me anymore, so never mind."

"What are you even talking about?" Samara glares at me. One can see why I've moved into the closet of our bedroom.

"Forget it, Sam. Go back to your innocent algebra. And keep one eye open when you sleep tonight." I dole out a helping of evil-eye fingers.

What is the point of having four brothers and sisters if I can glean no advice from any of them? Being first in the birth order sucks. Does Samara ever acknowledge how I helped her when she got her first period and Mom wasn't home? No. See if I help her when she has questions about losing her virginity. Although, chances are, she'll probably get there before me.

Ava and Asher continue to roll around on the kitchen floor. "You know, it would be a lot more comfortable to attack each other on carpeting," I suggest, trying to budge my way into the refrigerator for an apple and a mini Babybel cheese. I barely miss slamming Asher's head into the fridge door and make my way out of the kitchen and up to my room.

Curled up on my futon, I text Janina.

ME: I think I may have killed the cute boy from my film class.

JANINA: So he is cute?

ME: AND possibly dead

JANINA: Doubtful. It's not as easy to die from gym class as you think. What did you do to him?

ME: This sounds so stupid, but I just looked at him.

JANINA: I knew you were Carrie!

ME: That's what I said!

JANINA: I was kidding.

ME: Me too. Of course.

JANINA: So you looked at him, and he died?

ME: Well, he fell. On top of a bunch of other people. It was . . . awkward.

JANINA: OMG that was you?

ME: I think so? He turned around, and there was some tripping action and then they all went down.

JANINA: They all went down, huh?

ME: Is there a pervert emoji on here?

JANINA: Ha. Time will tell. If he lives.

ME: Tell what, exactly?

JANINA: Don't pretend that you aren't adorable and that you don't have the world's perkiest butt from walking everywhere.

ME: My butt is blushing.

JANINA: I have volleyball. Later.

I don't want to get my hopes up. In fact, I hate myself for even thinking of the possibility that someone may have been looking at me in a non-annoyed/disgusted/pitying way. It's too much reality to think of, so I turn on *Goblet of Fire*. Then I decide to mix it up a little and put on *Order of the Phoenix* because I like the way Ron looks longingly at Hermione by the fireplace. I consider whether or not I would like the boy from film and gym class to look at me that way and decide that I would definitely be very okay with that.

If he doesn't completely hate me at this point.

Dmitri

Reggie Reynolds is a total badass. Short spiky hair; dog chain collar; sleeveless shirts with things like "The Sex Pistols" or "The Dead Boys" on them; and chiseled biceps that make me, as a drummer, kind of jealous. And the best part is Reggie's a girl.

We've known each other since preschool, and even then she was all attitude. My first memory of Reggie was the day I created a skyscraper out of cardboard bricks. I was admiring my architectural masterpiece when this girl with a mop of black curly hair came screaming toward me on a tricycle. I leapt out of the way just before she crashed into my building, scattering the blocks everywhere. She skidded to a stop—I'm not kidding, she actually drifted the trike—and looked me dead in the eye.

"Sorry," she said, "but your little wall was in my way." What four-year-old talks like that?

I was not the kind of kid to take things personally (I'm still not), so I laughed. Reggie was so put off her game she was frozen. Her little trick was supposed to make me cry, but that's not me. After a long pause she laughed, too, and we've been friends ever since.

Reggie does gymnastics, and like those gymnasts you see on TV during the Olympics, her body is freakishly strong. She's barely five feet tall, and her neck and shoulders are a knot of pure muscle. So are her thighs. From what she tells me—and I believe her—the other gymnasts are afraid of her. "I like the tumbles, jumps, and spins, and it makes me strong. All the other little Debbies like the sequined bodysuits. Sometimes I hide their hair scrunchies just for fun. If I wasn't so good, I think the coach would kick me off the team."

Reggie comes to a lot of our gigs, and we eat lunch together sometimes, but it's not like *that*. I have no idea if Reggie is straight or gay. She has the sharpest tongue of anyone I know, and, the thing that matters today, she always seems to be up on everyone else's business.

REGGIE: Eliana?

ME: Yeah. She's in our grade. We take film class together.

REGGIE: Wait, is this girl the reason you tried to kill the whole gym class?

I'm lying on my stomach on the bed in my room, my phone in my hand, my laptop open in front of me. Reggie can't see me, but I roll my eyes anyway.

ME: Do you know her?

REGGIE: Dude. The whole school was talking about that. Seriously. What did you do, try to kiss her and there was a brawl?

ME: ☹ No. I was just looking at her. So do you know her?

REGGIE: Course I do.

Good old Reggie. She never disappoints.

ME: And?

Reggie waits a long enough time before answering that I wonder if she had to leave.

REGGIE: Since when do you like girls anyway?

ME: Since always? I mean, I don't have time to date, but I'm not gay.

REGGIE: You sure?

I know she's just messing with me.

ME: Reg . . .

REGGIE: All right, all right. What do you want to know for anyway?

ME: I just do! Are you going to help me or not?

REGGIE: Relax, lover boy. I'm just tugging your chain. Eliana Hoffman. She has like a hundred brothers and sisters and her dad used to own the video store in the strip mall by the post office. It went out of business about five years after the world started streaming. I guess some people just don't see the writing on the wall.

ME: Doesn't your uncle own a bookstore?

I don't get to tweak Reggie often, so I take advantage when I do.

REGGIE: Shut your face, Digrindakis. Books are different.

ME: So what else? What's Eliana into?

REGGIE: idk . . . She doesn't talk to a whole lot of people. Really, she seems like a grade-A nobody. Can't you find a girl with a little more spunk?

ME: Who says I'm trying to find a girl at all.

REGGIE: Hmm.

ME: Anything else?

REGGIE: There is one thing. She hangs out with this girl named Janina.

ME: The really tall girl? I think she's in our European Studies class.

REGGIE: If you mean the Amazonian nerd who wastes her time at beauty school and has really big tits, yeah, that's her.

Reggie knows I hate it when she talks like that. I guess at the end of the day, I'm kind of a prude. I need to get over that if I'm going to be a rock star.

REGGIE: Maybe she can help you. Hey, I gotta run. I'm playing Destiny in five and my squad has a massive raid planned. Good luck, Romeo.

And Reg is gone. She does that, sort of blinks in and out of the frame. Hey! That's a film metaphor! I'll have to use that in Mr. Tannis's class.

Anyway, maybe I'll talk to Janina tomorrow. Thankfully European Studies is before film class, which means I can be ready for Eliana. I have no idea what to say, so we'll see if I even take that step.

I close the laptop, put on my earbuds, tell Siri to play Titus Andronicus, and drift off to sleep thinking about Eliana as "To Old Friends and New" wafts into my brain.

Eliana

Some mornings I want to pretend my closet is a TARDIS and fly into outer space.

It starts around five thirty A.M., when the pipes squeak on for my mom's prework shower. After that, Samara destroys any hope that I will fall back asleep by turning on the outer bedroom light in order to get ready for swim practice. I used to stuff dirty clothes underneath the door crack, but somehow her putting on a bathing suit also requires her crashing into my closet door multiple times until she has sufficiently shimmied the skintight nylon over her body. I envy the ease with which she walks practically naked in public every day. Not that I want to be naked in public, but you get to a point when being in a bathing suit is a whole *thing* instead of just the outfit you wear in the water. I feel the same way about gymnasts and leotards. Maybe when you've participated in a sport since childhood, it doesn't faze you to wear so little in front of so many eyes. The only sport I've ever played professionally (and by professionally, I mean for three meets my freshman year) was badminton. I loved the slow-motion action of the game. I sometimes won. That's when my friends were still my friends, and we joined stuff together. I still don't understand how they justify to themselves that we aren't friends anymore. It's like they blamed me for my chemical makeup. It's not my fault things affect me the way they do. At least that's what my mom tells me. And if meds make me better, isn't that akin to a disease, like diabetes or high blood pressure? No one breaks up with their friends because of diabetes.

Friggin' depression.

Mornings and nights hit me the worst. At bedtime, it's dark and my brain turns on me. Mornings are rough because that's when you remember the things that made the day before difficult. You wake up, and there's a feeling: Something sucks. Maybe something is going to happen, and you have that sensation in your gut because that's how things always go. Or maybe something already happened, and sleep erased it for those eight hours or so. Then you wake up, feel okay for five seconds, until it hits you: Things *already* suck. Today I feel like that. My stomach gurgles with unease as I remember the pileup from gym class and my wussy exit. I know I have to say something in film class because if I don't, then I'm an even bigger wuss. I am not a fan of confrontation, but I also would rather confront my demons than let them fester.

Which leads me to think of Uncle Fester from *The Addams Family*, his bald head and buggy eyes, and I get all wigged out and eject myself from bed at rapid speed. I slam open my closet door, knocking over my sister, on one leg during her swimsuit routine, and she crashes to the floor.

Is this my new thing?

"Christ on a cracker!" Samara yells. Samara enjoys swearing like a seventy-five-year-old churchgoing granny.

"Sorry, dude. Have to pee," I blabber my apology as I beeline into the bathroom. It wasn't a lie. Who doesn't have to pee first thing in the morning? And if she didn't want me awake, she shouldn't have pounded into my door in the first place.

Mornings.

In the kitchen I pour Alpha-Bits and some blueberries into bowls for me and my two youngest siblings. It's the only sugary cereal my mom deems acceptable because of the possibility of learning something from the letters outweighing the sugar content. It's fast and easy, and it tastes only slightly sweeter than wood chips. I barely notice as I hoover it into my mouth and fret over having to make it through periods one and two before I can save myself from internal combustion upon entering film class during period three. My brain whirs as I go through the motions of morning routine: brush my teeth, tell my sibs fifteen times to brush *their* teeth, ensure my sibs have their lunch money, double-check my backpack for my schoolwork, get the sibs on the bus, walk to school.

On my way into the school building, I run into Daisy King. Daisy was my closest friend in second through fourth grade and part of the pack of girls I ran with in middle school. She was also the first of the friends to break it off with me after my shitshow that was the middle of freshman year. It's amazing how three weeks in a mental hospital can make such a difference in a friendship.

It's always a battle: Do I stare her down so she acknowledges what a buttress she was? Or do I walk past as though she does not exist to me anymore? She makes it easy by awkwardly (and obviously) pretending she has an important matter on her phone to attend to. Predictable.

After dropping off my bag at my locker, I meet Janina in our spot in the foyer near the vending machines. It isn't technically *our* spot, since half the school buys their breakfast with coins, but it has been one of the nice consistencies in my life since I started high school. Janina eats a bag of peanut M&Ms every day for breakfast. I don't know if my stomach could handle that, but she swears the peanuts are healthy. She is a goddess, so who am I to question her choice? Today she sports new purple highlights.

"I like your hair," I tell her, as she rips the candy bag open with her teeth and drinks in the contents.

"Thanks," she spits with a mouthful of chocolate mess. "It was supposed to be red."

"Purple looks good." Everything looks good on Janina.

"You want me to do it to your hair?" she asks. "I could use the practice."

"Maybe. Do you think it would look okay on me?" Color in my hair feels a bit too much like I'm trying to draw attention to myself, which I am not. Maybe she should make me go gray so everyone thinks I'm a little old lady and no one trips over themselves looking after me.

Janina and I sit down on a bench, waiting out the final moments before the first bell rings. She plays with strands of my hair, muttering colors and numbers and formulas. I bask in the sensation of someone touching my hair. I love the feeling. Even when I was a kid and the school nurse had to do a lice check because two of my siblings had the bugs (I escaped bug-free, thank you very much), I recall the tingling it caused all over my body. Then a kid walked into the nurse's office and puked four feet away from me, and that basically killed the moment.

"I'm going to apologize to that guy today," I mumble dreamily with closed eyes.

"From gym class?"

"And film," I note.

"Do you really have anything to apologize for? Aside from using your telekinesis to make him trip."

"Shut up! We still don't know that that *didn't* happen."

"Uh, yeah we do. Because we're not in a Stephen King novel."

"Feels like it sometimes, though, doesn't it?" I say, as I watch two freshman guys ogle Janina as she plays with my hair. She drops the strands and gives them the finger.

The bell rings, and we go our separate ways. I spend the next two periods having fake conversations in my head.

Me: *I'm sorry I made you trip. It's not easy being this beautiful.*

Him: *I couldn't take my eyes off you. Broken bones would be worth it.*

[Mood lighting and romantic music fill the gym. Making out ensues.]

I let a snicker slip from my mouth and have to cover it with a fake cough. I hope no one notices I'm blushing.

By the time I get to film class, I'm a wreck of nerves and clammy palms. The second I sit down, I know I need to use the bathroom or I will be shifting uncomfortably in my seat for the next forty minutes. Timed perfectly, in walks the boy. "Dmitri!" calls Ethan, a guy I know and dislike because of his constant mumbling class commentary, and I realize he's talking to the guy who sits next to me. Dmitri. I didn't hear that correctly when he first spoke to me.

Or maybe I was trying too hard not to listen. I actually thought he might have said "RiRi." I'm glad he said "Dmitri." It's a cool name.

The bell rings, and Mr. Tannis is talking before Dmitri gets to his seat. Turns out we have a pop quiz, and I have to pee really bad. This is not a pleasant combination. Plus, I can't very well apologize to Dmitri if we're taking a quiz because then Mr. Tannis will think I'm cheating. I painfully make my way through the basic questions about *North by Northwest*, strutting my film prowess a little bit just so Tannis knows who he's dealing with. I scribble essay answers at breakneck speed, leaving Tannis to decipher my illegible answers because the content of my bladder is about to make its way onto the floor.

Dmitri and I noticeably finish at the exact same time, evident by how he follows me up to Mr. Tannis's desk to turn in his paper. We make eye contact, and I want to talk to him, to apologize and smile, but if I don't get to the ladies' room this second I'll be apologizing for ruining his shoes. "Can I go to the bathroom?" I blurt out to Mr. Tannis, just as Dmitri offers me the cutest smile. Mr. Tannis nods, and I dash out of the classroom and down the hall.

Smooth moves, Hoffman. I'm sure Dmitri thinks you're a complete and total toolbox at this point.

Dmitri

I watch Eliana leave the classroom, turn to Mr. Tannis, and say, "Oh, yeah, I have to go, too." Like I'd forgotten and seeing someone else go to the bathroom reminds me. He cocks an eyebrow and kind of smirks as he hands me a hall pass.

My palms start to sweat as I walk down the hall. Eliana has enough of a head start that I can't see her.

I was able to corner her friend Janina last period, and I'm replaying that conversation in my head now. I went right up to her—damn, she really is tall, and her chest really is . . . also tall—and stuck out my hand.

"Hi, I'm Dmitri." For some reason her eyes went wide like something was wrong. Instinctively I checked my fly, but it was zipped. Over her shoulder—okay, actually, around her shoulder—Reggie was just taking her seat. She looked at me and used two cupped hands to make the universal sign for boobs. All the blood in my body must have rushed to my cheeks because I felt like I had a fever.

After a beat that was way too long, Janina took my hand and shook it. The girl has got a grip. "I'm Janina," she said.

"I know. I was hoping I could talk to you about Eliana Hoffman.

You're friends with her, right?" If I thought her eyes had gone wide before, I was wrong. Now they were like dinner plates.

The teacher, Ms. Sullivan, entered. She's the kind of educator who is overzealous about the subject she teaches, and who seems to really hate children. She's the same height as Reggie—which is to say, short—and always wears something pink. It could be a sweater, a dress, a pair of pants, a bow in her hair, it doesn't matter. Every day, something pink. I guess it's her thing. "Your attention, please," she said, and we all took our seats.

I usually sit on the other side of the room, next to Reggie, but today I dropped in the seat next to Janina. "So, hey," I whispered, "does Eliana have a boyfriend?" Shyness has never been a problem for me.

Janina shook her head. "No, but she needs one." Her voice underlined the word "needs," and her formerly wide eyes narrowed and bored a hole right through my brain, like she was trying to tell me something. *Wait*, I thought, *does Janina want to help me?* Fracking. Awesome.

"What does she like? What's she into?"

"Movies." *Perfect!* I thought. Janina paused. "And Harry Potter." *Boom!* Two for two. I love Harry Potter.

"Do you think you could put—"

"Mr. Digrindakis," Ms. Sullivan said, "why don't you take your regular seat." She nodded toward the corner in which I usually camped out, and it was not a question. Reggie covered her mouth to stop from laughing out loud. I had no choice but to gather my things and move across the room, but the intel I gleaned from Janina was enough for me to work with.

So here I am, one period later, sweaty palms and all, standing in front of the door to the girls' bathroom.

The message in every movie about a boy trying to get a girl— every single one—is to do the crazy thing. Steal the microphone from the PA system and dance on the bleachers while you sing a song to your soccer-playing true love on the field below; set up a brothel in your parents' house while they're out of town to win the affection of the prostitute with a heart of gold; stand outside the girl's house with a comically large radio over your head— while inexplicably wearing a *Matrix* coat—playing a meaningful song. The message is always the same: Take the chance, go for it.

That all makes a crap-ton of sense when I'm standing *outside* the door to the girls' bathroom. It makes a lot less sense once I'm inside, because somehow, without me knowing and without me thinking about it, I have stepped inside.

My first thought is *Where are all the urinals?* I mean, I know girls can't pee standing up, but after a lifetime of seeing public restrooms with urinals, it's jarring to have them suddenly disappear. It occurs to me that, really, guys don't *need* urinals. I'm just as happy to pee in a toilet. And since all the stalls have doors, it doesn't really matter that I'm in the girls' bathroom, does it? The part with the sinks is kind of like a waiting room. It's not like I'm going to see anything I'm not supposed to see. Isn't the trend in the world toward gender-neutral bathrooms anyway? The point is, it's totally okay I'm in here.

Totally.

Isn't it?

What is it about this girl? Is she even that pretty? Actually, yes. But I'm not that shallow, am I? It can't just be about looks. It must be whatever those things are that animals give off—homophones? pherodrones?—that make them attracted to each other. We learned about them in biology class, but I was writing lyrics in my notebook so I don't really remember the lesson. The point is, there is something larger at work here. Maybe Yia Yia cast some ancient Greek love spell on me. I wouldn't put it past her.

Well, too late for second-guessing now. Here goes nothing.

"Eliana?"

Eliana

I have to pee. I have to pee. I have to pee. This is all I can think as I scuttle to the girls' room. I slam open a stall door and can't get my pants down fast enough for my relief. A sink turns on, and I realize I'm not alone but appreciate the tinkle-masking spray from the water. Everybody pees, but I still would rather someone else not hear it. I'm not alone in this. I once read an advice column in a teen magazine where someone wrote in asking what they could do to make the sound of their pee less loud when they were in public bathrooms. The advice-giver, after mocking them mercilessly for caring so much about what others thought of the sound of their urine, suggested if they really couldn't handle the pee-dropping that they throw some extra toilet paper into the toilet before going. The advice-giver had to add in a dash of extra dig by telling the reader that this would be a waste of paper and destroy billions of trees per year just so no one could hear them peeing. I am still iffy on the matter and am glad when the hand-washer exits the bathroom through the whiny door.

I'm still midstream when the door squeals open again. But instead of slamming closed, a voice from the doorway bounces off the cinder-block walls. "Eliana?"

It's a dude.

I stop my pee. At this rate, I may be peeing into the new year. Maybe he didn't hear me. Maybe if I hold my pee long enough, he'll go away. And I'll have to go on antibiotics for a urinary tract infection.

Oh, please, just go away.

"Eliana?"

I think it's Dmitri. Calling my name into the girls' bathroom. This is not ideal.

I'm not going to make it much longer, so in order to move this highly awkward situation along, I answer, "Yes?"

"It's me. Dmitri. From film class?"

And PE, I think.

"Yeah?" *So awkward. So awkward.*

"Can I talk to you?" he asks from the doorway.

My screaming bladder makes me sound a lot less patient than I'd like to, and I blurt out, "In a minute, okay? Outside the bathroom?"

"Oh yeah. Sure. Sure. I'll just wait out here." And the door squeals closed again.

I breathe out heavily and finish the task at hand, flush, then wash my hands at the sink. I look at myself in the mirror. Why did I wear this t-shirt today? It's old, and the collar is worn away at parts, but it's so soft I can't help but wear it whenever it's clean. My navy hoodie from eighth grade could probably be culled from my clothing collection, too. The sleeves barely reach my wrists. But again, soft. It's like my clothes are giving me a snuggle. That's how other people choose their outfits, right? At least my hair looks good. I have Janina to thank for that. I remind myself to knit her a scarf. When I learn to knit.

I'm totally stalling. And I'm in a bathroom. Is that why they call it "stalling"?

If I don't go out into the hall soon, Dmitri will think I'm pooping in the middle of the day at school. For some reason, that's mortifying. Does he not poo? But I wasn't pooping!

Just go outside, Eliana.

I pull back the door handle using a paper towel like my mom taught me, and creep out into the hallway. School hallways during classes are so desolate. I wonder if this is what a film set is like: real location but with a surreal feeling.

Dmitri leans against a locker, thumbs on his phone, and looks up as the bathroom door slams. This is the first time I get a good look at him because I'm supposed to be looking at him. His eyes appear almost black, and I guess he's one of those guys who had to start shaving in sixth grade. I wonder if boys look at that as a good thing or an annoying thing, like getting armpit hair for girls. I'd considered not shaving mine, but I hate the peppery look of it in my armpits. Not that his face looks like my armpits. Unless my armpits are supercute and have a really strong nose. What? Armpits with a nose? I hope the conversation outside of my head goes a lot better than the one inside.

"Heeeyyyy," he drawls, and I catch him doing a quick once-over of me. Does he notice the holes in my t-shirt? The too-small hoodie? The gym shoes that are built mostly out of gummy bear duct tape?

"Hey?" I give Dmitri my "really?" single eyebrow. "You followed me into the bathroom."

"Oh . . . um . . . er."

"You know I could have you arrested. Or expelled." I don't know why I emphasized "expelled" second, like that's worse than being arrested. This boy has me all twisted up. Why am I being so mean again? Oh yeah. Because he walked in on me in the bathroom. "It's just not cool to come into the girls' bathroom."

He stammers through an explanation about boys doing crazy things to get girls' attention in movies, which naturally makes my ears perk. "What did you want, Dmitri?" I catch a little glow at the sound of his name.

For a second I think he might pass out or cry or maybe even drop to one knee and propose, but then he takes a breath and regroups. "I wanted to talk to you, and we never seem to get a chance in class."

"What did you want to talk about?" I ask, hoping I don't sound too defensive. I'm a little afraid he's going to give me shit for making him fall in gym class. Then I remember, I kind of made a guy fall in gym class, and I stand a little straighter. Which makes my hoodie seem extra small.

"This might seem a little forward . . ." Dmitri eyes his phone again, and I wonder if he has a planned speech typed in there. "Do you want to go to the football game with me this weekend?" He looks at me with his dark eyes, such direct eye contact, and I am completely taken aback. The scrunch in my forehead must be the giveaway because he continues, "It's supposed to be a big game, and I thought maybe you'd want to go together."

The only thing I like less than the idea of going to a high school football game is the idea of going to a high school hockey game. Losing a tooth is terrifying. Not that I would know what either game is actually like, seeing as I've never actually watched a sports game in my life.

My natural pause encourages Dmitri to continue selling, "So whaddya think? It'll be a lot of fun. I promise. We can totally make fun of other people."

That gets me.

"Sure," I blurt out. "I'll go. When is it?"

"Oh yeah, I didn't tell you that. It's this Friday. I understand if it's too short notice."

Yeah, I had planned on watching the last Harry Potter films and rereading the final book all weekend, but, "No, it's good. I'm free. It sounds fun." I nod and smile. He half smiles, then busts out into full beam. Which then makes me smile more. We must look like a couple of smiling dorks in the hall when the bell rings and billions of people stream from blown-open doorways. The din of the students makes it difficult to hear, but I'm pretty sure Dmitri asks me to put my number into his phone when he hands it over. I see he has already started a contact page for me, spelling my name with two Ls. I correct the spelling and type in my number. When I hand the phone back to him, our hands briefly touch. It's so stupid, but I feel myself blush like I'm living in Victorian times.

Dmitri shoves his phone in his front pocket and runs off, yelling down the hall to me, "Friday!" I watch as he crashes into a large senior, spins, and sprints away.

I'm in a daze when I shove my books into my locker. This is kind of a date. To a football game, no less. A twinge of panic hits me. Do I let him know I loathe football?

Dmitri

When Nicky and I were little, we discovered this old Claymation Christmas special on TV called *Rudolph the Red-Nosed Reindeer*. It's the sort of thing I imagine American parents share with their kids in an "I loved this when I was your age" kind of way. Not my parents. They'd never heard of Rudolph, and when Nicky and I made my dad watch, he was thoroughly confused. "What is with this reindeer's nose?" he asked, peering over the top of his glasses. Anyway, there's a scene where Rudolph asks if he can walk the little reindeer doe—reindoe?—home and she says yes. Rudolph is so excited he flies through the air screaming "She said yes, she said yes!" That's exactly how I feel as I run down the hall after getting Eliana's phone number. She said yes!

Of course, the scene where the doe says yes is also the scene where Rudolph's fake nose falls off, revealing his shiny red honker, and his entire life goes in the crapper. I manage to ignore that part.

I'm on cloud nine for the rest of the day. Every lesson from every teacher is brilliant, every joke told by every kid in the hallway is hilarious. I have literally never been this happy. Not even at band practice.

Eliana and I see each other across the gym during PE, and we exchange a knowing smile. This day is a grand slam home run. The only weird moment comes at my locker between sixth and seventh periods.

"So you're taking Ms. Wallpaper to the football game, huh?" Damn. Reggie does really know everything that goes on in this school. "You don't even like football."

Reg wears ripped jeans, a Ramones shirt, a black leather choker, and, in what I can only guess to be a show of irony or sarcasm or whatever, a shiny silver tiara with sparkly diamond things in her hair.

"Nice hat," I say, nodding at her head. She ignores the comment.

"Did you really go into the girls' bathroom?"

"How can you possibly know—"

"Super creepy, Digrindakis. You can get arrested for that shit."

"That's what Eliana said."

"Maybe she's not as dumb as I thought." There's a pregnant pause before Reggie adds, "You sure you know what you're doing, Digrindakis? You can do better than this girl, you know."

"I have no idea what I'm doing, and I don't want to do better." Reggie always makes me get my words twisted around.

"Oh, young Jedi, what to do with you."

"'Young Jedi'? I'm like four months older than you."

"Just be careful. I have a bad feeling about this."

"Two *Star Wars* references in one conversation?" I ask, recognizing the quote.

"Not *Star Wars*. Your life." Reggie pivots on her heel and leaves.

Somehow, she seems pissed at me. It's the only blemish on an otherwise perfect day, so I let it go.

The next morning, when I see Eliana in film class, I have a small panic attack because the aura she's projecting is like the previous day never happened. She shushes me three times when I try to talk to her, and ignores the notes I pass. I'm getting set to drop a pretty potent protest at her feet when the bell rings, but before I can open my mouth, she lays a hand on my forearm.

"Can we save the talking for Friday night? I don't like to get in trouble." She smiles at me and leaves the room.

The date is still on. Phew! That's all I need to know.

Eliana

Every Thursday I have therapy, thanks to a deal I struck with my parents after the hospital. My therapist is a Jewish woman in her forties. Thirties? I have no idea how to tell the age of adults. She wears high heels and stockings, so she is officially a grown-up. Her brown hair is blow-dried straight, something Janina taught me to spot by the nature of the frizz and something about how the ends of naturally straight hair still have a little "tweak" to them, as she says. I can also tell it's not natural because some days, usually when it's cold outside, she comes in with an unwashed ponytail, and the halo around her forehead is screaming to release its natural tethered curl. These are the things I focus on when I have to look at a person for hours of my life.

My therapist's name is Sheila Grossman, but I've never spoken it aloud to her. It's written on my calendar but I've never been in a situation where I felt compelled to look her square in the eye and frankly begin a sentence with her name. I don't know if she has ever used my name in a sentence, either, so we're even. Except for the financial piece. She doesn't pay me hundreds of dollars a month to regale her with stories of my depressing life.

Well, mostly depressing.

Today I'm not really in the mood to talk to Sheila. I feel like it's a waste of my parents' money to pay to talk to someone if I'm in a good mood. I can talk to Janina for free.

I take the city bus to Sheila's office, since I would never make the four-mile hike in time. The one day I did walk the distance, I was berated by Sheila for using walking as an escape mechanism (I was forty-five minutes late). That seemed ridiculous to me, seeing as we're always being told how beneficial exercise is for us and how lazy my generation is. But apparently, good old-fashioned walking just makes me weird. I'll add it to the list.

It was this observation that made me first question if Sheila really gets me, but she always has hard butterscotch candies in a dish in her office and I freaking love those. And it's mostly better than being home in my tiny closet bedroom. Mostly. I essentially do it because it makes my mom worry less about me backsliding into a deep depression and needing hospitalization again.

Sheila crosses her legs and takes out her laptop. She types the entire time I'm speaking, and I want, just once, for her phone to ring in the middle of one of our sessions so I can wrench open her laptop and catch her in the act of sending emails to a secret lover. Or playing solitaire. Or ordering pantyhose. Why can't she just listen to me? Why does she have to type everything I say? She can't possibly do both. And now there's this record on her computer of everything that she thinks I say as she types. As though that couldn't be used against me someday. Not that I'm running for president or anything, but you never know. People are overly harsh on female candidates.

Her typing, in addition to her attitude toward walking and pantyhose, is why I barely tell her anything real. Sometimes I even make stuff up. Sheila still thinks I hang out with Daisy King.

If I told her the truth, that Daisy thought I was too complicated to have as a friend and most of our other friends followed suit, then we'd have to look deeply into why and examine things and *snoooooozzzzzeee*. So I try to keep it light and impersonal, or I talk about my parents, which therapists love to hear. Yes, Sheila, I know it is not my fault that my dad has no job and my mom keeps the family afloat and I have to be more responsible for too many siblings than I'd like to. I appease her with the look of revelation, as though what she said is meaningful and powerful and has changed the course of my existence. Therapists love that look.

So why is it that I am so compelled today to tell her something real? To talk about Dmitri?

I sink into the too-soft couch across from Sheila in her black leather chair. Her laptop screen sets her silky smile alight in blue, and she begins our session in the same way she always does: "So how are things?"

Normally I answer with a standard "Fine," and we sit for several minutes in silence while she types grand sentences about how we are sitting in silence. Today, and I immediately kick myself for doing so, I say, "Good, I think. I'm going to a football game with a boy from my school."

She types. I hate her. "Is this a date?" she asks.

"I wouldn't call it a date. We barely know each other. It's more of a social get-together with a bunch of other kids. Plus football."

Sheila goes into a long lesson in boys and dating, which I immediately tune out in order to have a conversation with myself. Would it be too obvious if I put my earbuds in? I nod a lot, "Mm-hmm" a bit, and hope she doesn't realize I have blocked her out completely. I'm too busy thinking about what is actually going to happen when Dmitri and I have hours of time together in a sporty place. Will it be fun? Romantic? Will we bond over women's professional wrestling? I'm kind of excited about the whole thing. Which makes me smile, which makes Sheila smile, and I gather I've responded in a way that satisfies her for this session.

"Next week?" she offers, as I hand her the check my mom gave me for the appointment.

"Yep. Same Bat time. Same Bat channel," I say.

"Bat?" she asks, and I groan inwardly that she doesn't get the basic Batman reference.

On the bus, earbuds in, I envision me and Dmitri on the bleachers, wind blowing through our hair, the sun setting dramatically behind us. Then a football soars through the air and breaks my nose. Or I try to casually stand and cheer for the home team, and I accidentally forward roll down the bleachers. Or learn Dmitri just asked me out as a friend.

It's possible that this is the Jewish side of me, the part who repeats (but never says aloud because I'm not ninety-three years old) "keinehora," a Yiddish expression used to ward off bad luck. It feels greedy to think that I only deserve good things, so I automatically assume something bad has to follow anything good. Yin and yang. Which is totally not Jewish. I've found, in my vast fifteen years of life experience, that bad stuff always follows the good stuff. Always. Period. End of discussion.

It's the when and the how that keeps me guessing.

Dmitri

"*D*oes anyone know anything about football?" The panic in my voice is a living, breathing thing. I've ridden the high of Eliana saying yes to our date all the way to Friday morning, without actually stopping to think how the date will go. I woke up realizing I know absolutely nothing about football. What if she's an expert? I'm going to look like an idiot.

My mother is doing her whirling-dervish thing through the kitchen; my father sits at the table looking like an antique statue of a twentieth-century man, reading an actual paper edition of the *Star Tribune*; Nicky munches on cereal while reading a different book from last time, the cover of this one sporting a handgun in a colorful crocheted knit thing set against a black background; and Yia Yia leans against the door frame, sipping the mud she calls coffee. They must sense my anxiety, because they all stop and look at me.

"Όχι." *No*, my mother says.

"Now you want play football?" My father is confused. "You music already take too much time. You need focus on schoolwork."

"I don't want to *play*," I answer. "I just want to know something about it."

"Why?" Nicky looks up over the top of his book.

"I'm going to the game tonight."

"The Vikings?"

"What? No! The high school game."

This piece of information makes Nicky cock one eyebrow—damn, I wish I could do that. "Why?" he asks again.

And there it is. Do I tell them I have a date? It's the only plausible explanation for wanting to see the Mondale Cropdusters play the . . . the . . . crap! I don't even know who we're playing! Anyway, I don't think I'm ready to open the "Dmitri has a date" can of worms yet, so I lie. "Some friends are going and they invited me."

Nicky holds my gaze for an extra second before going back to his book, as if he's already figured out my secret. Sometimes it's like having Yoda for a brother.

"Refrigerator Perry," Yia Yia says. We all turn our attention to her, waiting for more. She doesn't disappoint. "Super Bowl Shuffle," she says, and then she does this strange little dance.

What.

The.

Hell.

I want to go back to bed.

I open my mouth to say something, but nothing good is going to come out, so I shake my head and say, "Never mind, I'll Google it."

It's not like I've never watched football before, I've just never paid attention. The Wikipedia entry—which I try to decipher on the way to school—confirms what I already know: Football is a ridiculous and confusing game.

I'll just have to make sure Eliana and I are so deep in conversation about movies and Harry Potter that we don't even notice the action in the field.

Not much of a plan, I know, but it's all I've got.

I smell my pits as I enter the building for first period; I hope I used enough Axe body spray.

Eliana

"*It's* cool, Mom, you don't have to drive me." I shove my feet into my Converse, wondering if I should be wearing some kind of furry boot matching my school's hideous green-and-gold color combination instead. I have zero knowledge on what to wear to a football game, and even less about what actually happens during the game. Based on commercials, I assume there will be something to do with giant foam fingers and scoop-shaped chips. Also, shirtless dudes with paint on their stomachs.

None of these facts are making me want to go to this game. What if Dmitri is a massive sports enthusiast, and we have nothing to talk about? What if he takes his shirt off midgame to reveal his green-and-gold tribute art? What if everyone we are meeting secretly knows that I am a football virgin, and they pour pig's blood on my head from above?

If only I had Carrie's telekinesis.

Envisioning myself destroying the football field with my brain powers isn't getting me out the door any faster.

My mom approaches me with my Hufflepuff scarf in hand. "You should probably bring this. It gets cold sitting still for hours."

I take the scarf and wrap it around my neck several times. "Like, how many hours are we talking?" I ask.

"No idea. I've never been to a football game, either. The good thing about a high school football game versus a professional one is that the stands won't be filled with drunk idiots. At least I hope not. Call me if they are, and I will come get you."

A text from Dmitri told me to meet him outside the game entrance on the home side of the field. The only times I've been near these grounds were on the infrequent occasions when a gym teacher wanted us to run laps outside. Not a common occurrence in Minneapolis.

It feels wrong to be here, like everyone knows I'm a sports imposter. Or worse, like I'm entering the Hunger Games. I would suck as a tribute. I would absolutely, no question, be the first kid killed. Maybe even eaten. I have no discernible skills except for walking quickly, watching mass quantities of movies, and getting good grades. What will good grades get me when I'm attempting to outwalk a kid who's been trained to poison me with a blow dart?

"Hey!" Dmitri greets me from behind, and I jump. I hope he doesn't have any darts. I turn around quickly and lightly shove him.

"You scared me!" I say. He looks shocked.

"I did not expect you to be that strong." He rubs the spot on his chest where I pushed. Maybe I'd do better in the Hunger Games than I thought. Also, does that mean he has already spent time assessing my strength attributes?

"I lift weights the second I get home from school. And when I wake up. I'm actually training for the Olympics," I joke.

"Really?"

"No."

"I'm both relieved and disappointed."

"Then we're off to a great start!" I enthuse.

Surprisingly, Dmitri looks charmed. Maybe there is actually a boy in this world who finds awkward conversation and brute strength appealing.

"Ready to go in?" he asks, and offers up a bent elbow.

I carefully link my arm through his and announce, "We're off to see the wizard!"

"What wizard?" Dmitri looks at me blankly.

"You seriously don't know that reference?" I'm appalled, until he breaks into a huge grin to let me know I've been played.

"You scared me for a minute there," I admit.

"Then I'm two for two." He nods proudly.

"Is that a sports reference?" I ask.

"Why don't we go in and find out?"

Together we skip between rows of bleachers until we hear a chorus of "Dmitri! Up here!" from the top row of seats. I look up and barely manage to contain the "ugh" that escapes my lips. Amid the sports fans I spy with my little eye is one Daisy King, also known as my-ex-friend-who-dumped-me-because-of-my-depression. Ugh again. Dmitri attempts to lead me up the stairs, but I give an involuntary yank on his elbow. "You cool with this?" he asks. "Those are some of my friends. And their friends."

"How well do you know these friends?" I can't help it; the question just flies out of my mouth.

"Like on a scale of one to ten?"

I shrug and Dmitri shrugs back. Then he points to each person in succession, one eye closed for precision, and names them off. When he reaches Daisy he claims, "And that's a blond girl I don't really know. So those are all of the people!"

"All of the people," I repeat. From the looks of it, Daisy is in full-on ignore mode, pretending to be engrossed in whatever is happening on the field. I'll take it. The space left for me and Dmitri is one row down and several seats away from her, so I suppose I can handle it for one game.

We sit down, Dmitri's shoulder close to mine but not quite touching. I try to watch the game, but there is a buzz emanating from Dmitri. Or maybe that's the dry autumn static. Either way, I feel compelled to look at him every few minutes. Most times he's looking back at me and smiling. Is this normal?

"So who are you rooting for?" Dmitri asks.

"I have a choice?"

"Of course. I think we should scream out random names. Like, 'Go, George! Get 'em, Ronaldo!' Stuff like that."

"You don't come because you like football?" I ask.

"Nah. Aggressive sports aren't really my thing. Unless we're talking WWE ..."

"Oh my god! I love WWE! It's like staged, but real at the same time. And they're such crazy-good athletes. Can you imagine standing on a bunch of ropes and throwing yourself off them to land on another person? Sick! In another life, that's totally what I'm going to be."

"So you believe in reincarnation?" Dmitri asks.

"I don't know if I believe in it. I don't quite know what I

believe, actually. I think it's important to imagine there is something else, something good at least, after we die. Not necessarily because that's where we're going to go but because that's where people we love end up. But reincarnation or heaven or hell? I haven't made up my mind yet. What about you?"

"I believe I'd like a hot pretzel."

"Dmitri." My voice is the audible equivalent of an eye roll.

"Okay, okay. My parents are pretty religious. They make me and my brother go to church every week, and I went to Sunday school for ten straight years, so I guess I've been brainwashed."

"So you're a believer?"

"See, that's the thing. I'm not really. I *know* I've been brainwashed, indoctrinated. It's like a cult. And really, when you think about it, the whole bearded-white-guy-in-the-sky thing just seems silly. And if he is real, where's he been for the last two thousand years? I mean, if there was a God, wouldn't football be less stupid?"

That makes me laugh out loud.

"But," he continues, "they got to me young, and drilled their ideas into my brain for a whole lot of years, so while I don't *intellectually* buy it, I sort of *feel* it. Confusing, I know."

"Confusing," I agree.

The audience around us lets out a group "Ohhhh!" and I see a player from the other team writhing on the field in agony.

"You got this, Sampson!" Dmitri yells.

"Sampson?" I ask.

"Poor guy." Dmitri shakes his head sympathetically.

"Poor Sampson," I concur.

"Hey!" a voice calls from above. It's Norm, one of Dmitri's friends. Who still names their kid Norm? "We're going to head to Denny's. You want to come?"

Dmitri looks over at me. I want to say yes. I want to spend more time with him because I'm having a really good time despite, you know, sports. But when I watch Daisy stand up and I catch her eye, there is no friendship there. No kindness. I can't deal with that. I can't pretend it doesn't hurt.

"Off to Denny's, then?" Dmitri puts his arm over my shoulder, which makes what I say next painful.

"I think I'm going to go home."

"What? Why?"

"It's kind of late. I'm really tired. I have to pray for Sampson," I joke.

Dmitri offers a half smile. "You sure? How are you going to get home?" he asks.

"My mom. We live close. It's cool."

"You sure?" he asks again. I can tell he's disappointed. And probably confused. I don't blame him, but I'm not about to tell him why I won't go with the group.

"Yeah. Totally. You go and have fun. Tell me all about your lukewarm coffee and breakfast potatoes when I see you on Monday."

"Okay, I guess. You want me to wait with you until your mom gets here?"

"Nah. I'll sit in the stands until she lets me know she's here."

"That doesn't feel right. How about I sit with you and make everyone else wait to leave for Denny's?"

"Really? I don't know..."

"I insist."

Dmitri walks up the steps to discuss the delay with Norm. He throws out a thumbs-up signal, which makes me shiver the tiniest bit at the chivalry of it all. I text my mom to pick me up, and she replies that she'll be here in five minutes. Two of those minutes are spent waiting for Dmitri to make his way back to me while he discusses things with his friends. I play a Jumble game on my phone until Dmitri slides next to me with a pleasant shoulder bump.

"I'm going to wait by the pickup circle," I tell him.

"I'll come with you!" he enthuses.

Dmitri walks ahead of me down the metal stairs, and I envision myself tripping and rolling down the stairs, into Dmitri, and onto the field. Surprisingly, this does not actually happen. Does this mean I officially don't have telekinesis? If I did have it, why would I use it to throw myself down the stairs? I really hope Dmitri isn't a mind reader.

Can you imagine what dating is like in the X-Men school?

We arrive at the pickup spot, hands in pockets, closed-mouth silly smiles on our faces.

"Thanks for inviting me tonight. Sorry to bail so early. Big group activities aren't usually my scene."

"I get that. Maybe next time we get together it can be more intimate." I look away and blush. "I mean, not like that, but like a smaller group. Or just a group of two?"

"Yeah, that would be good," I agree. My mom pulls up, and I silently curse her for being so prompt. "That's my mom." I nod toward the car.

"Cool. Thanks for coming tonight," he says.

"Thanks for having me," I say, then think to myself how stupid that sounded. *Having me?* Ugh.

With my mom in the car next to us, we both ruminate on how to end the night. I have no idea what to do, and I can tell by Dmitri's furrowed brow that he's not sure what to do, either. I thrust my hand out for a good-night handshake. He laughs, takes my hand, and we shake one, two, three times.

"Good night," I say.

"Good night, Eliana." Even though it's my name that I've had forever, hearing Dmitri say it now gives me goose bumps.

Inside the car, my mom asks, "How did it go? Did you root root root for the home team?"

"I think that's baseball, Mom. And no, I did not. I rooted for Sampson," I say, and laugh to myself.

Dmitri

"S o how was your date?"

Dammit. I don't ask Nicky how he knows I was on a date. I just accept the fact that my brother is in tune with the universe in a way most of us can only aspire to be.

"I'm not sure?" His patented raised eyebrow asks the question for him. "Well, I think we were having a really good time," I continue. "We totally have the same sense of humor, she hooked her arm in mine, we have a similar view of the afterlife—"

"You talked about the afterlife?"

"Yeah, isn't that what people talk about on dates?"

"How would I know?"

I'm reminded Nicky, his wisdom aside, is two years younger than me and has never been on a date in his life. Or at least not that I ever heard about. On the other hand, he's so mysterious that for all I know he has a wife and two kids in Iowa.

"Anyway, it was going good, but then it ended really abruptly."

"How?"

"Some of my friends were going to Denny's and invited us along, but she slammed the door pretty hard."

"Maybe she doesn't like Denny's."

"No one likes Denny's. That's not the point."

"Then what is the point?"

That's actually a good question and I'm not sure I have an answer, but I try anyway. "It kind of felt like she was done hanging out with me. Like she just wanted to go home."

"Did you kiss her good night?"

"We shook hands."

Now Nicky's other eyebrow joins the first, so they're both in an elevated state of . . . what? Surprise? Pity? Comedy? "Did you ask her for another date?"

Damn. Another really good question. Maybe next time I should bring Nicky with me.

"No."

"I think you're supposed to do that."

"Yeah."

We're both silent for a minute. Nicky looks at me expectantly, like he's waiting for me to catch up. And I do. "You think I should ask her now?"

He looks at the clock on the wall. It's ten P.M. Not too late. I nod and pick up my phone, and then stop.

"Where should we go? The movies?"

"The Greek festival is next weekend."

You know the scene in the movie where the protagonist somehow doesn't see the really obvious thing everyone in the audience sees? Like in Percy Jackson, when the entire audience knows that some random person is a demonic creature sent to destroy him, but Percy is just oblivious? That's what it was like with the suggestion of the Greek festival. Not only will Eliana have to meet my family, and not only is it the complete opposite of the quiet two-person date she suggested, it will absolutely shine a spotlight on the overwhelming Greekness of clan Digrindakis; I will be exposed for how weird I am.

But I think of none of that. Instead, I tell Nicky, "Good idea," and start typing my text to Eliana.

Eliana

$\mathcal{I}$'m snuggled under my blankets replaying the football game when I hear my phone buzz. Janina and I already finished a quick debriefing of the evening while I brushed my teeth.

JANINA: How was the game?

ME: Oh, you know, gamey.

JANINA: So you didn't kiss him?

ME: How did you know?

JANINA: No exclamation points.

ME: Ah.

JANINA: Will there be another game?

ME: I don't know. I bailed kind of early. He probably thinks I'm a freak who doesn't even like him.

JANINA: But you do, right?

ME: Yes. Which means I'll probably never hear from him again. Sigh.

JANINA: On that cheerful note, I really have to rinse this bleach off my lip.

ME: Say what?

JANINA: Moustache issues.

ME: Uhhhh . . .

JANINA: Good night!

When I hear another buzz, I roll over and paw for my phone, which always somehow creeps slightly out of arm's length away. The effort of having to roll over, thus unwrapping my burrito-like state, annoys me, and I'm about to curse whoever texted me when I see it's from Dmitri.

I sit up sharply.

DMITRI: Hey! Since football isn't your thing (or mine), I was wondering if you wanted to go to a Greek festival with me next Friday. Rides, food, Greeks . . . and me!

I sit with the text a moment, nearly cuddling the phone. With a burst of energy I type:

> ME: yed

and hit the send button before autocorrect or I manage to fix the spelling.

I scramble to edit and end up sending the exact same wrong word.

> ME: yed

Crap.

> ME: YES

I text. All caps.
After a minute, I receive a reply.

> DMITRI: I am glad that yed, yed, and YES you can come.

> ME: Good night, Dmitri.

It feels brazen to type his name.

> DMITRI: Good night, Eliana.

Dmitri

J'm not really sure how I'm supposed to act when Eliana and I see each other at school on Monday. Are we boyfriend and girlfriend? Are we just friends? We have a second date, so I figure we have to be *something*.

I keep looking over my shoulder as I drop my stuff in my locker, scanning the hallway for Eliana—I don't want to have to wait for film class—but there's no sign of her. I wish our lockers were closer. Damn, I think I really like this girl.

"You shook hands good night?"

Reggie can be ninja-like in creeping up on people. Even with me surveying the hall, I didn't see her coming. It must be all the gymnastics. And the fact that she's under five feet tall.

"How did you know we . . . ," I start to ask, but honestly, I'm not in the mood for Reggie and her ring of information. "Never mind."

"Seriously. That's lame even for you."

"Don't you have someone else to bother?"

"Not at the moment." A smile loaded with mischief plays across Reggie's face, and it makes me soften. This is classic Reg. She'll dig at a person, like she's picking a scab on their arm—too personal, too invasive, and kind of gross. But she does it in a way that is somehow charming and endearing. Although I might be the only person to see it that way. She doesn't have a lot of friends.

"You know you're supposed to *kiss* the girl good night, right? Do I need to teach you everything?"

"Not that it's any of your business, but her mother was right there."

"Yeah, okay, probably a good choice not to kiss then. But a handshake?"

"*She* shook *my* hand." I'm feeling exasperated. "Look, can you just let it go?"

"Whatever, lover boy, whatever." And then Reg, as she is wont to do, wanders off.

A second later there's a tap on my shoulder. I turn around, and for an instant, I think no one's there. Then I see Eliana on the other side of me. The old fake shoulder-tap trick; I cannot believe I fell for that.

"I cannot believe you fell for that," she says.

It doesn't matter. It's Eliana. She's here. She sought me out. I feel like the Grinch when his heart grew three sizes that day.

And she's smiling. Wow . . . that smile.

"That girl is weird," Eliana says, nodding down the hall just as our last view of Reggie is swallowed by the growing mass of students heading for homeroom.

"Don't I know it," I mutter.

"A former girlfriend?" Eliana tries to pass the question off as playful, but doesn't do such a good job of it. This is my first-ever encounter with anything that even remotely smacks of jealousy.

"Huh? Oh god, no. We've just been in school together for like a million years is all." I feel kind of bad for downplaying my relationship with Reggie—she really is one of my best friends—but right now I need to remove any reasons for Eliana not to like me.

"So what does a non-Greek girl wear to a Greek festival?" she asks, noticeably changing the subject.

"Hmmm . . . Well, my grandmother wears nothing but shapeless gray dresses, so maybe that?"

Eliana's eyes dart to the side for a second before landing back on my face. In poker this would be called a tell. She doesn't know I'm kidding. Part of me wants to see if she'll actually find a shapeless gray dress to wear. While that would be a pretty funny prank, I have to believe doing so would be an unforgivable offense.

"I'm kidding," I tell her.

Where she shoved me at the football game (when I startled her), now she punches me. Hard. Really hard.

"Hey!"

"If I had shown up dressed the same as your grandmother, only to find out you were kidding, I probably would have killed you. Just so you know." But she's still smiling.

The bell rings, and on instinct—just like that Russian guy's dog and the dinner bell we learned about in science last year—we turn in opposite directions to head to class.

"Dress like you would for a state fair," I tell her over my shoulder.

"I've never been to a state fair!"

"Oh. Then go with the gray dress."

"Dmitri!" She's laughing now and I grab her arm to stop her.

"What period do you have lunch?" I ask.

"Sixth."

The air goes out of my sails a bit. "Oh, I'm fifth."

"It's okay. I don't eat lunch with people who don't take fashion seriously."

I pause for a second to look Eliana up and down. Faded blue jeans, navy blue sweater with loose threads, Converse that have seen better days. "Really?"

She sees me evaluating her fashion sense and then blushes. "Don't push your luck, buster." And she punches me, again. I rub the spot on my shoulder, which will very likely be sporting a bruise later today. I might have to talk to her about these random acts of violence. "And no, not really. See you in film class."

And with that, she's gone.

Eliana

I wish I could live through a shopping montage. Like in the movies when one person tries on outfit after outfit, and their friends shake their heads no, until the perfect outfit rears its fashionable head and then everyone is all, "That's it! That's the one!"

Instead, Janina is crammed into my room-hole, attempting to coerce me into buying something—anything—online other than a black t-shirt and skinny jeans.

"Look at this sweater. It's pink and fuzzy! Like a pink baby bunny!" Janina rotates the laptop to expose a ridiculous cotton candy explosion of a hoodie.

"Why would anyone want to wear something that looks like a skinned, dyed animal? Plus, pink?"

"You would look nice in pink. And in something without a hole in it."

"Some of us don't have the luxury of buying new clothes all the time," I argue.

"I'm not even saying new. We're thrifty. Hell, you can rifle through my closet. This is a date *plus* parental units. I'm merely looking out so you make a strong first impression." Janina swishes my bangs out of my face.

"Do I really need to woo them with my clothes? It's a festival in fall. We'll be wearing jackets. Why do you care so much about this anyway? You're usually pretty chill about me being my old, surly self."

"You're right. I'm sorry. You just seemed so excited after your football thing—"

"I did?" My face warms.

"You're blushing! See, pink does look good on you!"

I smack Janina on the arm.

"Dude. You may need to tone down the random acts of violence." Janina rubs the spot where I so lightly tapped her.

"But then how will I show Dmitri that I'm dominant?" Janina scrunches her forehead at me. "I kid. Ha. See how light and funny I am? Not a care in the world. Now help me pick the least worn-out shirt to wear to the Greek festival."

I try on six different t-shirt and hoodie combos while Janina checks her phone, managing to give me five thumbs-down and one side-to-side "so-so" hand gesture for the final one.

"We have a winner!" I decide.

Greek festival, here I come. With or without my montage.

Dmitri

My father's view of American culture is frozen somewhere around 1957. That doesn't really make sense, since he was born in 1960 and came here in 1982 to attend graduate school. He should be fascinated with Bon Jovi, DeLoreans, and President Reagan. And while he does put Reagan on a kind of pedestal—we have a framed portrait of Ron and Nancy in our living room—the rest of his worldview is from an older time. Case in point: the Cadillac.

It wouldn't be so bad if Dad had a cool, vintage, convertible Caddy with tail fins. No, we cruise the streets of suburban Minneapolis in a black 2008 Cadillac DTS. It looks like it belongs to a fleet of cars from a limo service that's fallen on hard times. Like you call 1-800-WE-RIDE-U (because who else would still use a 1-800 number) and this is the car they send, complete with a geriatric driver with a white shirt, black vest, and one of those stupid caps. But because it's a *Cadillac*, Dad believes it makes him seem important. Like he's Frank Sinatra.

I hate this car.

When Eliana asked if we could meet at the festival, a wave of relief washed over me. Having her ride with my family, in the

Caddy, would be worse than dental surgery. And dental surgery, in case you didn't know, sucks.

We're in the "land-boat" (Nicky's name for the Cadillac) on the way to the church when I spring the news on my family that I have a date.

"Dimmi-moo!" Yia Yia exclaims. That's something Greek grandmothers do. They add a "moo" syllable to the end of someone's name to show affection; Nicky-moo, Yani-moo . . . you get the idea. It always sounded normal to me—I used to even kind of like it—until friends caught wind and made it a focal point of teasing. There are only so many times you can hear your bandmates call you Dmitri-moo before it starts to get under your skin.

"It's not a big deal, Yia Yia," I say. "She's just a girl from school."

"Who this girl? Does she go our church?" My mother's question underscores a certain kind of prejudice that exists in our community, and that probably exists in other immigrant communities, too. My mom starts with the blind assumption—no, not an assumption, a core belief—that this girl is Greek. It's inconceivable that she could be anything else.

"No, Ma, she doesn't."

"What church she go to, then?" I can hear the confusion as my mother tries to sort out the location of the next closest Greek Orthodox church, and, doing the math, wonders how I could have met a girl from so far away.

"She's not Greek."

Lesson Number One from Dmitri Digrindakis's forthcoming bestseller, *How to Stop a Conversation in a Greek Family Dead in Its Tracks*: Tell them your girlfriend is not Greek.

The only sound is the whine of the DTS's balding tires against the blacktop.

"Then what is she?" my father finally asks. The wariness in his tone suggests he's wondering if I'm dating someone from another species.

"I'm not sure. I think she might be Jewish."

A longer silence, the sound of the wheels somehow louder now.

"Jewish? Like Sammy Davis Jr.?"

I only know who Sammy Davis Jr. is because next to the framed photo of Ron and Nancy is a framed photo of the Rat Pack.

1957.

"Sure, but she's not Black." The collective exhale from my family—well, not Nicky, he's reading a book and doing his best to ignore this exchange—fills the car with stale breath and too much carbon dioxide. I crack a window and do my best not to vomit in shame.

I once tried to have a conversation with my parents about tolerance, about how America is a great melting pot, how people here are just people, how the color of their skin or their religion doesn't matter. (I left gay people off the list, because, you know, Rome wasn't built in a day.) It was right after my father had uttered a racial slur, thankfully in Greek, to describe the young Black woman who had been waiting on our table at Chili's. The girl didn't understand what my father said, but I think she picked up on the tone and I wanted to die. It's true, she wasn't the best waitress, but she just as easily could have been an inept white, or heaven forbid and forgive all that is holy, Greek, waitress. I made that point to my parents, too.

"Of course, Dimmi," my mother said in English. "Of course." But she was just saying that to shut me up.

"Please," I beg now, "if you meet her, don't make a big deal, okay? Just try to be normal."

"What? I am most normal guy you know!" My father's Trump-like protest is left unanswered as he turns our 5,347-pound Cadillac (I looked it up) into the church parking lot.

We're here half an hour before the time Eliana is supposed to arrive. As my parents bark unheard instructions at our backs, Nicky and I take off to scope things out.

The church, Prophet Elias—and now that I think about it, the names Elias and Eliana must come from the same root; I suppose that's kind of cool—hires an outside company to run the festival, which means it has all the trappings of any other carnival or county fair. There are games (shoot the clown in the mouth with a water gun to explode a balloon, throw basketballs into a hoop too physically small to allow the ball to pass through, knock bottles over with cruddy old baseballs), rides (a small roller coaster, bumper cars, and of course, the granddaddy of them all, the Ferris wheel), and food concessions, these provided by the congregation rather than the carnival company. There are gyros (pronounced "year-ohs," not "jie-rohs," oh, ye uninformed), souvlaki, moussaka, and an assortment of Greek desserts, including my favorite, loukoumades, fried dough balls dripping with honey.

I'm checking my phone every twenty seconds to see what time it is, and to see if Eliana has texted to cancel. Reality is moving forward at a glacial pace, but at least there is no text. I should be less nervous for our second date than our first, but the proximity of my family, and the overwhelming Greekness of my surroundings, are kind of freaking me out.

"How do I look?" I ask Nicky. He's wearing jeans that stop two inches above his ankles and a denim jacket with an "Eat Sleep Read" button on it, so maybe he's not the best person to be giving me fashion advice, but he's all I have. I spent an hour trying on every piece of clothing I own, winding up with my favorite gig outfit: black jeans, white Johnny Cash t-shirt, gray sweater with a hood, and black sneakers.

Nicky looks me up and down, is about to say something, then shrugs. "I don't know. Good, I guess?"

"Thanks." I hope he hears the sarcasm in my voice. "You've been helpful."

"How is it going, Digrindakis boys?"

We whirl around and are standing face-to-face with George Parikos; he's Nicky's age, my height, the weight of a sumo wrestler, and sports a heavy five o'clock shadow that probably started rearing its ugly head around one thirty this afternoon. Someday George will win Olympic gold in weight lifting. He moved here with his family five years ago, and we see him every week at church and in Sunday school. He's kind of a cretin.

"Hi, George," I say. "Where's your other half?" I ask, nodding at his "I'm with Stupid" t-shirt.

"Huh?"

"Your shirt. You're supposed to walk next to someone with a shirt that says 'Stupid.'"

"I am? I thought this meant anyone next to me is stupid." He repositions himself next to me and cracks up.

Checking my phone again—T-minus five minutes—I turn to Nicky. "I have to go." He nods and I make my exit with Sumo-George still cackling.

I head for the festival entrance, wallet in hand, ready to pay Eliana's admission. I smell my armpits and breath a few times, and all is good there. The cool fall air is helping keep the flop sweats at bay.

A nice, normal Honda CR-V—it's a burnt orange kind of color—pulls up, the door opens, and out steps my date. My heart does that thing where it jumps to the right in my chest and then immediately back. It hurts, but in the best kind of way.

Eliana is wearing black pants and a gray sweater, too; we look at each other and laugh.

The man driving the car calls out that he's going to pick her up at ten o'clock and starts to say hello to me. I walk toward the car, extending my hand to meet the person I presume to be her father, when Eliana closes the door behind her and walks past me to the entrance, saying, "Let's go" as she does.

I shrug my shoulders and give a small wave to the man in the Honda. He looks at me, smiles—it's the same smile as Eliana's, so this *must* be her dad—and shrugs his shoulders, too, before driving off. I like him.

Eliana grudgingly lets me pay her entrance fee and is given a wristband, and finally we're at the festival together. So far the date is going really well.

Then my parents and grandmother walk up.

"Dmitri!" my father's voice booms, even louder than normal, echoing off one of the festival rides. His smile is so wide, and so clearly fake, I wonder if he's going to need surgery to remove it later.

"Hi, Dad. Mom, Yia Yia, this is Eliana." I don't know if my family or Ellie hear the dread in my voice, though I'm not sure how anyone can miss it.

Eliana is a perfect lady. She extends her hand and steps forward. "Nice to meet you."

My father takes her hand and shakes it so hard I'm worried he's hurting her.

"Nice to meet you, too. You are Jew girl, yes?"

My eyes go wide.

Eliana's eyes go wider.

My grandmother hangs her head and shakes it from side to side.

My mother smacks my father in the arm, making him yelp. "What?" he squawks. She admonishes him in Greek.

"Ah . . . ," he says. "Signomi." That's Greek for excuse me. "I mean to say," he corrects himself loudly and deliberately, "nice to meet you. You are Jewish girl, yes?" He emphasizes the "ish" as if this were his mistake. He and my mother both smile like idiots. I join my grandmother in hanging and shaking my head.

"Yes," I hear Eliana say, as if nothing is wrong. This is followed by a silence I can only describe as awkward.

"Come," Yia Yia says, taking us each by an elbow and leading us away.

"What?" I can hear my father's voice receding in the distance. "What I do?"

When we're a safe distance from my parents, Yia Yia, wearing one of her many gray dresses, stops and turns to face us. "You make nice-looking couple. Here." She presses a twenty-dollar bill into my hand. Yia Yia never gives me money. Until this moment, I wasn't even sure Yia Yia knew what money was. "You go on Ferris wheel and maybe magic happen, eh?" She winks, turns, and is swallowed by the crowd.

"Well," I say, desperate to say something, "that's my family." I pretty much want to die.

"C'mon," Eliana says, catching me by surprise. "We can't disappoint Yia Yia."

I follow her to the Ferris wheel.

Eliana

*D*mitri and I walk side by side toward the Ferris wheel, the bright lights of the midway rides and games creating fluorescent blobs as I blink. I stuff my hands into my hoodie pockets, something I often do while I walk, but then regret it since that would deter Dmitri from trying to hold my hand. Or maybe it's a defense mechanism if Dmitri doesn't actually want to hold my hand. No matter, we're about to ride a Ferris wheel and make magic happen.

She didn't mean have a baby, right?

Bad, old hard-rock music blasts from enormous speakers outside the Rotor, which makes it difficult to attempt talk, small or otherwise, with Dmitri. I catch him looking at me and smile inside. When we reach the Ferris wheel, a sign reads "Two Tickets per Rider."

"I forgot to get tickets," Dmitri acknowledges, not like he made a mistake but more like, whoops, no big deal. And it isn't a big deal, but I'm rather amazed at how he can be so cool about it. I feel like a bumbling fool no matter how insignificant my mistakes may seem to someone else. I start to wonder if it's possible Dmitri is too cool for me. I drop my hand out of my pocket to try to scratch an anxious itch on my elbow, and Dmitri practically rips my hand off grabbing for it.

His face reads something I can only assess as admiration, but that feels too presumptuous. He is holding my hand, however, before I have managed to scratch that itch. Since the itch is on my elbow, I kind of need my other hand to scratch it. But I don't want to let go for fear of Dmitri never holding my hand again. I fix the problem by lifting Dmitri's hand with mine and using both our hands to scratch away the sensation in my elbow. "Sorry," I say.

"Not a problem. Let's go find those tickets." His smile is so warm and adorable. He seems in his element. Then I rack my brain to think of which piece of this could possibly be someone's element. Is it the Greek piece? Is he a carny lover? Is it that his family is nearby, and he feels loved and supported? Or is he a serial dater, and he just knows what he's doing?

"Eye of the Tiger" blares through the air, and Dmitri leans in close so that I can hear him say, "Don't tell anyone, but I kind of love this song."

"It will be our little secret." Did that sound cool? Confident? Creepy? This boy confuses my brain. In a good kind of way.

The ticket booth line is short, and we wait behind a family with at least five children. I almost revert to big-sister mode when two of the kids run between and around us as though we're part of the fun house.

"Cute kids," Dmitri says genuinely.

"Meh." I shrug.

An older woman in a Greek church baseball cap sits inside a windowed box, taking money for tickets. She is the only one in there, a panic-inducing thought for me. What does she do if there's a line and she has to go to the bathroom? Does she go in a bucket? Is there a secret basement room underneath? I kind of have to go to the bathroom now.

Dmitri hands over the twenty-dollar bill from his Yia Yia, and he and the unable-to-pee-when-she-pleases lady exchange some pleasantries in Greek. I assume it's Greek. It's not Hebrew or pig Latin, my other two languages, although my Hebrew has become pretty rusty since I had to memorize my Torah portion for my bat mitzvah. I'll try and brush up on it next time I go to a Jewish carnival. If those exist. I went to Purim carnivals when I was a kid, but those are more throw-a-ping-pong-ball-in-a-goldfish-bowl games than actual midway rides. And we don't really speak Hebrew to each other.

Why does the fact that he can speak a different language make me insecure? My face must show some sense of this, because as we walk away from the ticket booth, Dmitri re-holds my hand and gives it a squeeze. "Twenty dollars buys twenty tickets. Back in my day, you could get four tickets for a quarter!" I think that was a joke. I don't laugh.

"That was stupid. Do you want to put these in your purse?" Dmitri asks me, holding the string of tickets up like a character in a movie brandishing a string of connected condom packets.

I did not just think that.

"I don't carry a purse," I answer, hoping I'm not blushing from the condom thought. "But I can put them in my pocket," I suggest.

"That's okay. I can, too. I just thought maybe you had a purse, but I shouldn't have assumed. That's cool that you don't carry a purse. Girls seem so obsessed with their purses, like they conceal secrets that only you are allowed to know."

"Maybe those girls have their periods, and they just don't want you to find their tampons," I suggest. Periods: always an on-point topic for a date. I quickly change subjects as we walk. "When I was little I went to this summer camp where I didn't have any friends, and we went on a field trip to a carnival. Which, looking back on it now, seems a bit unnecessary when you're already going to summer camp. Anyway, because I didn't have any friends at the camp, I wandered around this carnival all by myself and I came upon a tent with 'Snake Woman' written on the flap. I was terrified of this, imagining a woman with a human head and a snake body. I'm guessing now that it was probably just a woman holding a bunch of snakes, but that's not where my mind went. As scared as I was, I really wanted to peek inside that tent, but I didn't have any money."

Dmitri doesn't reply but grabs my hand once again. Our hands fit together nicely, comfortably, and it's cool enough outside with a slight breeze that I'm not worried about sweaty palms.

Back at the Ferris wheel, Dmitri hands a carny four tickets. The man, in a sleeveless shirt showing off sinewy arms with countless muddied tattoos, holds open the chair's gate. "Ladies first," Dmitri says, as he gestures to the seat. I don't tell him that I find that phrase antiquated and unappealing. Not wanting to hold up the rest of the wheel's riders, I slide into the chair. Dmitri follows, bumping against me, then scooching away to allow for a little space. The Ferris wheel starts with a lurch, and we're off, wind in our hair and the fair bustling below. Both of my hands are on the lock bar, because even though we are traveling at probably five miles per hour, it still feels better to hold on to something. I will never be one of those people who raises my hands above my head on a roller coaster. Has anyone ever lost a limb in that situation?

"So," I say, my words swallowed in a pocket of air we leave behind, "Yia Yia, huh?"

Dmitri chuckles and explains, "She's my mom's mom. She's old-school Greek, but for some reason seems to be much more open-minded than my next-gen parents. She must sense something good about you because she never gives me money."

"Even though I'm a Jew girl?"

"I'm really sorry about that. My dad has foot-in-mouth disease sometimes."

"No, it's okay. I am a Jew girl. Is that a bad thing to him?"

"Not bad technically. But like if we were to, you know, get married or, god forbid, have kids, it might be a big deal."

"I'll be sure not to propose tonight," I assure Dmitri.

"I thought that might be a ring box in your pocket." Dmitri nudges my shoulder with his, and we both laugh. I'm not doing so badly.

When we reach the bottom of the wheel rotation, and the sleeveless man is about to open our gate, Dmitri suggests, "Want to ride again? I figure we'll have less of a chance of running into my family if we stay aloft."

"Sounds good," I concur, and Dmitri fishes four more tickets out of his pocket.

On our second go-round we talk about movies, starting off

with ones we remember taking place in part at carnivals (my contributions are *Zombieland*; Tod Browning's 1932 black-and-white classic, *Freaks*; and *Supergirl*).

"*Supergirl*?" he asks incredulously. "Wasn't that ubercheesy?"

"Cheesy as a delectable pizza. She was played by Helen Slater, who also played badass film hero Billie Jean in *The Legend of Billie Jean*." I flex my movie muscles.

"Fair enough. Did you know *Freaks* was made—"

"Using actual sideshow people? Of course I know that. A movie like that could never be made today. Even if it is a brilliant statement on how we fear what we don't understand," I explain.

"Hmmm," Dmitri considers. "I always thought it was more of a take on how ugly beautiful people can be."

I think for a moment before nodding. "Yeah, that, too. Amazing so much can be said through a black-and-white horror movie."

"Now, have you seen *Freaked*? That's a whole other freaky ball game."

Words pour out of us, and we ride the wheel three times before we decide to get off and head over to play Skee-ball. There we run into Dmitri's parents once again.

"Dimmi, Yia Yia not feeling well. Her heartburn acting up. She wait for us in car. We need head home now. Say goodbye you . . . friend," Dmitri's father says.

"Um . . . ," Dmitri stutters. "At least let me wait with Eliana until her dad can come get her?" Dmitri sounds unsure around his father, and his dad gives him a solemn nod. I text my dad, who says he'll be here soon. Dmitri and I walk to the gate with his parents following behind.

"It's cool," I assure him. "I would have kicked your butt in Skee-ball anyway. It would have been humiliating, you never would have asked me out again. Really, it's better this way."

"So you want me to ask you out again?" He grins.

"I'm not saying that. I'm just saying that now you have the opportunity without your pride getting in the way."

"I was going to let you win anyway," he says. "To be chivalrous."

"I would have ensured you lost. I don't need chivalry."

"That's a relief because I kind of suck at Skee-ball. Next time we can find a game I'm good at, so I can impress you with my skills."

"Croquet?" I suggest.

He elbows me gently, and I feel my cheeks warm.

We arrive at the fair gates, and Dmitri's parents sidle up directly next to us while I wait for my dad. Kind of a banter-killing moment.

We pass the time by playing I Spy.

"I spy something brown."

"That guy's teeth."

"You're good."

My dad pulls up a few minutes later, and I hastily say to Dmitri, "See you in school?" before I dive into the passenger seat. Lest my dad actually try to interact with Dmitri's parents. Me meeting his family was momentous enough, but let's not pretend my dad is the type of dad who would impress Dmitri's parents.

"Did you have a good time?" my dad asks as we drive away.

"I did." I nod. But that's all I say. I don't want to overthink it, but I may have just had a really decent date. With the definite possibility of another one on the way.

Dmitri

Unexpected Turbulence rents a room at Ace Studios for our rehearsals. It's a cramped fifteen-by-fifteen box with amps, mics, and most of a drum kit. I have to bring my own snare, cymbals, and, of course, sticks. For practice I use a pair of plain wooden sticks; for gigs I use these very cool translucent sticks that glow each time you hit them. They were a Christmas present from Nicky.

We're on our second run-through of the set list for the Seventh Street Entry gig and things are going well. I haven't missed a cue; my stops, starts, and fills have been crisp; and the rest of the band is in the zone. It's kind of fascinating to me that we can have so much musical chemistry and so little personal chemistry. That's true of so many bands, I guess, which in some weird way gives me added hope we're going to make it someday. I mean, how can we not?

I texted Eliana as soon as I got home from the festival last night. I know, I know . . . you're supposed to wait a day so you don't seem needy or desperate or something. But that's not me. Doing things for the sake of appearance is just dumb. Plus, she texted back right away, which she sometimes doesn't, so I don't think she minded.

ELIANA: How's Yia Yia?

ME: She's okay. She gets this bad heartburn thing, and last night antacids weren't really helping. She liked you, by the way.

ELIANA: How do you know?

ME: "Dimmi-moo, I like this Eliana girl." Lol

ELIANA: Lol, indeed.

We chatted for a little while more and then I asked her what I'd been dying to ask her. What I'd planned to ask her at the church, but never had the chance because we had to leave early.

ME: So my band has a really important gig next Saturday night—it's at the Seventh Street Entry in downtown Minneapolis—maybe you could come?

ELIANA: Like a date? Or like a groupie?

I couldn't tell if she was joking or insulted, which put me back on my heels, but only for a second; I recovered.

ME: What's a groupie?

ELIANA: Ha! Well played. Let me check with my parents. I'm not sure they want me going to clubs downtown. How are you getting there?

ME: I have to go with the band. Chad uses his parents' SUV for our equipment, so I would need to meet you there.

ELIANA: Hmmm . . . I have to drive myself downtown to be your groupie? This is sounding more and more appealing.

She threw in an eye roll emoji for good measure.

ELIANA: I was kind of thinking our next outing might be a movie, you know, since we both are so into movies.

My heart skipped a beat because I was pretty sure Eliana had just asked me on a third date.

ME: OMG, I would love that. As soon as this gig is behind us, my time will be more my own. Until then, we have a crap-ton of practices scheduled, like every night this week. And really, it would be awesome if you were there. At the gig, I mean.

We left it that she would check with her parents, and we would try to go to the movies the weekend after. It wasn't exactly how I wanted the conversation to go, but Eliana didn't shut me down, and hey, now I have plans with her for two more weekends. I don't think it makes her my girlfriend yet, but . . .

After we signed off, I was so filled with emotion I did something I like to do, but almost never do well: I wrote a song.

(Verse 1)
You glossed over the point of your story,
The one about the lady with the snakes in the tent
It's not about freaks, sideshows and faded glory
It's that you didn't have any friends
(Bridge)
But how can that be?
Don't they see what I see?
(Verse 2)
You're hiding something, tucked away behind the curtain
A secret so deep and dark it might break you
You may be an enigma, but of this I'm certain
I'm not giving up until I break on through
(Bridge)
How can it be,
That they don't see what I see?
(Chorus)
Our fate is sealed

With the things you make me feel
Girl
Girl on the Ferris wheel

There's another verse I don't like as much, but really, I'm proud of this song. I want to share it with the band, though that has never gone well in the past. (Chad. Ugh.) Still, if Eliana is ever going to hear it, the song is going to need music and I don't have the chops for that.

We finish the second run-through of the set list, including an encore—Chad insists we keep an encore in our hip pocket, and while it kind of seems like a jinx, I guess it make sense—then it's on to new material.

We always end rehearsals with new material and today is no different. Chad has a fast, angry song called "Build the Wall." It's this anti-immigration screed about a Mexican drug smuggler. He wrote a rudimentary guitar part for it, too, and plays it for us on Kyle's Strat.

Chad is super conservative, like even more than my dad. I'm not at all political, but since I don't really like what Chad or what my dad have to say most of the time, I figure that makes me a liberal. (Maybe there's something wrong with people whose name ends with an "ad" sound. Mental note to avoid guys named Brad.)

When Chad is done, the three of us just stare at him in silence. Drew gives voice to what I'm thinking:

"No. Fucking. Way."

"What? Why not?" Chad is pissed.

"First," Drew responds, "it's too political. And I for one don't agree with what it has to say."

"Me neither," Kyle adds. I keep my mouth shut.

"Illegal immigrants are taking—"

"Second," Drew continues, steamrolling right over Chad, "the song sucks."

Chad opens his mouth to argue, but really, there is no comeback for "the song sucks." And really, the song sucks.

"Fine," he says after a moment. "We need to focus on the set list anyway."

Kyle takes his guitar back from Chad and is starting to put it away when someone says, "I have a song." What's really surprising is that the someone is me.

"Oh brother," Chad mumbles.

Kyle stops what he's doing and looks at me. "Okay," he says, "let's see it." I can't believe I'm doing this, but I take a folded piece of paper out of my back pocket and hand it over.

My mouth goes completely dry, like Sahara Desert dry, while Kyle is reading it. Chad, his mouth a sharp line across his face, sticks his hand out for the paper when it's apparent Kyle has finished, but Kyle hands it to Drew. "Hey, Dimmi, this is pretty good. Who's the girl?"

Drew reads it and nods and then hands it to Chad, who, predictably, laughs out loud. "This?" he says before he's even had time to read it. "You guys wanna do *this*? I'm not singing it." He drops the paper, letting it float down to my mounted tom as he struts out of the room.

Drew shrugs and starts to put his bass away.

"You really like it?" I ask Kyle.

"Yeah. It's got some nice imagery."

"Can you help write music for it?"

Kyle raises one eyebrow—I must be the only person in the entire world who cannot raise just one eyebrow—as he thinks for a minute. "Yeah, why not. But I'm not sure we can ever get Chad to sing it."

Chad is not the person I'm thinking about right now. I hand Kyle the paper and smile at the thought of having a song, a real song, to give my almost girlfriend. Is there any better gift in the world than writing a song for someone? This has been like the best weekend, ever.

"Her name is Eliana," I say to Kyle. "The girl's name is Eliana."

Eliana

I spend the majority of the weekend in my room-hole watching movies and reliving moments from the festival. The Ferris wheel seemed like the ideal spot for a kiss and to solidify Friday night as a quote, unquote date, but at the same time, "It's kind of uncomfortable to kiss someone you are sitting next to while tethered in with a metal seat belt," I explain to Janina over Facetime.

"Yeah, I get that. Ferris wheels have romantic intentions, but the practicality of it all is highly suspect."

"Have you ever kissed anyone on a Ferris wheel?" I ask.

"No. I have kissed someone on a Tilt-a-Whirl, but that didn't end up so hot."

"I can imagine. Was that when you had to replace your tooth?"

"Maybe," she answers coyly. "I still think it can be construed as a date if you didn't kiss. You held hands, right? That's practically considered married in some cultures."

"I missed that in our World Cultures class last year," I say.

"That's because you were too busy mourning the death of Cedric Diggory."

"It was Fred Weasley, and Ms. Leff never talked about holding hands. I got an A in that class, by the way," I note.

"Who are you going to believe? A teacher who wears brown shoes every day, or a person your age who has held many a hand in her day?"

"You make yourself sound like an old lady, you know."

"Wise, my friend, it's called wise." Janina lowers a fake pair of glasses onto her nose.

"Keep telling yourself that, Nina." I work my way back to the real question. "So was it a date or not?"

Janina looks at me through the screen with incredulous eyes. "Obviously, El. He asked you out. You went to a freaking festival. You rode a Ferris wheel three times. And there was purposeful touching. Hell, you met his parents. I can't say that for most guys I've dated."

"He was just kind of sketchy when I tried to be all cool and ask him to hang out again. He made it sound like we weren't going to hang out again for weeks because of his 'band'"—I throw an air quote—"and that the next time we'd actually get together would be me getting myself to their show. Along with, you know, all the other people that he probably invited to see them."

"Why did you air quote 'band'? He *is* in a band. You and me saw them last year when I was going out with the guitar player from that shitty group, Monkey Stick. It was right before . . ."

"Oh yeah. Right before the hospital. I guess I forgot. Did I look horrible back then? Do you think Dmitri remembers?"

"You had much longer hair. And it was after I tried to bleach it, and it was all growing out and you had those grunge roots. I thought it looked cool. But if you don't remember and you were in the audience, I'm guessing he doesn't remember from his stage vantage point. Or maybe he's been pining for you this whole time, and it's taken him this long to ask you out! Wouldn't that be cute? You hand-holding darlings." Janina places her hand over her heart sentimentally.

"I swear you had to be my grandma in a past life. Or in my current one."

"Your superhot grandma, right? Like Helen Mirren?"

"Sure." I nod dramatically.

"How about this: I'll go see his band with you, get you all gorgeous, and I'll read his cues. It's not like you aren't going to see him every day at school for the next couple weeks, right? I'm sure he'll drop some scorching remarks about your butt, and everything will be crystal clear."

"Why is it always my butt?"

"Indeed," is all Janina says before she hangs up.

I lie back on my futon and shove my headphones over my ears. With eyes closed, I listen to *Harry Potter and the Half-Blood Prince* as it plays on my computer. When I feel like it, I answer some math problems on my homework. When it's time to eat, I go downstairs and soak in the din of my family. I want to ask them what they think, but I also don't really want to know. The more I talk about it, the bigger deal it will be when I figure out he has no interest in me other than as a partner on a series of Ferris wheel rides and as his newest groupie. Am I going to have to pay to get in? Or will there be a list? And what does it mean if I'm on it? Or not on it? Life is so much clearer under my covers.

Dmitri

The next six days pass in a blur of school, homework, and drumming. Not only is our rehearsal schedule relentless, I have three papers due, two tests, and a crap-ton of reading. (If you say it right, you can make "crap-ton" sound like a French word—craptonne.) If someone were to ask me what happened during the week, I probably couldn't recount any details . . . except for three VERY notable events.

NOTABLE EVENT #1: Eliana tells me she's coming to the gig. The Art and Craft of Cinema is normally a no-contact zone (Eliana is a very focused student, which I respect and admire), so I'm really surprised when a folded piece of paper lands on my desk. I look around to see who might have tossed it. Everyone has their eyes trained on the front of the room, so I shrug and unfold the note.

> *Okay, I'm in. Janina and I are coming to your gig on Saturday night. Your band better be good.* ☺

I sneak a peek at Eliana, but she doesn't look in my direction. It doesn't matter. I write "awesome" with eleven exclamation points on the note (eleven is my lucky number), wait until Mr. Tannis has his back to the class, and toss it on Eliana's desk. She scoops it up and tucks it into her notebook without reading it. This girl is a riddle wrapped in a mystery. Damn, I love that.

I'm so happy I worry I'm going to start cackling like a lunatic, so I ask Mr. Tannis for a pass to the bathroom. I secretly hope Eliana will follow me, but she doesn't. She also bolts class when the bell rings, before I get a chance to talk to her about her note, but that's okay. She's coming to the gig.

She's coming to the gig!

NOTABLE EVENT #2: At band practice on Wednesday, after we've gone through the set twice—and man oh man are we tight—and it's time for new material, Kyle says he has a song.

Kyle writes about half our lyrics and almost all the music. Chad is a loudmouth who likes to think he's the leader of the band, but really, it's Kyle. We learned about Teddy Roosevelt in history this year: "Walk softly and carry a big stick." That's Kyle to a T.

Anyway, Chad and Drew look at him with anticipation. A new Kyle song is always a big deal at our practices. Kyle takes a second to retune his guitar; as he does, he turns his back on the room and faces the drum kit. Then he winks at me. Huh?

He turns back around and launches into this slow, chunky, and completely infectious riff. It's got a bluesy feel with what I've learned over the years are seventh chords and minor chords. I can already hear the drum part I'm going to put to this in my head. Simple, straightforward, hi-hat and snare, three-four time.

Drew and Chad are both nodding along with the guitar, both smiling, when Kyle starts to sing.

"You glossed over the point of your story,
The one about the lady with the snakes in the tent"

My first thought is *wow, good lyrics, but they're kind of familiar.* Duh. It takes a second to realize this is my song. MY SONG!

Kyle's voice is better suited to background vocals, but he's doing my words justice. The melody is lonely, expansive, filled with longing, and a perfect fit for the lyrics and music behind it. I'm so moved I have to sniff a few times to stop from crying. It's the truth.

I look to Chad and Drew to see if either one realizes what Kyle is up to, that's he's snuck my song into the room. Drew shoots me a glance and smirks. Yep. He knows. But Chad—nodding, swaying, and smiling along with the music—just watches Kyle, proof he never read my lyrics in the first place.

Kyle strums the last chord, letting it ring and fade. Chad, Drew, and I all clap, and Chad even whoops. "Damn," he says, "we have to get that into the set for this weekend."

"Really?" I say. I'm so surprised I can't help myself.

"Yeah," Chad says. "We've been practicing the set so much I'm worried about it being over-rehearsed. I was going to suggest we take Friday off just so we come at the gig fresh on Saturday. But adding a new song will keep us on our toes. Can you give me the lyrics?"

Kyle smiles and hands Chad what I recognize as the piece of

paper I gave him a couple days ago. Chad looks at it, looks up at me, and then looks at Kyle. "Wait, is this . . . ?"

"The song Dimmi wrote? Yeah, you fucking tool. If you'd read it the first time you would've seen how good it is."

Chad is about to protest, but realizes he's been played and has lost. And I have to give him credit because the next thing he says is "Okay, let's work it up right now. Drew, can you add a bass part?" As much of a dick as he can be, Chad really is committed to the success of the band.

"Already have," Drew says. He was in on this, too? I put my hand in front of my mouth to stop from laughing out loud.

Chad turns to me with a "well, what about you?" look on his face.

"I had no idea this was going on," I protest, "but I love what Kyle has done with it and I think I already have a good drum part for it." Chad nods.

Kyle runs through the song a few times, teaching Chad the melody, refining Drew's bass part, and helping me tweak the drums. Twenty minutes later, "Girl on the Ferris Wheel" is officially added to the set list for Unexpected Turbulence's upcoming gig. It sounds amazing.

NOTABLE EVENT #3: Janina corners me in the hallway between third and fourth period on Friday, the day before the gig. Eliana is absent for the second straight day. I texted and she said it was a stomach thing but didn't say anything else and wouldn't really talk. I've been worried, so I'm glad to see her friend.

"How's Eliana?" I ask before Janina can say a word.

"She'll be fine," she answers. "But listen—" She pokes me in the chest. She actually pokes me. "Don't fuck around with her."

"Huh?" Does she mean sex? We haven't even kissed yet!

"I mean don't fuck around with her feelings, okay?"

"What are you talking about?"

"You seem like a nice boy, Dmitri, so I'm trusting you to not hurt her."

"Hurt her?" This is the weirdest conversation I've ever had. "Why would I hurt her? I want her to be my girlfriend."

Janina smiles at that. "Well, I'm glad to hear that. But still, sometimes people hurt other people without meaning to or even knowing they're doing it. Just treat Eliana right. She's my best friend and she's the best person I know."

I kind of feel like I'm having a conversation with one of her parents and it freaks me out. At the same time, I'm really happy to know someone else sees in Eliana what I see, and feels strongly enough to want to protect her like this.

"I promise," I say, holding up three fingers in a Boy Scout salute, "I am *not* going to hurt your friend. Just the opposite . . . if she lets me."

"Good boy," Janina says, and pats my shoulder like I'm a family pet. Then she turns and walks away. Standing right behind her, lost in the shadow of Janina's tall frame, is Reggie. Her sudden appearance startles me.

"You are such a tool, Digrindakis," she says. "Such a tool."

I'm so taken aback that I have no idea how to respond, so I blurt out the first thing that pops into my head. "Are you coming to the gig?"

Reggie—who is wearing her black leather jacket, a short blue skirt with a black stripe down the side, ripped tights, combat boots, and something I've never seen before, makeup—hangs her head and mumbles, "Of course I am." Then she turns and goes, too. The whole encounter leaves me unsettled.

And then, it's Saturday.

Gig day.

Eliana

I don't know what's wrong with me.

That's not true. I just hate that there *is* something wrong with me.

All through film class Monday, Tuesday, and Wednesday, I could barely keep my focus. I kept wondering: *Is Dmitri looking at me? If he is, how is he looking at me? Like a friend? Like more than a friend? Like a fangirl member of his entourage who is one of many he has invited to a gig?*

"Gig" is such a stupid word. Like, who does he think he is?

I can tell I'm depressed because I'm getting mean. It's my defense mechanism. One of many. Some people eat a lot. Some people cry. I get mean and lock myself in my bedroom-hole and watch movies until my eyes bleed. Well, almost until they bleed. I'm assuming that's the next step anyway.

Why am I depressed, though? I had a really nice time at the festival. Grades are still aces. My brothers and sisters are neither more nor less annoying than usual. My dad remains unemployed and mostly in his basement. My mom is rad but never around. Nothing all that new. But I'm not myself. For starters, being myself has never involved a guy liking me. It's so confusing. I feel like an idiot saying that a guy likes me, because it seems so presumptuous. How does one know concretely if anyone likes them? At least with my female friends, they are straight-up awesome or straight-up awful. With Dmitri, it's like I'm supposed to be able to read all of his cryptic boy code. Was he holding my hand because he wants to, or am I living the plot of *Carrie* and it's all some big ruse that will culminate in a bath of pig's blood at the gig? Bloody gig.

I'm so worked up in confusion on Thursday that I stay home from school with a stomachache. And I do actually have a stomachache. But I'm not sick. Sick of my brain, maybe. Was that kind of funny? I can't tell today.

At breakfast my mom presses her lips to my forehead, her way of gauging my temperature without a thermometer.

"You don't have a fever. But your stomach hurts?" I nod vigorously, and she looks at me dubiously. Her brow crinkles, and I know what's coming next. "We're not starting this again, are we, Eliana?"

My stomach really begins to crush in on itself. I know what she means. Over a year ago, I started getting stomachaches. And bouts of insomnia. And long periods where I wouldn't leave my room-hole. Eventually I acquiesced and went into an inpatient program for teenagers. It was a few weeks of my life I will never get back, and everything changed dramatically in that short time span. I lost friends, started my long walks, went into outpatient therapy, and began my drug regimen, which continues today. I had hoped the drugs and mandatory office visits would quell any future outbreaks of depression, like Proactiv does for acne, but the pain in my stomach and doubt in my brain make me think otherwise. Which makes me feel even more depressed. The spiral begins . . .

I attempt to reassure my mom—and myself—that this is a temporary setback, based purely on situation and not chemical makeup. "I'm okay, Mom. School has been kind of stressful, and I ate this burrito thing at lunch yesterday. It was a bad choice. But I promise I'll go tomorrow." I hear myself say the p-word and cringe. It's such a fake, bullshitty concept, and I regret it. She's heard that word a million times before, and it has lost all sense of truth and meaning.

It's enough to get me out of school for a day, at least. "You can stay home if you meet Ava and Asher at the bus stop. And put in some laundry." Mom hustles around the kitchen, tucking plastic sandwich bags into lunch boxes and screwing lids on water bottles.

I consider asking her why I need to be the one to do either of those tasks when her husband is home all freaking day doing god knows what in the basement, but I got out of school with an empty promise and don't need to push it.

After everyone is out the door (except, as always, my dad), I escape to the cozy confines of my room-hole and plunk down on the futon. If I pause for two bathroom breaks and bring up a Pop-Tart for lunch, I can get through three and a half Harry Potters before the wee ones' bus lands. The movies have a trancelike power over me, and the day flies by without me thinking much about my actual life.

I curse the clock at 3:20, close the lid of my laptop, shuffle halfway into my Converse, and trudge to the bus stop across the street. The sun is blinding after a day spent with only a small octagonal window of light for seven straight hours. I shield my eyes with a hand salute until the bus arrives and the shadow looms over me. Asher and Ava seem relatively excited to see me, with big hugs from both and a sloppy kiss from Ava. I summon enough energy to make them an after-school snack of Goldfish, almonds, and Panda Puffs cereal (my patented snack mix). Isaac and Samara walk in twenty minutes later, offer indifferent hi's, and head straight to the puzzle table for homework. I pop in a DVD of Scooby-Doo for Asher and Ava and Facetime Janina, who should just be leaving cosmetology school.

She answers as I plop myself down at the kitchen table. "Hey!" She smiles warmly through the phone. "Where were you today? I swear I saw lover boy looking around forlornly for you."

I feel a twinge of hope at that but also know she's kidding. "I stayed home. Stomachache. Didn't really feel like going to school." I detect a drop in the smile from Janina and know she's thinking just what my mom was: Is this happening again? So I lay on the smile extra thick. "No worries. I'm okay. You stay home sometimes. Everyone does, and they don't get guilt-tripped about it."

"True. You'll be back tomorrow, though, right? It's Friday. Dmitri's show is Saturday." Janina singsongs this information, as though tempting me. It's not tempting, though. It's traumatizing.

"I don't know if I want to go," I sigh.

"You want to go. You will go. Even if you don't actually want to go. We're going."

"Um. Okay." We stare each other down through the phone

screen until Janina cracks and laughs lightly. "Gotta go! I'll see you tomorrow. Promise?"

"I promise." And there it is again. Right after I say it, I know I won't go to school. It's a terrible feeling. It's like I'm stabbing myself in the face over and over and I know it hurts and is bad for me, but I can't stop doing it. And even while I'm doing it, I'm telling myself, "You should really stop because stabbing yourself in the face is probably going to leave scars and think of all the blood you'll have to clean up and you'll look so much better if you don't have a face full of stab wounds and you, you know, still have eyes and all." But I can't stop doing it.

If I go to school, I'll have to see Dmitri. I'll have to explain why I wasn't in school today. That's humiliating.

I spend the hours until my mom comes home trying to concoct a story that will get me out of school tomorrow, one that won't feel like I'm backpedaling or breaking promises. And then, like a gift from the heavens above, Ava throws up on me. Three hours later, I'm praying to the porcelain gods alongside her.

It's a vomit-filled miracle.

Dmitri

"**D**ude," Chad says, "stop calling it the *Seventh Street* Entry. Everyone cool just calls it the Entry."

Drew rolls his eyes. "Do you call it the Entry?"

"Yes, that's what I'm telling you!"

"Then not everyone cool calls it the Entry." Kyle laughs.

"Ha. Ha," Chad answers, drawing out each syllable. "I just don't want us to seem like Podunks."

"Just be yourself, Chad," Kyle says, "and relax."

We're in the cramped backstage area of the club. There's some graffiti on the cinder-block wall, some ratty old furniture, and that's pretty much it. Drew and Kyle are using electric tuners to get their instruments in sync and Chad is doing push-ups. He wants us to think he's some kind of buff god, but I'm pretty sure he only ever exercises when other people are watching. As for me, I'm pacing.

It's five minutes to showtime and I'm starting to freak out. There are like 250 people here. We're used to playing for audiences of twenty or thirty, so this feels huge. For the most part they're not here to see us; the headliner, Pig Pimples, won't go on until 10:30, and it's only 8:25 now. (It was Kyle who figured out the name Pig Pimples was a play on Hogwarts. I wish we'd thought of that. Genius.)

The stage lights, which are low, scatter illumination on the row of people right up front and since we're first on the bill, that's mostly our crew. There's Kyle's girlfriend, Drew's girlfriend, Nicky with his friend Jason, and Reggie, who I'm blown away to see is wearing all white—white Sex Pistols tee, white skirt, white tights, even white go-go boots. The way her outfit contrasts with her black hair and thick black eyeliner, she looks kind of amazing.

The one person I don't see is Eliana.

I've been checking every few minutes for the last hour, but there's no sign of her. I even looked outside the front door by the legendary wall of stars, and nothing.

The wall of stars outside the door to *the Entry*—there, I said it right—is like the Hollywood Walk of Fame for notable bands that have come through the Twin Cities. Hanging just above the upper left-hand corner of the door, in a spot of what I think must be supreme honor, is Hüsker Dü. Someday Unexpected Turbulence is going to have one of those stars. I can just feel it.

Anyway, when I don't find Eliana anywhere, I text her. No surprise that she doesn't text back. I'm stewing over this as I pace a groove into the floor of the green room when a thirtysomething man pokes his head in. "Unexpected Turbulence, let's get this started."

"Bring it in." Chad does this before every gig. He has us form a small circle, or, since there are four of us, I guess a kind of square, put our hands in the middle, and chant "U.T., U.T., U.T.!" Then we break our hands apart dramatically. It's a dumb ritual, but I think each of us likes it in his own way. And by now it would be bad luck *not* to do it.

Showtime.

There are some whoops and hollers from our friends up front, along with some half-hearted claps from those farther back, as we take the stage. The spotlights are now on full, so any hope of finding Eliana is lost; everyone beyond the first row of people standing up against the stage is in silhouette.

Chad takes the mic out of the stand, puts it to his lips, and lets out a booming "Helloooooooo, Minneapolis!" We practiced this over and over; it's my cue to start the thundering beat of our first song and I don't miss it. I begin with fast-paced eighth notes on the floor tom and alternating quarter notes on the bass and snare, all with a ferocity I didn't know I had. Two measures later, Chad, Drew, and Kyle thunder in and we're off and running.

I've read stories about athletes getting in the zone during big games—there's a scene in this dumb Kevin Costner baseball movie where he's on the mound in Yankee Stadium and shuts out all external stimuli other than the batter and umpire, and just pitches—and that's what happens to me. Everything outside the music melts away; the four of us become one with the audience and I experience a kind of high I've never felt before. Is this what sex feels like?

By the time we've played through most of our half-hour set, the smattering of applause has swelled to a torrent. The entire room is shimmying and shaking and practically convulsing to the music. People seem infected with the groove we're laying down. I feel powerful and humbled and grateful and euphoric all at once.

When we finish a song called "Tire Swing"—a Kyle-written love song with a very sad and dark undertone—it's time for "Girl on the Ferris Wheel." Chad looks to Kyle to start the guitar part that leads us in, but before he does, Kyle turns back to face me.

"Eliana," he says, "right?"

What? Why is he asking me this? I nod.

Kyle turns back to his mic. "Our unassuming drummer—" Before he can finish there's some spontaneous applause. "That's right, give it up for Dmitri!" There are more cheers and I'm pretty sure I blush. "Anyway," Kyle continues, "Dimmi wrote this next song for the girl of his dreams. Is Eliana in the house?"

What. The. Fuck. He did not just do that.

There are murmurs and questions and heads craning this way and that, and I think I'm going to die of embarrassment because Eliana didn't show, when a loud, "Here! She's right here!" booms from somewhere near the back. I know right away the voice belongs to Janina. There's some tussling in the crowd, the front row parts like the Red Sea, and a large, long, elegant hand shoves Eliana forward until her shins bump the stage. The lights fall on her like stardust.

She's wearing a black shirt, blue jeans, and Converse high-tops. It's a simple outfit she's worn to school before, but somehow she looks different. I think maybe she's wearing makeup, and her hair has definitely been tended to. One of the colored lights catches her eyes, which are crazy-wide with embarrassment, and they twinkle.

She.

Looks.

Beautiful.

And she came.

She's here.

"Welcome to the Entry, Eliana," Kyle says to her. "Dmitri wrote this next song for you." Before Eliana can react, before I can say anything, he starts that captivating guitar riff. Part of me wants to kill him, part of me wants to pay him a million dollars.

Eliana, with Janina right behind her, stands dumbfounded as we play the song. Chad half sings to her and half sings to the crowd. I concentrate on the drums, but can't take my eyes off Eliana. She looks back and forth between me and Chad, like maybe she's confused as to who is actually singing to her, which kind of freaks me out. *It's me*, I try thinking loudly, *it's me!*

When the song is over, while the audience goes nuts with appreciation, Eliana mouths "thank you" to me, takes a step back, and is swallowed by the sea of people. We play the last song in our set, and, like Chad predicted and hoped, we're called back for an encore.

This gig was everything I'd dreamed it would be and more.

When we're done, the stage lights dim and we move quickly to get our gear out of the way for the second opening band, a three-piece that was famous in the 1980s (kind of a nostalgia act now), called the Scar Boys. I'm looking everywhere for Eliana while I move gear, but I don't see her. I have a sick feeling in my stomach that the song was too much and she left.

As I'm taking the last piece of my equipment—a crash cymbal—off the stage, I turn around and Eliana is standing three feet away, like she appeared out of thin air.

"Hey!" I say with enough excitement that I probably sound deranged.

She pauses just long enough to make me wonder if she's okay, then steps forward, takes my face in her hand, and kisses me, hard, on the mouth.

Someone kill me now, because I could never, ever, EVER die happier than this.

Eliana

"We'll be fine, Mom. Great, in fact. The house will probably be standing when you get home. We promise. Right, guys?" Mom and Dad stand in the doorway, about to leave for their first date in forever. Dad somehow managed to put on a button-down shirt for the occasion (I'm surprised he remembered how to manipulate a buttonhole), and Mom is wearing a skirt reserved for the Jewish High Holidays. I look toward my siblings and Dmitri, who is here to help me hold down the fort. Or so I told my parents. My actual plan is to pay off Samara to give me and Dmitri some alone time in the basement while we watch a movie.

It was my idea to put in *Psycho*, partially because, as it's an Alfred Hitchcock gem, I have the excuse to give the parentals that it's for school; but mostly because I love it so much.

"Why did he call the movie 'Psycho'?" Dmitri asks, as we dump my dad's collectibles off a hideously brown-and-orange-plaid couch, once a fixture in my Grandma Eddie's rumpus room. My dad refuses to get rid of the couch because it holds "special memories." My standard retort for that is "and special couch bugs." Is that a thing? Couch bugs?

"It's such a perfect title! Kind of random and not once referenced in the movie, but it sounds so good!" I argue. "Can you imagine what it was like to see a movie with a person brutally murdered and stuffed into the trunk of a car back in 1960? It must have been terrifying!"

"Spoiler alert," Dmitri coughs.

"I thought you've seen this," I say, plopping down onto a lumpy cushion. Dmitri plops down next to me, arm hairs tickling my own.

"I have. Of course I have, but I can't be expected to remember every little detail."

"Being stuffed into a trunk is hardly a little detail. I'm guessing it's all a shower scene blur in your man brain."

"I should be offended by that," Dmitri says, "if it weren't true." I dole out an elbow to the rib. Sometimes I worry I'm too physically aggressive, but Dmitri never responds with anything but a jokey retort. So I think I'm safe. I hope.

The opening credits tear across the screen like knife blades, the violins striking over and over. "Brilliant soundtrack," Dmitri notes. I concur.

The movie opens with a shirtless man and woman, dressing after a midday hotel rendezvous. I wonder if Dmitri's uncomfortable watching this gorgeous and endowed woman in her massive bullet-boob bra while sitting next to me. The onscreen couple kisses, and the way Hitchcock filmed it allows you to hear every smeck and peck of the lips. It's extremely intimate compared with today's music-swelling, mood-lighting, faker-than-fake smooching we put on film. It also makes for a lot of empty airspace.

"Did you know that actress is Jamie Lee Curtis's mom?" Dmitri asks.

I try not to roll my eyes. "Uh, yeah, everyone knows that. And it took her years to be able to take a shower again. Which is kind of strange, you know? I mean, if you're in the movie and you know that you were not actually killed while taking a shower, what would be so scary about it, then? My mom had a college roommate who would never take a shower unless she knew someone else was home at the time." Should I stop talking about women taking showers?

There's at least a good half hour of suspense before someone finally gets offed, and it's every bit as brilliant as I remember.

"Anthony Perkins is beautifully creepy, isn't he?" I ask Dmitri. His arm is now around my shoulder. I both really want it there and really want to focus on the movie, which is confusing.

"What exactly do you mean by beautiful?" Dmitri asks.

"Do I detect a hint of jealousy?" I say. "After I had to watch Bullet Boobs McGee gallivanting around in her skivvies?" Dmitri chokes on my ridiculous choice of nicknames. "Yes, Anthony Perkins was crazy hot in that skinny, David Tennant, black-and-white kind of way. That makes him all the more unsettling in this movie." Dmitri kisses my cheek, and now *I'm* unsettled.

"I've heard he was so good in *Psycho* that it completely ruined his career," Dmitri explains.

"Did you pull up the *Psycho* Wikipedia page before you came over?" I tease.

"Maybe . . ."

There are moments that pass where I know Dmitri is looking at me, breathing on my ear in a way that suggests he's not really paying attention to the movie. But what if my brothers or sisters burst into the basement to ask for a snack? What if they catch us mid-lip-lock and I have to explain that to my parents and I'm never allowed to watch a movie with Dimmi in my basement again? I don't want him to think I don't want to, though.

"Hey." I turn toward Dimmi, his face close enough that our noses touch. I kiss him, and the room is electrically charged. He leans in for more kissing, and I swear my siblings can hear our smacks, as though we're part of a Hitchcock film. I push Dmitri lightly away. "I don't want my brothers and sisters to catch us," I say.

"Do you think they would?" Dmitri asks. "You paid off Samara, right?" He goes in for another kiss. I hesitantly give in to him.

"Does your brother ever interrupt you when you're doing something, even when you ask him not to?" I ask, and his eyes click with recognition.

"Good point." Dmitri folds.

Toward the end of the movie the know-it-all shrink explains the entire psychiatric reason for Norman Bates's killer instinct.

"This is so boring! I wish Norman Bates as Norman Bates's mother would just kill this guy!" I shout at the screen. "Do you think people back in the day of *Psycho* shouted at the screen like people do today?"

"I doubt it. Society was so much more polite, in a sort of racist, sexist, homophobic way," Dmitri notes.

"Once I went to a movie where a guy's head got chopped off,

and someone in the audience yelled, 'His head hurts now! His head hurts now!'" Dmitri and I laugh, and it sets off a tickle fight that has us tangled up in a knot of arms and legs. We kiss again because it's pretty much impossible not to when we're this close.

And then the basement door squeaks open. "Ellie?" It's Asher. "I had an accident, and Samara won't clean it up!"

From behind him, Samara yells, "I didn't sign up to clean up your pee, Asher!"

"See?" I say to Dmitri, as we undo our snuggly pretzel.

"Think Isaac would clean up the pee if I gave him twenty bucks?" Dmitri asks, pulling me back down to the couch as I attempt to stand up.

Then we hear the sound of the front door squealing open, and Mom and Dad are home again. Shortest date ever.

"Welcome to my life, Dmitri."

He smiles, and I'm so glad he's in it.

Dmitri

My three favorite things about Chad, in order, are:

1. The knowledge that someday he's going to die.

Nope. Nothing else. That's all I've got.

This is the first time Eliana has come to rehearsal, and Chad decided to be Chad the second we walked through the door.

"Oh cool, it's the girl on the Ferris wheel. How'd you like the way I sang that song to you?" Then he blew her a kiss and started cackling.

I was about to say something to put him in his place, but Kyle beat me to it.

"You'll have to excuse Chad, Eliana, he has a medical condition called penilopia."

I could see the twinkle in Ellie's eyes. She knew where Kyle's joke was going before the punch line but played along anyway. "What's that?"

"He's a dick."

"Whatever," Chad muttered, turning his back on the communal laughter and pretending to scribble lyrics in his notebook.

In addition to the band, Kyle's and Drew's girlfriends are here.

They're sitting side by side on a crappy little couch shoved against the only unoccupied space of wall in the room. It reminds me a bit of the couch in Ellie's basement, the one she claims has an infestation of "couch bugs." (That hasn't stopped us from snuggling on it to watch movies.)

Ellie and I have had exactly seven dates since the day I followed her into the bathroom. While she has repeatedly made sure I understand the error in judgment that propelled me into the girls' room in the first place (and I do, I really do), and even though we haven't said it out loud yet, we're definitely boyfriend and girlfriend. I mean, I visit her locker between every period, even though my locker is really far away; we hang out on weekends; and I text her almost every night. Aw, who am I kidding, I text her *every* night.

Anyway, it's gotten serious enough that I figured I could invite Ellie to see Unexpected Turbulence practice. I think she must really want to, because she asked me last week, "What the hell do you do at rehearsal anyway? Tell stories about your female conquests? Sneak beers? Have pillow fights?" That last one made me laugh out loud. It seemed like she wanted to see how the sausage was made, so to speak, so I asked, and she said yes. (Well, she said no the first two times I asked, but I figured she was being polite.)

The room at Ace is so small that there's really no physical space for Eliana other than on the couch. And that's where Ellie sits, between DiDi (Kyle's girlfriend), and Gwen (Drew's girlfriend). They scooched apart when Ellie sat down, to make room, but really there wasn't room. I think it's kind of cute the way they're all smooshed together. I'm sure Ellie and I will laugh about it later.

DiDi and Gwen are both super nice. They're seniors at Walter Mondale and hang around with this clique of popular girls. They groom themselves in the vein of Janet Leigh from *Psycho*— what did Eliana call her? Bullet Boobs? Not that they have big boobs or anything, just that they're really well put together. Not that Eliana's not well put together. Arrrrgggggghhhh! Being a boyfriend is a lot harder than the brochure makes it out to be. Anyway, seeing Ellie between DiDi and Gwen is cool. It feels right.

"All right, everyone, saddle up." This is Chad's cue that he wants us to run through our set. As I'm counting us in, I see DiDi and Gwen put their earplugs in. Crap. I forgot to tell Ellie to bring earplugs. The look of panic on her face is a palpable thing. The nanoseconds of time between each of the four clicks of my drumsticks, setting the tempo for the song, unfold in some weird, altered state of time. Part of my brain wonders if I can tap some inner Flash superpower and leave between clicks three and four to get earplugs for Ellie. Then I snap back to reality and bring us in on the crash cymbal.

I think Ellie screams, "Oh my god!" but we're so loud I can't be sure. I'm the only one who notices. She squeezes her arms from between the Bullet Boob girls, elbowing DiDi's actual boob in the process, and plugs her ears with her fingers.

Unfortunately, the way UT runs through a set at rehearsal, we don't stop for thirty solid minutes. But Eliana is a trouper. She's all smiles when we're done. It's not a smile I've seen on her before—more teeth than usual, and her eyes are squinted a bit—but she's smiling, and that's what matters.

Damn, I think I'm really falling for this girl.

Winter

Eliana

"You want to drop out of your film class?" Mr. Person has on a hideous red-and-green sweater that I can only hope is in on the joke. He seems more annoyed than usual. The day before winter break should not do that to a person. Or a Person.

"Maybe. I'm not sure. And it's not dropping out if I do it at the semester, right? It's just a change in schedule. I remember this from last year. I can get my A and then switch into a different class, first day of the new semester in January. Easy peasy lemon squeezy." I spread on a cheesy smile for extra "eezy."

"What's wrong with film class?" Mr. Person leans back in his chair and attempts to pull a pencil with a filthy eraser nub out of a mug reading "You Got to Coordinate." He tugs too hard, and the mug topples its contents all over the floor. I lean down to help him pick up the pencils and stretched-open paper clips.

"Nothing is wrong with it, per se. I just need a change. I've already seen all of the movies anyway."

"What would you take instead?" Mr. Person attempts to act casual by placing the pencil in his mouth, then realizes it's the pencil tip and pulls it out with disgust. He eyes the eraser side, and seeing it is no better, flings the pencil across his desk.

"You tell me. What's available?" I consider picking up the

pencil and putting it back in the "You Got to Coordinate" mug, but Mr. Person did have it in his mouth. Would it help convince him I need to change classes?

Initially I had tried to convince Mr. Tannis that he should mix up the seating assignments in film class. But he was very confused and asked way too many questions. I wasn't about to tell him that I just needed a little bit of space from my boyfriend because sitting next to him during film class and having him whisper sweet nothings in my ear is crazy distracting. Dmitri doesn't always want to take my not-so-subtle ignoring him as a hint, but I also don't want to have to directly tell him that it is kind of embarrassing to be the girl in the back of the classroom with her boyfriend staring at her instead of the movie. Switching classes is the obvious right choice here.

Mr. Person squints at his desktop and clicks around. "The sheer variety of options is staggering," he drolls. "You have study hall A, study hall B, shop, and yearbook."

"You know I can't waste my time in study hall, although B sounds complex with a hint of mystery." Mr. Person does not smile. What would he rather be doing with his time? "If I join yearbook, would I have to, like, talk to people?" I wonder if the Person family call themselves People when there is more than one of them around.

"You could just sit there with your mouth shut for the next five months. I don't know if anyone would mind. Perhaps they'd even appreciate it."

"Yowch, Mr. P. You are extra sassy today. What I meant was would I have to do interviews and walk around the school with a camera around my neck, taking pictures of exciting things like kids leaning against lockers and running in track meets? Because I see myself as more of a behind-the-scenes type of gal."

Mr. Person is the king of the extra-long beat. He pauses first to the point of humor, and then he extends it to the maximum for discomfort. Did I overstep with the "sassy" remark?

"These are questions for Ms. Wendell. I'm sure she will shove you into a corner by your lonesome, if that is what you so wish."

"Going anywhere for winter break, Mr. Person?" I cheerily ask.

"My in-laws are coming in tonight to stay with us. For two whole weeks."

"You must be overjoyed," I note, although he clearly is not.

"That's one way to put it." Mr. Person turns toward his desktop and poises his hands for typing. "So are we making this change official, or would you like to mull it over and come bother me again after winter break?"

"By 'bother,' you mean make your day a little brighter, right?" I smile, but Mr. Person isn't breaking the facade today. I was hoping he'd encourage me to make this choice, tell me how smart it is for someone of such a young age to want to expand my horizons with a subject out of my comfort zone. And that it is totally, completely not a sign that Dmitri and I should break up just because I want to move out of one measly class we share together. It's not like I'm telling him I can't spend Christmas with his entire, ginormous Greek family for my first Christmas ever as his Jewish girlfriend of a few months.

Did I just shudder?

"I'll take yearbook for five hundred, please," I tell Mr. Person.

"Five hundred what?" he asks as he types the change into the system.

"That was a *Jeopardy!* reference. I assumed you watch *Jeopardy!*. You have that Alex Trebek–moustache look about you."

Mr. Person stares straight at the computer screen and answers, "He shaved his moustache."

"Aha! I knew you watched his moustache."

Mr. Person dramatically bounces his middle finger on the enter key.

"'So let it be written, so let it be done.'"

I guffaw at Mr. Person's *Ten Commandments* reference. "I knew you wouldn't disappoint me, Mr. Person."

He offers a half smile, and I know he still loves me. In that guidance counselor, totally platonic and usually annoyed way of love. Love.

Now how do I break the news to Dmitri?

Dmitri

"*W*eird how?"

"I don't know, just weird."

Nicky and I are sitting across from each other on the floor of his bedroom, a chessboard between us. I have only four pieces left (king, knight, bishop, and pawn); Nicky has ten pieces left (enough, including his queen, that it's not worth naming them all). He's going to win. He always wins.

My father likes to claim that chess was invented by the Greeks, but it wasn't. Nicky researched it and found out chess originated in India, long after ancient Greece was dead and buried.

"India?" my father blustered when presented with the evidence. "όχι!" *No.* Don't try to confuse prejudice with the facts.

"So Eliana was just weird?" Nicky makes air quotes around the words "just weird."

"Like every time I tried to hold her hand or put my arm around her, she found a way to, I don't know, disentangle herself."

Nicky looks up. "Good word." I'm pretty sure my brother sees me as a complete moron. I suppose next to him I kind of am. "Where were you?"

"The mall."

"The mall?" He says the word like it tastes bad.

"Yeah."

"Ellie wanted to go to the mall?"

"I don't know, I guess so."

"You don't know?"

My brother can be relentless with his questions. "I mean, I suggested it, but lots of kids go to the mall to hang out."

"Dimmi, Eliana is not lots of kids."

Sometimes I think Nicky knows Ellie better than I do. The times she's been to our house, the two of them seem to get on really well, like they understand each other better than I understand either one of them. That's probably why I've asked for Nicky's advice tonight.

I move my bishop across the board to challenge his rook, but Nicky shakes his head. "That will put you in check." He's right. The bishop is protecting my king from one of his aggressive little pawns. I move it back.

"Things were great for a while after we kissed that first time, at the Seventh Street Entry gig, but now it's like something's changed. Like maybe I'm doing something wrong."

"Like taking her to the mall."

"Would you forget about the stupid mall!"

Nicky looks up at my little outburst, smirks, and shakes his head. "Why don't you just ask her?"

"Ask her what?"

"Ask her if something's wrong."

I think about this for a minute as I stare at the chessboard. The advice seems so simple that it has to be true. But asking her would feel like walking naked into a minefield with no metal detector or bomb-sniffing dog. I don't want to get blown up, especially if I'm not wearing any clothes.

There are only two moves I can make on the board: my king one space to the left or my pawn one space forward. The walls are definitely closing in. I move my pawn.

Without time to blink Nicky moves his rook all the way down one of the ranks. He could have put me in check with his queen; since he doesn't, I can only guess he's setting me up for the final kill. He's really good at thinking two or three or five steps ahead.

"That's just not how relationships work," I tell him, trying to play the I'm-dating-someone-and-you-never-have card. But even as I say it, I know it's BS. Truth is, I'm too scared to ask Ellie what's wrong.

So, of course, my brain, being my brain, goes in the opposite direction. "Maybe I should tell her I love her."

Nicky looks up at me. I mean really looks at me. He squints his eyes and cocks his head a bit to one side. He even sniffs like he's trying to smell something. It's unnerving.

"What?" I ask.

"I'm trying to tell if you're on drugs."

"Very funny."

I move my pawn another space. I have only one space to go before I get my queen back. Nicky moves a bishop in a way that doesn't seem to be helpful to him at all.

"Do you love her?"

"Yes!" Even I can hear that my answer has too much force. "I mean, I think I do." My pulse starts to race. "I mean, yeah, of course I do."

"Look," Nicky says, "you're right. I've never been in a relationship. But if you ask me, and you did, it sounds like maybe Eliana just needs some space. Like this is all new to her, and she's still figuring out what it all means. Telling her you love her will be like trying to hold her hand or put your arm around her times a billion." He pauses and watches me for a moment. How did my little brother, with his too-short corduroy pants and his too-small polo shirts, get this wise? It must be all the books. Then he adds, "That or she just really hates the mall."

"Jerk," I answer. I move my pawn forward. "Queen, please." My voice is smug, my comeback in the game about to get underway.

He replaces my pawn with a queen, then slides his bishop—the one that seemed useless—backward across the board, and captures the newly rescued queen. I see now this was his plan all along, as the bishop now threatens my king. I have nowhere to go.

"Checkmate," he says. I can only shake my head.

"I'm going to bed." I get up to leave.

"Dimmi," he says when I'm at the door.

I turn to face him. "Yeah?"

"Eliana's a special girl, but I think maybe a fragile girl, too. Just try giving her some space. Don't rush things."

Hmm. I don't *feel* like I'm rushing things, or crowding her. Am I?

No, I can't be. I didn't even text her tonight. Well, I did, but only once. Maybe I should text her again now, just to say good night.

Nicky's words evaporate in the air and get left behind as I take my phone out of my pocket and head back to my room.

Eliana

"The mall?" Janina is on the other end of Facetime, wearing an expression that mirrors my own incredulousness.

"Right?"

"Does he know you at all?" she asks.

"To be fair, there was a valid reason for being there. He was looking for a Christmas gift for Nicky."

"That at least makes a little sense. But the mall? Who even goes to the mall anymore except old ladies who walk around it five times in giant white gym shoes before they hit their Weight Watchers meeting?"

"That was quite an image, Nina."

"Thank you."

"Yeah, it was weird. It felt so of another era. Like, what's Chico's? And why would anyone voluntarily enter it?"

"My grandma loves her some Chico's. Don't knock it until you've worn one of their color-blocked jackets."

"Did you chug a tureen of coffee today or something?" I ask.

"Maybe. Or two. Did you have fun at all?" Janina's image joggles as the background moves up and down, up and down.

"What the heck are you doing?"

"Squats," she answers. "Fun. Did you have fun?"

I consider the question. "What is fun, really? Were there Ferris wheels? No. Mass quantities of kitties frisking about? No. Bungee jumping? Maybe."

"You can have fun without doing actual obvious fun things. Did he at least hold your hand?"

"Yes," I say, exasperated. "Like, the whole time. I couldn't even pick my nose if I'd wanted to."

"A." Janina squats on each point for emphasis. "You have a second hand. B. Why would you want to pick your nose in the middle of a mall?"

I shrug in loose agreement.

"Let's try this: What did you enjoy at your mall date?"

I ponder. Maybe a tad too long.

"Ellie . . ."

"Okay okay. I liked talking with Dmitri about how our families spend the holidays and his favorite toys when he was little. He secretly has a massive Transformers collection."

"Aw."

"But I swear when he was gushing to me about Optimus Prime, he was checking out this girl who walked past us. Like a complete up-and-down once-over. And he kept talking to me about Transformers like he didn't just picture this girl naked."

"Are you sure that's what he was doing?"

"It was blatant and yet oblivious. He actually leaned over to kiss me a minute later. All I could think was that he was imagining kissing that other girl."

"Doubtful. Boys have terrible memories. I'm sure he was thinking of you and only you."

"Are you? Are you really sure?" I ask suspiciously.

"No." Janina stops squatting. "I wish I were. Dmitri can be a dip-shit sometimes, but not all the time, right?"

"No, I mean, we did go to the mall to find his brother a Christmas present. So that was kind of sweet."

"What did he end up getting him?"

"A pop-up book of fancy chess sets."

"Thoughtful," Janina assesses.

"Yeah. And he bought me a Jamba Juice, which was tasty?"

"Why do you always sound like you're asking a question when you talk about Dmitri these days?"

"That is the question," I reply. I'm not sure if I know the answer yet.

Dmitri

"*P*lease," I say, "not the asparagus."

"What?" my mother answers. It's more of a complaint than a question. Everything my mother says is more of a complaint than a question. She's standing on the small stone ledge in front of the fireplace, using a pushpin to hang a bouquet of asparagus from a metal wire. "It keep kallikantzaroi away. You want them in you house?" She turns and winks at me, like of course I want to keep the bad spirits away, how could I not want to keep the bad spirits away?

"Ma, I'm not sure there are any kallikantzaroi in America; I think they're only in Greece."

"No, no," she says, putting a second and third pushpin into the wood of the mantel. "They smart. They find you, 'specially if you bad boy."

I sigh at the battle already lost. Hey, it was worth a try.

I suppose the tapestry of cultures from all over the world is part of what makes America great. Right now the fireplace asparagus—a tradition akin to Italian people eating fish on Christmas Eve, or Americans hanging mistletoe to steal a kiss— feels like a billboard screaming that my family is different. I'm already nervous enough about Ellie coming over Christmas Day and the asparagus isn't helping. The civilization that gave us Aristotle and Pythagoras also gave us asparagus—a coincidentally weird hybrid of the words Aristotle and Pythagoras—as a guard against clawed, hooved elves. Really? Some days I wish I were Irish.

I wanted to take Ellie out for a movie and Chinese food—she told me this was called a "Jewish Christmas," which I thought was funny and sounded like a nice way to spend a day—but my father wouldn't hear of me not being home.

"You invite Jew girl—"

"Ah!" my mother interrupted.

"Sorry. You invite Jew*ish* girl here."

"Can we please start calling her Eliana?" I ask.

"Okay, okay. You invite Eliana here. She should meet you family." My mother's invitation sounded final enough that I didn't argue.

Ellie's already met my parents and Yia Yia enough times to get a sense of who we are, but Christmas Day ratchets it up to a whole new level: Uncle Gus and Aunt Vi will be here with my cousins George and Aspasia—not first cousins, but some number cousins some number of times removed—whose identity is almost completely defined by our ancestral culture, which means George is going to try to flirt with and hit on Eliana, and Aspasia is going to spend the day in the kitchen with the older women. Aunt Stella, my mother's younger sister, also known by me and Nicky as the Cheek Pincher, is coming with her new (and third) husband, Spiro. The Pappas family, friends from church, are coming with some of their distant relatives in tow. (Really, they're the only bright spot. Alex and Meg Pappas are as American as me and Nicky, so we usually try to sneak off and hang out and watch movies.) And, of course, Aunt Maxine, Yia Yia's older sister, will be here. Maxine is older than dirt and has this weird disease that makes one of her eyeballs bulge out of her head. Nicky refers to her as Mad-Eye Maxine. She wears big old-lady sunglasses to cover it, which somehow makes it worse; you can still see the wonky eye through the tinted lenses, and indoors, at night, it's downright creepy.

It's not only the cast of *My Big Fat Greek Wedding* that has me feeling anxious. We go the whole nine yards—the lamb on the spit in the backyard, the singing of traditional Greek carols, the decorating of boats (a big tradition in Thessaloniki, the city from which my family hails)—and I'm just positive this is going to make Ellie question our whole relationship. (And shouldn't that expression be the whole *ten* yards? A first down is ten yards, not nine, I think. I don't get it.)

Anyway, the only saving grace is that I've got a secret weapon to protect against all the Greekishness Ellie is going to be clobbered with: I am one thousand percent sure I have completely nailed it with my Christmas present for her. Well, Christmas presents.

First, Janina helped me pick out this very classy necklace. It's a single polished pearl, Ellie's birthstone, on a silver chain. I think it's pretty and Janina assures me Ellie is going to love it. My initial plan was to get a "D&E" tattoo someplace my parents wouldn't be able to see and to surprise Ellie in private, but Janina suggested this wasn't the best idea. I think her exact words were "What are you, stupid?" When you're in love, you do stupid things, I guess. I knew she was right as soon as she said it.

Second, I made a book of gift certificates for Dmitri Back Rubs. There are ten of them. I saw it in a movie once and thought it was fun. Ellie loves when I rub her neck, so I think this will be a hit, too.

But the best present, the one that will show Ellie how much I really do treasure her, is that I paid Joe Loskywitz fifty dollars to switch lockers with me. Starting January 3, our first day back from Christmas break, I'll be Ellie's locker neighbor. Now she and I can see each other in between every single period. She is going to flip.

My mother finishes with the asparagus and starts on the thistle. I give up and go to the kitchen.

Yia Yia is sitting at the table. Her two hands, which are wrapped around a mug of thick black coffee, are shaking a little. She looks drawn-out, thinner, like maybe she's fading away. But then she sees me and lights up, and she's Yia Yia again.

"Dimmi-moo! Come. Sit." I do. "I hear you talking to you mother."

"I know, Yia Yia, it's just . . ." Yia Yia puts a hand up and I stop.

"Dimmi, this who you are. Who we are. We hold on to this to remember where we from, ναι?" I nod. "You honor you ancestor by remembering. You honor me. This girl, she love you, then she love *all* of you." I gloss over the fact that I still haven't grown the stones to tell Ellie I love her. When I texted her after my chess game with Nicky, she never wrote back; I guess she'd already gone to sleep. By the time the sun had come up the next morning,

I'd lost my nerve. I know that I *want* to tell her, but what happens if she doesn't say it back?

Since I'm too chicken to tell Ellie, I do the next best thing.

"I love you, Yia Yia." I stand up and kiss my grandmother on the forehead.

"Of course you do, Dimmi," she says, patting my wrist. "There is lot to love." And then she breaks out laughing and I can't help but join her.

Eliana

J am knitting. Mrs. Weasley made it look so easy when she whipped her wand into the air and two knitting needles clacked together to make the beloved Weasley letter sweaters. I can barely finish a pot holder. Or is this a scarf? I need to get good fast because my whole plan for a Christmas gift for Dmitri relies upon my knitting prowess.

Knitting is supposed to be something that relaxes people, or so I've read. But all this anticipation of meeting Dimmi's entire Ancestry.com family tree for a holiday I don't even celebrate is uberstressful. The beginning of winter break should be a time of rejoicing for any normal teenager. I guess that makes me—surprise!—abnormal. There is so much together time during vacation, and when you live in a house with four kids and two parents in Minneapolis in the dead of winter, together time is essentially a scene from *The Shining*. I half expect my dad to break through the basement door at any minute with an axe, shouting, "Here's Johnny!" It's bad enough he's brandishing his shiny new résumé.

"I'm ready to rumble!" He rolls his Rs and draws out "rumble," as though his next job will be as an announcer at a local monster truck rally. I can't decide if that would be cooler than being the ex-owner of a defunct video store. Anything that gets him out of the house would be cooler than our current situation.

Isaac, Samara, and I sit on the living room couch watching *The Dark Crystal*, an old movie that is masterful in its ability to terrify my younger siblings with puppets. Instead of parking himself in the perfectly available squishy lounge chair, my dad squeezes himself in between me and Samara, draping his arms over our shoulders. I try my best not to flinch. Dad is annoying, self-absorbed, and clueless, but he is Dad. In his hands he holds his résumé, and I pray he doesn't ask me to read it. Aside from being highly boring, reading someone's résumé feels akin to reading their online dating profile. I don't want to know what things you think are awesome about yourself. My aunt once had me help her upload pictures to a dating site, and it was disturbing. I did not need to see her in a vinyl miniskirt.

"This is the future of your dad, kids. The new me. The new life . . ." Dad is mumbling many sayings of "new," as though he will convince himself that he will find a job and all will be well with the world.

I don't know why I'm being so hard on him. I think everyone is getting on my nerves today. Janina Facetimed me this morning, and I assumed it was so we could get together and she could help me with my present for Dimmi. Nope.

"I can't hang out today. I have to break up with Jeremy before my family leaves for Hawaii tomorrow."

"So you're abandoning me for a boy?' I accused.

"I'm abandoning you for the absence of a boy, so then I'll have all the time in the world for you. To deal with your boy troubles," Janina argued.

"But you're still abandoning me for the entirety of winter break to go to Hawaii while I am forced to alternately lock myself in my room-hole and meet all six hundred fifty-seven members of Dmitri's extended family while they judge every Jewish inch of my body."

"How did you manage to say all of that without a single breath?"

"I practice diaphragm breathing when I'm not freaking out about things. So, actually, never."

"What's to freak out about? You have a great boyfriend, right?"

"Right?" I should have sounded more certain, I know. But I wasn't only trying to convince Janina of my feelings. "It's complicated."

"Have you finished his Christmas present?"

I held up the drumstick warmers I am attempting to knit. I found the pattern online and assumed they would be easy to make, thoughtful, and useful gifts. If his drumsticks get cold. But the warmers weren't quite as polished as I had hoped.

"Have you started?" Janina squinted into the phone.

"Ha ha. It's a delicate pattern. I'm sure he'll like them. It's the thought that counts, right?"

"Oh, he'll like them. He'd like if you gave him a paper bag puppet. He's madly in love with you, El."

For some reason, this made me cringe. "Don't say that. I mean, he likes me a lot. But he's not madly—we've only been together a few months."

"You don't recognize that mad look in his eyes whenever he sees you like I do. You're not getting rid of this guy easily."

"Why would I want to get rid of him? He's great. He's fun and nice and plays the drums well." I stumbled through a list of what makes Dmitri such a good guy. Who was I trying to convince? This should have been a no-brainer, but I was anxious about it. I hate being anxious. I changed the subject.

"I wish you weren't going away for break. Why does your family have to go to Hawaii? I hear it's horrible and ugly there. And cold. Really cold."

"Yeah, I think that's the other Hawaii. The one we're visiting is essentially paradise. I'll bring you back a lei."

"Hide me in your suitcase?"

"If only. I better go pack. Kisses and happy Hanukkah!" Janina blew a kiss at the phone and hung up.

Now I'll be left in the cold prison of my bedroom during December in Minneapolis. Life is a turd. My dad has escaped the basement. Janina is leaving the continental United States. And I get to spend Christmas with seven hundred Greek family and friends of my boyfriend who is "madly in love with" me. That last one should feel better than it does. Maybe it's the close quarters that are getting to me.

I excuse myself from my dad's grip and return to my roomhole. There I prop myself up on my futon, and attempt to knit the drumstick warmers while watching the first Harry Potter. It's a lighter film, filled with fun and hope and tons of magic. Damn, I wish I were there right now.

Dmitri

"*O* w!" Ellie turns to scowl at the eight-year-old on her right, who just stabbed her with the wooden wand we were each given with our dinner.

This night is not going well.

It's T-minus three days to the Night of the Living Digrindaki Christmas—a lot of people don't know, but Digrindaki is the plural of Digrindakis, as in one Digrindakis and two Digrindaki; okay, not really, but I think it's funny—and I wonder if Ellie is as nervous about it as I am. I doubt it. She's so determined, so nose-to-the-grindstone, that I'm not sure anything fazes her. I have this recurring nightmare of Aunt Stella getting a wad of both my and Ellie's cheeks at the same time and pinching until she rips the flesh off our faces. Well, not an actual nightmare, more like a terrifying daydream, but I'm pretty sure it could happen.

Anyway, Ellie and I agreed that exchanging Christmas presents—sorry, holiday presents; she reminded me that not everyone celebrates Christmas—in front of my extended family on Christmas Day would not be the most comfortable thing in the world, so we decided to celebrate by exchanging gifts over a nice dinner out.

This date needed to be perfect, and that started with the selection of the restaurant.

Yelp and Google showed a bunch of choices in the small downtown of our little suburb, but none was quite right. There was an Italian place called Tri Colore, but most of the reviews talked about the wine cellar, which wasn't going to be any use to us. There was an Indian restaurant called the Bombay Club, but Ellie isn't big on spicy food. I was totally stressing out over it and was about to text Janina for help, when, on page three of the Yelp listings, I found my answer.

Away from downtown, closer to the mall and in a little strip center with what has to be the last Radio Shack in America, is a brand-new Harry Potter–themed restaurant called the Great Hall. The pictures on Yelp—and it's so new there were only five—showed two long tables like the ones at which the different houses eat in the Harry Potter movies. The only review posted so far said "Definitely more of a Muggle experience. Stay away from the bangers and mash." I wasn't really sure what that meant, but it didn't matter. This felt like fate.

When I texted Ellie the restaurant choice, she didn't respond other than to say she would meet me there.

"*Expecto Patronum*," the little brat next to Ellie says now, pointing his wand right between her eyes. The kid's mom finally notices her son is up to no good, mumbles a "sorry, he's just so excited" to Ellie, and turns the boy's chair to face his family.

Now that we're here, I'm not sure this was the best idea. The only seating is at one of two long tables, you're forced to dine with the people sitting on either side of you. Any sense of intimacy or romance is out the window. It doesn't help that we're the only couple here. The other diners are all frustrated and angry-looking parents with children too young to really appreciate or understand Harry Potter. It's also the only thing actually open in this strip center. The Radio Shack is dark, empty, and out of business, and with both the nail salon and tae kwon do studio currently closed, the vibe here is more Halloween than Christmas.

The Patronus spell is the third one Ellie has had to endure from what is clearly the most hyperactive kid in the restaurant. She's bearing it with style and grace, but I'm wondering when she's going to crack and use her own wand to brain the little rug rat.

"So . . . ," I say.

"So."

"I kind of thought this would be a bit more, you know, Harry Potterish."

Ellie's eyes soften a bit. I think she knows I tried and that has to count for something.

"It's okay. I liked the idea of it when you told me, but I'm always wary of things that try to pass themselves off as part of the wizarding world." She pauses to take a sip of her "polyjuice," which tastes an awful lot like Kool-Aid. "You know, I stayed up the entire night of my eleventh birthday waiting for an owl or a Hagrid or something." She smiles, but it looks more sad than happy.

Conversation usually flows pretty easily between me and Ellie, but tonight it's just awkward. Besides the restaurant, I'm totally amped up over the presents in the plastic bag at my feet. We need to get the gift exchange over with so we can go back to enjoying each other's company. It's now or never.

"Here," I say, plopping the bag on the table.

Ellie stares at it and pauses for a second before asking, "You got me something from Target?"

"What's that?" The little boy next to Ellie uses his wand to point at the bag.

"Harry, stop," the mom says. "Let these nice young people eat their dinner."

"Wait." Ellie turns to face the family, looking from the mom to the kid and back again. "Is his name *actually* Harry, or are you just calling him Harry because you're here?"

"Actually Harry." The mom smiles. "We're kind of big fans."

Ellie's eyebrows go up and stay up. She turns back to me and mouths "okay" in a way that suggests maybe it's not. The mom's back stiffens and she swivels young Harry back toward his dinner yet again.

"So, Target?" Ellie asks, nodding at the bag.

"Huh? Oh, no!" I insist, recovering from the interruption. "This is just the bag I used to carry your presents here." A nervous, lunatic kind of laugh bubbles up from my throat.

"Did you say presents, as in plural?"

"Um . . . yeah . . . is that okay? I mean, it doesn't matter if you got me only one." Crap. That came out wrong. "I mean, I just wanted to get you these things."

Ellie has that look she gets sometimes where her mouth cuts a straight line across her face, separating her eyes from the rest of her body, like she's two different people. "Really, Dimmi, you shouldn't have."

"No, El, I wanted to." I reach forward and take her hand in mine, and for a minute, she lets me. Then she pulls back again. "And really, only one of them is a *present*, as in an actual thing."

"What?" Her confusion in this moment is exactly what I'd hoped for. I want her to be surprised.

"Okay, let me explain. First, the present," I say, and pass her the wrapped jewelry box. Ellie takes it and kind of weighs it in both hands. "Open it."

She tears the paper off and flips the lid of the box up. "A pearl. That's my birthstone," she says, looking up at me.

"Yeah."

"Thanks, Dimmi, it's beautiful." Ellie takes the necklace out and puts it on. She's wearing a black sweater, and the lone pearl set against a silver pendant really stands out. It looks great. She looks great.

"Janina helped me pick it out."

"Hmm," she says. "Should I be nervous about the two of you?"

"What? No!" I'm about to go to DEFCON 1 when Ellie laughs.

"Relax, you goober, I'm kidding."

"Oh, good, okay."

I'm about to give her gift number two when Ellie says, "Wait! I have to give you my present." She reaches into her backpack and pulls out a small, soft package. The wrapping paper has the words "Punk Rock" in the colors of the British flag.

"Where did you find this paper?"

"Online. Go ahead." She smiles and nods at it.

I carefully peel the tape back and unfold the paper.

"Oh my god, Dimmi, just tear it," she laughs.

"I don't want to ruin it."

Ellie rolls her eyes, but it's more playful than not.

Inside I find what look like two long, freaky glove fingers. I have no idea what they are or what they're for. But I look up at her and smile anyway. "Thank you! Where did you find these?"

"I made them."

"What? Really?" If I had any doubt that Ellie loved me, it just evaporated. I want to get up, go around the table, and hug her. Maybe I don't know what these things are for, but she *made* them. For *me*!

"Cool!" Harry the scamp says. Before I know what's going on, he reaches across the table, grabs one of the finger blankets out of my hand, and sticks his wand in it.

Is that what this thing is, a blanket for my wand? But why did she make two?

Harry's mom, who now seems as annoyed with us as she is with her own kid, snatches my new wand warmer out of her son's hand and looks at it before she passes it back across the table. "What is it?" she asks.

At the same instant I say, "A wand blanket," Ellie says, "Drumstick warmers."

Drumstick warmers? Huh. I don't think I've ever noticed my drumsticks getting cold. Still, she made them and that's all that matters.

I laugh, trying to act like my wand blanket comment was a joke, but I catch Ellie looking at me through squinted eyes, trying to figure if maybe I didn't really know what her present was supposed to be. I want to tell her that it doesn't matter what the present is, the fact that she made it for me is . . . everything. Really. Everything.

But I don't. Instead, I steamroll ahead.

"Okay," I say, trying to move us past this, "time for my next present."

The coupon book is really just a few sheets of paper stapled together. Each one says:

```
This coupon entitles the bearer to one
free back rub from Dmitri Digrindakis.
Expiration date: Never.
```

I'm not the best artist in the world, and now, looking at it through Ellie's eyes, I can see how amateurish this gift must seem. Too late; the cat, or in this case coupon book, is literally out of the bag, so I hand it over.

Ellie's mouth scrunches up into a weird little circle, like she's trying to figure out what this is supposed to be, as she flips through the pages.

"I saw it in a movie," I blurt out. "I thought it would be cute."

"It's very sweet," Ellie offers without a lot of emotion.

This whole evening has felt off-kilter from the start. The restaurant, the kid, my not knowing what the drumstick warmers were, and now my dopey coupon book. I'm feeling embarrassed and I just want to get things over with so I hand Ellie her third and final present. This is either going to be what saves this date, or buries it once and for all.

Ellie feels through the wrapping paper and tries to guess what's inside. "It's a picture frame?"

I nod.

"Did you get a picture of us framed? That's very sweet, Dimmi."

I shake my head no. "Open it."

Ellie squints again—god, she's cute when she does that—clearly wondering what I'm up to now as she shreds the "A Joyous Holiday Season" wrapping paper. She stares at the photo for a long minute before looking up at me in confusion.

"Um . . . you got me a school locker?"

"No, that's a picture of *your* locker."

"You're giving me my own locker?" she laughs.

"No! I switched lockers with Joe Loskywitz. You and I are neighbors now, for the rest of the school year!"

Ellie's laughter peters out and her jaw goes slack. She doesn't say a single word; she just stares at me in disbelief. I have rendered her speechless.

BOOM!

Nailed it!

Eliana

In the sanctuary of my room-hole, I look over the gifts from Dmitri:

- *One coupon book for massages. (Do I even like massages? Enough to get a coupon book full of them? I hope he doesn't mean the type of massage where he oils me up and lights a bunch of scented candles and plays music with whales dying in the background. Will he notice if I "forget" to use the coupons?)*
- *One necklace with a pearl. (This was kind of sweet, but I also kind of hate my old-lady birthstone. How often am I expected to wear this? Necklaces make me feel like I'm choking.)*
- *The locker. The mother-effing locker.*

Things I like to do at my locker:

1. *Remove and/or insert my books*
2. *Store items, such as my backpack, jackets, and a light snack*
3. *Look into my minuscule mirror to make sure I don't have a stray booger*

4. *Spin the lock at precisely the right frequency so that I land on the correct numbers to open it. This works approximately 9.2 percent of the time (not an actual statistic).*

Things I don't like to do at my locker:

1. *Linger*
2. *Hang out*
3. *Chat*
4. *Make out*
5. *Stay any longer than is necessary, thus making me late to class*

I already have my schedule perfectly planned out: how long it takes to walk from one side of the school to the other, which passing periods I can use the bathroom on a normal day and which passing periods I can use the bathroom when I need extended time. Having Dmitri at the locker next to me is going to mess all of that up. What if he wants to cuddle? Whisper sweet nothings in my ear? Make me cash in my massage coupons? I will be perpetually late for class and will lose all of my valuable bathroom time. I'll end up with boogers in my nose, a bladder infection, and anemia for lack of snack eating time. This is terrible.

Stressful.

Panic inducing.

I start to call Janina, then remember she is in Hawaii. I try anyway.

No answer.

I wish I had someone else to call.

In the past month, some of my old friends, the ones who couldn't handle Depressed Eliana, started coming up to me at my locker (and you know how I feel about locker time). I didn't know what to make of it. They wanted to talk about Dmitri. They wanted to giggle. They wanted details. Part of me felt really good having these people, these once-ago friends, show interest in me. But the bigger part of me, the one that I'm wielding as a protective metal shield, says not to trust this. Sample conversation:

"Hi, Ellie! You look so cute! Did Nina do this to your hair?" Daisy King greeted me at my locker a week before winter break. She leaned forward and futzed with my bangs, as though it were a totally normal occurrence and not the first time she's said two words to me in six months. I'm sure my flinch was noticeable. I felt both embarrassed and justified. I don't like people who make me feel two emotions at once. Maybe that's why I'm so conflicted about Dmitri.

"Uh, yeah, she cuts my hair. It's kind of her thing." I slammed my locker, not in any sort of dramatic fashion but with enough force to punctuate my need to move to my next class. Daisy wasn't getting the signal. Perhaps in her estrangement she forgot about my propensity for punctuality and perfection in a school setting. Also, alliteration.

"So you and Dmitri . . . ?" She said this as a question to which I knew the answer.

"Yep." I nodded and sidestepped a bit, trying to get the message across that class was happening for us all and it was time to move on. No such luck.

"He's pretty hot. How did . . ." She started the question I knew she wanted to finish with "*you* get him?" ". . . you guys meet?"

"We sort of bumped into each other, you could say. We have a couple of classes together."

"Think you can get us into Unexpected Turbulence's next show?" "Us," I assumed, was the group of girls who once occupied space on my floor for slumber parties and would have known the story of me and my first boyfriend if they'd hung around.

"I don't really have that kind of clout. I mean, with Dimmi, yeah, but the clubs are all run by weird old dudes with dangly earrings. The shows usually only cost a few bucks anyway." I worried that sounded bitchy. Not that I had any reason to worry, when Daisy totally shat upon me and probably was only interested in speaking to me now because I am part of the dating pool.

"Cool. I get it." And she smiled, like she didn't want me to think she was being bitchy. Like she cared what I thought about her. It was all so 180.

"I really have to get to class." I thumbed down the hallway and started up on my toes to walk.

"I know how you hate to be late." And just like that I felt that connection we once had. When she knew my favorite foods and how I never slept in pajama bottoms because of how they scrunched under the sheets and where I stored my replica Golden Snitch. It was too confusing, so I ran off toward my math class with a quick "Gotta go."

We had several exchanges like that recently, and I don't know what they meant. Does she want to be friends again? Does she miss me? How much of it has to do with Dmitri?

Back to Dmitri and my locker.

His locker.

His-and-her lockers.

"Ava!" I call to my littlest sister, and she stumbles up the stairs in quick response.

"Yeah?" She peeks her head into my closet door, her cute round face dimpled with grape jelly.

"Can you walk on my back, please? It's bothering me again."

"Yes!" she exclaims. I lie on my futon, stomach down, hands flat by my sides. Ava carefully pads her bare feet up and down my back. I don't know how much longer we will be able to do this. Ava already feels heavier. I listen for the necessary cracks, and the tension begins to ease.

"Okay!" I scream out for her to stop, a little crushed but definitely relaxed. Ava jumps off me, the extra pressure pumping a breath of wind from my lips. She bounces to the floor and kisses my cheek, leaving behind a sticky calling card.

As I lie deflated and loose, I remember the massage coupons. Dmitri's massages never leave me feeling like this. When Dmitri massages me, there are always those moments where his hands slip forward a bit, and I wonder where they're headed. Instead of relaxing me, I'm left contemplating how far we are going to go.

I tuck the coupons and the locker picture underneath the sweaters-I-never-wear section of my closet shelf. I'll worry about them later. For tomorrow is Christmas at the Digrindakis house. I think I have enough to worry about.

Dmitri

"*N*o, like thees: spaaaahn-ah-koh-peee-tah." My mother draws out each syllable as she tries to get Ellie to say the word with the proper accent.

"Spanikahpita," Ellie says, the first "a" voiced like the "a" in "plan" instead of the "a" in "father." I'm not sure, but I think Eliana might be screwing with my mom, which in one sense is pretty funny, but in another makes me uncomfortable. If she is, my mother misses it.

"You good girl," Mom says, chuckling as she pats Ellie on the shoulder.

At my insistence, Ellie arrived early. I wanted her—I wanted us—to have a chance to settle in before the rest of the company got here. I figured it was better than having the entirety of the Minnesota Hellenic Society surround and smother Ellie the second she stepped through the door. Now Ellie can establish a dominant position, like an army defending a beach. (I have no idea if this theory will work.)

BING! BONG!

Our doorbell is So. Freaking. LOUD! Nicky and I have begged Dad to replace it, but he says the bell has gravitas, though that wasn't the word he used. "We want peoples to know we are family to take serious." He puffed his chest out when he told us this. Whatever.

"Dmitri, you answer door." My mother nods in the direction of the deafening sound.

"C'mon," I say to Ellie, but don't take her hand. Holding hands in front of my family feels too intimate. For the first time I understand her feelings about not being affectionate in public. Though I do wish we could be more affectionate than we have been in private.

BING! BONG!

"We're coming," I scream, the stress of the day starting to make me crack.

The late afternoon sun is directly opposite our house, so when I open the door we're greeted by a short but hulking mass of shadow; a slightly misshapen head tapers to puffy arms as if the beast's shoulders don't exist. It—the gender can't yet be discerned—is breathing heavily, like Darth Vader, only the sound is tinged with a phlegmy rasp, like it isn't getting enough air.

"Dimmi-moo!" Aunt Maxine steps into the light of the foyer and Ellie lets a small peep escape her lips; the bulging eye—Aunt Maxine's sunglasses failing to shield it from view—is even bigger than usual. Damn, I forgot to warn Ellie. "This moost be you girlfriend!"

Aunt Maxine stretches her arms forward to grab Ellie's face, leaning in and preparing to kiss Ellie on both cheeks as she does. While I can't smell Aunt Maxine's breath from here, I've been victimized by this move enough times in my life to know what Ellie is about to experience. Oh god, she is going to dump me for sure.

But then Ellie pulls a quintessentially (thank you, PSAT prep) Ellie move. Just before Aunt Maxine's tentacles can snake their way around the back of Ellie's neck, locking her in an old-Greek-lady death grip, my wonderful, beautiful girlfriend steps back and sticks her hand out. "Hi, I'm Eliana. It's nice to meet you."

It seems such a simple and obvious counter to the Maxine Maul that I'm stunned no one has thought of it before. So is Aunt Maxine. She stands there with her arms straight and perpendicular to her body in a full Frankenstein pose, completely unsure of what to do next. Eliana takes it a bit further when she clasps one of the two hands hovering in front of her face and shakes it.

"Um, yes" is all Aunt Maxine can manage to say.

This time I do take Ellie's hand—survival trumping embarrassment—and pull her out of the foyer and toward the back of the house.

"Where are we going?" she whispers, a hint of nervousness in her voice, probably wondering what horror awaits her next.

"Away from here," I mutter in response.

I glance over my shoulder and see Aunt Maxine has finally lowered her arms. She remains standing there in a state of utter confusion.

BING! BONG!

Another guest. Someone else can get it this time.

Eliana

The eye. The GIGANTIC eye. W.T.F. "Dude, you should have warned me. Seriously. Was that some kind of a joke?"

Dmitri chuckles at this, then sees my face of resolve. His lips straighten immediately. "No! I wouldn't do that! I'm just so used to her bulging eye, I didn't think it was an important detail."

"Dimmi, all details are important. Your family is testing me. And I don't like to fail a test."

Dmitri and I are hiding out in the basement. And not the finished, shag-carpeted, couch-bearing section of his basement. We're talking laundry room, granny panties hanging from a line, concrete floor replete with hidden mousetraps, crawl space filled with melting cardboard boxes covered with giant Sharpie scrawl. It's cold even though we're standing next to the furnace. Every time the heat kicks on, I jump at the sound of flame hitting gas.

"I'm sorry. I promise to tell you every last detail about my family from now on. From my uncle Gus's missing testicle to my cousin George's tattoo of his mom's face on his butt."

I attempt to read Dmitri's face. Is he kidding? I give him my question eyes.

"TMI?" he responds.

"Oh my god, Dimmi. I can't do this. My stomach hurts. And

they're going to make me eat more of the spanakopita. Which is delicious, but how much feta cheese can one consume?"

"That's not a question you should ask out loud when we get upstairs. I'm just saying."

I shake my hands, trying to flick away the nerves that are devouring my body. Dmitri comes up behind me and wraps his arms around my center. At first I tense, not wanting to be surrounded any more than I already feel I am with his family. But he nuzzles my neck and sways us to an imaginary rhythm, and I eventually relax. Until the sound of at least a dozen children in hard-soled dress shoes clamber above our heads.

"Can't we stay down here? It's a lot of a lot. They wouldn't notice."

"Are you kidding? My aunt Vienna is practically planning our wedding."

Is that supposed to make me want to go back upstairs?

Dmitri

*B*ING! BONG!

The doorbell rings again just as we hit the top of the stairs; the volume of it makes Ellie jump.

Nicky has dragged us back to the party; Mom complained to him that "Dimmi and his girlfriend need be with guests." The spotlight on our whereabouts made Ellie visibly cringe.

The entry to the basement is geographically closer to the front door than is almost any other point in the house, so on instinct I turn to answer the door.

"No!" Ellie's shriek is simultaneously a scream and a whisper, like the word was coming from deep in her throat and lost some of its steam on the way out of her mouth. Our friends from church, the Pappas family—including Meg and Alex, the only other kids at the party not right off a boat from Athens—look over at us from the living room, concern in their eyes. I offer a nervous smile and laugh.

"I'll get it." Nicky, who was right behind us, gives me a reassuring pat on the shoulder. I love my little brother.

Ellie and I stand back, watching as Nicky opens the door. She and I are somewhere on a continuum between deer in headlights and studio executives in a private screening room watching a really bad horror movie unfold before them. Either way, we're rooted to the spot. Ellie throws caution to the wind and grabs my hand.

The sun is a little lower in the sky now, so the silhouette at the door is immediately recognizable as Aunt Stella.

The Cheek Pincher.

No. Not now. Please, God, not the Cheek Pincher. Not now.

Stella steps in, grabs Nicky's shoulders with her hands, and holds him at arm's length, sizing him up. "Look at you. Getting to be such big boy." Then in one swift move, her thumb and forefinger are squeezing a wad of my brother's face.

"Hi, Aunn Shtella," he manages to mumble. I see a tear form at the corner of his eye as he swallows the pain.

"Dimmi-moo!" she exclaims as she spots me standing behind him. Then Aunt Stella sees Ellie and her eyes go to our hands, which are still clasped tight. Ellie catches this and lets go. "And this moost be you girlfriend." Stella's voice is gentle, even sweet. But still, her claw starts to rise.

Oh no. Here it comes.

"Brace yourself," I whisper so softly I'm not sure Ellie hears me.

Stella steps forward, and . . . and . . .

She shakes Ellie's hand. "I'm Dmitri's aunt Stella. It nice to meet you."

Ellie must be as surprised as I am, because it takes her a beat to realize how normal this interaction is. She shakes my aunt's hand back and chokes out, "Hi, I'm Eliana."

Stella leans in and gives me a gentle hug. "Where you mother?"

"Kitchen," is all I can manage to say.

"Spiro, έλα εδώ," Aunt Stella says over her shoulder. For the first time I notice my much older uncle—the third in what will be a string of many, I suspect—behind Stella. He looks a bit shell-shocked but obediently enters the house; nods to me, Ellie, and Nick; and follows his new wife to the kitchen. I watch them retreat down the hall, my hand going to my unmolested cheek.

It's the first time in my living memory that Aunt Stella has not performed her signature move on me. Maybe it was seeing me with a girl, knowing I'm more of a grown-up than not, that stopped her. Or maybe she didn't want to embarrass me in front of Ellie.

Either way, it's the end of an era. While I'm relieved, some part of me is—inexplicably and oddly—sad, too.

Eliana

*D*mitri's family is so different from mine. My dad has three sisters, and my mom has two sisters and one brother. I have a lot of cousins, but everyone lives in different states and we only see each other when someone has a bar or bat mitzvah, a wedding, or a death. And in each of those occasions everyone is so serious, so composed. Our only way of greeting is a kiss on the cheek, which is so grown-up and uncomfortable. I don't want to be kissing cheeks, so close to people's mouths. What happened to a nice hug or pat on the head? Even though I'm terrified of Dimmi's family and their aggressive physical affection, I'm also a little jealous that they seem to love each other so damn much.

Not that I doubt my family's love for me. My parents aren't nearly as hands-off, mouths-on as the extended family. But I don't know if Samara would ever have my back the way Nicky has Dimmi's. Hell, I think he'd even have *my* back. What an odd feeling.

At first I was nervous that Dimmi's family would shun me, being Jewish and all, but instead they offered me a game of twenty (thousand) questions about Jews. The easiest to answer were those with historical references. I fielded queries on everything from holiday meals to my religious education. People were polite and stayed away from the more philosophical and belief questions. The only one that really threw me was when Aunt Maxine busted out with, "What you think, Ellie, on soocumceesion?" Her accent was so thick, it took me a minute to realize she was asking about circumcision.

First off, she called me Ellie, which is not a nickname I accept all willy-nilly. I was seriously close to shutting her down with an "Eliana," but I know how severe that would have sounded. Instead I focused on the foreskin at hand. "I was at the bris of both of my brothers, and after they sucked some wine off the mohel's fingertip, they didn't even cry when he did the ol' snip-snip." Out of the corner of my eye I could have sworn Nicky did that thing where someone spits all of their drink out in a dramatic spray. Or maybe I imagined it. Then Dmitri started coughing so loudly I thought there might be a little Grecian Heimlich action. Aunt Maxine, however, seemed to find my answer perfectly acceptable and raised a glass of ouzo. "To soocumceesion!" she declared. "To soocumceesion!" The rest of the family chanted. All 750 of them. Then I spent the next hour wondering if Dmitri is or isn't circumcised. Then I spent the hour after that wondering how I would even know. After that I panicked about if and when I would find out. Could Dmitri see my upper lip sweating? Was he thinking about circumcision? Would I end up spending my entire first Christmas party thinking about penises?

I can't imagine that's what Jesus intended.

Dmitri

*A*n hour later, Alex, Meg, Nicky, Eliana, and I are in my bedroom listening to music.

Ellie bore the Greek version of the Spanish inquisition with grace. After Aunt Maxine asked about the "Jew custom" of circumcision—which is ridiculous, because Nicky and I both got snipped at birth—I called an end to it, inviting the other kids upstairs. (Even Yia Yia winced at Maxine's question.)

After a forty-five-minute game of Yahtzee (a Christmas tradition), which Nicky won (another Christmas tradition), I'm sitting on the bed between Ellie and Meg, with Nicky and Alex on the floor. Hüsker Dü is on my turntable.

It's been months since I've seen the Pappas twins, and while Alex is pretty much the same, this is a whole new Meg. Usually when I see her, at Christmas and Easter gatherings, she's wearing an ankle-length plaid skirt with a white shirt, her dark hair pulled back into a tight ponytail. Today Meg's hair is wavy and wild with blond highlights and hangs down past her shoulders; her skirt, still plaid, stops a whole bunch of inches above her knees; and now it's her shirt, not her ponytail, that's tight. She looks so different I can't stop staring at her.

"This is great!" she says about Hüsker Dü, and slides a couple of inches closer to me. "You're in a band, aren't you, Dimmi?"

It doesn't take a lot to get me to talk about Unexpected Turbulence, so I angle myself toward Meg to answer.

Nicky gives a single loud cough. It's the "danger ahead" cough we use with each other when Mom or Dad is on the warpath. My parents aren't here, so I look at him confused; he catches my gaze and shifts his eyes to Eliana. I glance over my shoulder, but Ellie just smiles at me.

Huh. Maybe it was a real cough.

"I'd love to see you play sometime," Meg says.

"That would be awe—" I start to answer.

"Dmitri, I have to go to the bathroom," Ellie interrupts. She doesn't usually call me Dmitri anymore, preferring Dimmi. She's already off the bed and walking out. When you gotta go, you gotta go, I guess.

"Okay. You know where it is," I tell her half over my shoulder.

Ellie closes the door with a little more force than might be necessary as she leaves. Once she's gone, Meg slides closer, meaning her knee is now touching mine.

Nicky winces and covers his face with his hands, and Meg laughs. Alarm bells are going off in my brain, but I'll be damned if I can figure out why.

Thankfully Alex looks clueless, too, so maybe I'm just being paranoid.

Yeah, that's it. I'm definitely just being paranoid.

Eliana

*H*ow long can I hide in the bathroom before Dmitri notices? I look at myself in the mirror, at my basic outfit of blackness, and compare it to Meg and her short skirt and desperately tight shirt. Is that what Dmitri wants in a girl? If so, why did he go after me in the first place? Am I just some placeholder until he finds bigger boobs?

I wash my hands, even though I never actually peed. I don't want to go back to Dmitri's room, don't want to watch him pretentiously spin records because he thinks it makes him look cooler than everyone else. News flash: It doesn't. One can just as easily press a tiny button and make the sound come out of a phone as they can take seven hours to delicately place the round black disc onto a turntable and ever-so-carefully drop the needle onto the fragile record.

Instead of returning to the den of music and ogling, I tiptoe down the stairs to get a peek at the family action in the living room. One of Dmitri's younger cousins plays the violin (or possibly the viola; she is very small, so the size comparison is way off), and most of the relatives surround her to watch. The tune is painfully screechy, but any music is better than Hüsker Dü for the eight hundredth time.

I slink along the wall until I find an empty seat next to Yia Yia. As I lower myself into the chair, Yia Yia grabs my hand and places it onto her lap in a warm gesture. There we sit, listening to the girl with two long braids in her black hair play an unfamiliar tune, close enough that my arm reaches the floral fabric of Yia Yia's Christmas dress. At first I sit stiffly, unsure of what I am supposed to do. Do I reciprocate and put my other hand on top of her hand on top of my hand and make a hand sandwich? My family hasn't prepared me for this moment at all. Thankfully, the cousin finishes her rousing solo, and Yia Yia removes her hand from atop mine to clap. I clap as well, then latch my hands together in my lap. The buzz of conversation builds quickly throughout the room, as do the clinks and clatters of utensils and plates. I strain my brain to think of a conversation starter for Yia Yia, but she beats me to it.

"So you and my Dimmi are happy, yes?"

That depends on your definition of happy. Maybe you should ask him and that skank upstairs. "Yeah, we're good," I say, and I don't manage to even convince myself.

Yia Yia now places her hand on my lap. I study the blue bulges of her veins. "Dimmi is a boy. Boys, not so smart as girls. They brains only know how to small focus. We have the big focus, big picture. You understand?"

"Kind of." I shrug.

"That girl upstairs. Meg. Dimmi know her many years. She good girl, but she testing the world. Testing her clothes. Testing her mother's patience." Yia Yia laughs, a tinkly, fairy laugh that infects me and pushes a smile onto my face. "She not better than you for Dimmi. She just show things you too smart to show. Dimmi is dumb, like all boys. You let him know he being dumb. You tell him with you pretty smile, and he will figure it out."

I can't help but smile more when Yia Yia tells me my smile is pretty. "I don't know if I'm the right person for Dimmi. He is so happy all the time, and people like him so much. I'm not really that type of person."

Yia Yia squeezes my hand with unexpected strength. It's actually rather painful as my finger bones crush into each other. "Eliana, you the perfect person to be. For you. If Dimmi too stupid to see, you make him see. And if he still too dumb, you tell me and I smack brains back in his head."

I do not doubt that Yia Yia's smack could change the composition of someone's head.

"You go back upstairs. Dimmi probably wondering where you are."

Yia Yia releases my hand and pats my cheek in a gesture that is somewhere between affection and a smack. Yia Yia is kind of a badass.

"Thank you," I offer her, and I walk back up the stairs to the bedroom. Hüsker Dü emanates from a crack in the door, as does Meg's laughter. I attempt to shake off my feelings of jealousy and inadequacy. Yia Yia is right. If Dmitri is more interested in that, then screw him (I'm paraphrasing Yia Yia, of course).

I push the door open more aggressively than I meant to, and it slams into the wall behind it.

I am here.

Dmitri is still on the bed, Meg practically on his lap. My stomach lurches, but I play it casual and sit next to Nicky on the floor. I grab a deck of cards, ignore the scene on the bed, and ask Nicky, "Want to play War?" I am fully aware that War is a two-person game. Just as sitting on a bed next to a girl is.

Nicky doesn't hesitate. He dumps the cards deftly into his palm. He shuffles and divvies up the cards, then declares, "Let the war begin."

I glance up at Dmitri, who is looking down at us, smiling obliviously, and concur. "Indeed."

Dmitri

"She's a special girl, you know." Nicky is lying on the floor of my bedroom, dealing himself a game of solitaire.

After he and I helped Mom and Yia Yia clean up from the party—Dad doesn't do "women's work" but he doesn't seem to mind his sons doing it—we retreated to my room to hang out and listen to music. Bob Marley's *Legend* is on the turntable. It was Nicky's Christmas gift to me. It's supercool because the vinyl is the colors of the Jamaican flag. Nicky said the album was on *Rolling Stone*'s top 100 records of all time and he figured I would like that. I never gave reggae a chance before, but really, it's great background music, perfect for a late night after a long day.

"Who? Meg?" I ask in response to Nicky's statement. Ever since she slid next to me on the bed, causing her skirt to ride up so I could see her underwear, I haven't been able to get Meg off my mind. It was royal blue. The underwear, I mean.

"No, Einstein. Eliana. Your girlfriend?"

"Oh."

"Oh?"

"I mean, yeah, of course she is."

"Dude. Think with the head on your shoulders."

"Funny. You just make that up?"

"Nuh-uh. I read it in a book."

At first I think he's kidding, but Nicky does read a lot of books.

"Did Ellie seem weird to you today?" I ask. Something about the way Eliana was acting toward me was off. And the way she and Yia Yia hugged when Ellie's dad came to pick her up, well, I'm not sure what to think.

I'm lying on my bed scrolling through ChatteringFaces, looking at Christmas pics posted by kids from school. It's mostly Christmas trees and kids in pajamas oohing and aahing over presents.

Reggie introduced me to ChatteringFaces. It's kind of like a kids-only Instagram; you can't join unless you're on a preapproved list of high school and middle school students. It's so much better than the other social media platforms. Reg said most parents hate it because they can't keep tabs on their kids, but my parents are so clueless about technology it's not an issue for me and Nicky.

"Yeah, of course she did."

"Whaddya mean, 'Of course'? Ellie *did* seem weird to you?"

"Dimmi, she had to endure the entire Digrindakis family today."

"I know. I was really nervous, but I thought she handled it pretty good."

"Pretty well. Handled it pretty well." Nicky is a stickler for grammar. I'm used to it, so I let it go. "But that's not really the point. She was off-balance because of meeting the family, yes. She seemed *weird"*—Nicky makes air quotes around the word—"because you were flirting with Meg."

I sit up so fast I fall off the bed.

"Ow! What? I wasn't flirting! It's just, you know, Meg." Nicky stares at me, giving my brain time to roll back the footage from the afternoon.

Me next to Meg.

Me turning my back on Ellie to face Meg.

Me not seeming to care when Ellie left the room.

Meg's short skirt.

Meg's underwear.

Meg's *royal-blue* underwear.

"Oh shit."

"Yeah," Nicky says.

Bob Marley, singing about a "Buffalo Soldier," whatever the hell that is, is masking my breath, which has grown short and heavy. I'm freaking out.

"What should I do?"

"How should I know? I've never even had a girlfriend." Nicky flips over a queen of hearts and places it on one of his piles. I take that as a sign, grab my phone, and compose a text to Ellie.

ME: Hey, El. I miss you. Thanks so much for coming over today. I hope you had a nice time.

I can't jump right into the matter at hand. I have to ease into this to find out what Ellie is really thinking. She's like a cat; if you approach her from the wrong direction, you can get scratched.

While I wait for a response, I lie back down on my bed and replay more of the day: Aunt Maxine's awful greeting; Aunt Stella's normal greeting; the courtroom cross-examination on the subject of circumcision; the basement; that strange—and now that I think about it, meaningful—hug from Yia Yia; Meg; Meg's underwear; Meg's royal-blue underwear.

Nicky falls asleep on the cards after a few minutes—he looks so much younger when he's asleep—and I'm just starting to doze off, too, when my phone vibrates me back to full consciousness.

Ellie.

REGGIE: Merry Christmas, Dmitri.

My head flops back on the pillow. Reggie. I don't know if I can handle Reggie right now.

ME: Hey. Merry Christmas.

REGGIE: So how'd it go?

I had told Reggie about Eliana coming to meet the Digrindaki. *The Digrindaki.* That makes it sound like my family is some kind of mythical creature from ancient Greece that spits fire and eats goats whole. Not really far from the truth when you think about it.

Anyway, Reggie has a tradition of stopping by on Christmas night, after her own family's celebration is over. She joins me, Nicky, Meg, and Alex for board games or whatever it is we're doing. Reg, for whatever reason, is totally at ease around my family. Though she did once pinch Aunt Stella's cheek in some kind of weird retribution. There was a tense moment before Stella burst out laughing. Then we all laughed and she hugged Reggie. Go figure.

When I told Reggie about having invited Eliana this year, she deflated for a second. I could see it. She paused for a long minute, waiting, I think, for me to ask her to join us. I didn't. This would be the first time in a few years, and I'm guessing it threw a wrench into Reggie's plans for the day.

I know. I'm a jerk.

ME: I don't know.

REGGIE: You don't know how it went?

While the text is incapable of expressing the smirk buried in Reggie's question, I see it for what it is. The trailing "dumbass" is implied.

ME: It's just been a long day, okay?

There's a strained pause before Reggie responds.

REGGIE: You all right, Digrindakis?

I think for a minute before answering honestly.

ME: I don't know.

REGGIE: Did you do something stupid? No, wait. Don't answer that. Of course you did.

I can see exactly how this conversation is going to unfold, and honestly, I'm not up for it. Reggie will tease and badger me until I tell her every sordid detail, and in the end, I'll not only realize everything I've ever done—in my entire life—is wrong, but I'll feel even worse.

I see the little dancing dots letting me know Reg is typing more. I cut her off.

ME: I think I need to go to sleep. Talk to you tomorrow, okay?

The dots stop and start again.

REGGIE: K. Good night.

Reggie's texts are usually full of exclamation points and swear words, so I can tell she's pissed or hurt or something. Whatever.

I rest the phone on my chest. I'm not anywhere close to sleep when it buzzes again.

Finally, Ellie.

MEG: ♥

I turn my phone off without answering and lie there for a long time, unable to sleep.

The only thing I see when I close my eyes are splotches of royal blue.

Eliana

I want to die. No, I want to barf. I want to die barfing. Barf dying? Ugh. I just don't want to feel this way is what I really want.

After the Greek Christmas Where My Boyfriend Decided Hot Greek Girls Are Better Than Complicated Jewish Girls, I am glad to have a week and a half left of winter break to curl up in my closet and lock the door. The outside world = bad. Harry Potter fanfiction = good.

I scroll through all of the Bill Weasley stories I have already read 10 million times. Why aren't there more of them? I need escapism. Now. Am I being greedy?

Greedy.

Like, say, having a girlfriend but thinking you can look—leer might be a better word—at other girls and it doesn't mean anything unless you act on it. But it does mean something. I know guys are helpless when it comes to their utterly basic need for eyeball stimulation, but Dmitri could try to be more subtle about it. Or he could at least not do it while I'm there. Like the last time I saw his band, it took him three songs to find me in the crowd. He was too busy staring at this girl in the front row with a very sparkly tube top on. Who wears tube tops? And a sparkly one at that. He's like a freakin' crow. "Ooh! Shiny!" Maybe I should roll around in glitter to get his attention.

Do I even want it?

Is that what this is even about?

Maybe all of the time I have spent carefully crafting the art of subtly sneaking away from Dmitri is manifesting itself in his interest in other girls.

Is it my fault?

Am I not attentive enough to his needs? Do I not laugh enough at his jokes? Swoon enough over his song lyrics? Take off enough clothing for his liking?

Do I not sparkle enough for Dmitri?

I slam my laptop lid closed. I don't want to cry over something that could be nothing. I don't want to start the tears that I know could last for days. Weeks. The tears that stain my eyes red and swell the dark circles underneath.

My phone buzzes. Another message from Dmitri.

DMITRI: Where are you? I miss you.

He feels guilty. That means he has done something wrong.

But has he actually *done* something? Like, actually something more than used his eyes as weapons against my soul?

Stop being so dramatic, El. You were the one who wanted to switch classes. You were the one who didn't want to hold hands every time they swung close enough to touch. You were the one who denied him a kiss in front of his brother when it felt too showy. Again.

Maybe it *is* your fault.

You push him away. You don't give him enough of what he needs. You are grumpy. You wear ripped black t-shirts. You barely crack a smile.

It is you.

I throw open my laptop screen in order to drown myself in a Harry Potter marathon, but my screen freezes.

Even my computer hates me.

I attempt to text Janina in Hawaii, but she has been practically MIA since she left. I don't blame her. But I kind of hate her at the moment.

I shove my phone to the side and flop onto my stomach. Soon enough my face is slick from crying. My pillow darkens with my pathetic tears.

I don't want to be this person again. I want to be the happy girl with the cool boyfriend who adores her and writes her songs and wants to touch her constantly. I want to be that girl who will bask in the glow of his admiration and kiss him passionately and spontaneously, who wears quirky dresses and glasses and makes him proud to be seen with her.

I want to be someone else. Somewhere else.

Anywhere but on this tear-soaked futon mattress in a closet.

Dmitri

"I'm not gonna get up
I'm gonna stay on my back
I'm not gonna get up
Unless you take me back
There's nothing that's worth doing
Since you said goodbye
Until you forgive me
I'm gonna lie here until I die."

Chad reads the lyrics to my latest masterpiece out loud; it's called "Apology to El." He delivers each line with extra flair, like he's Norma Desmond from that movie we watched in film class. Jerk.

We're in the rehearsal space at Ace Studios on the last afternoon of our holiday break. We have to be back at school tomorrow morning, and I wanted to get this song written for Eliana before I saw her.

"Really?" Chad's voice is dripping with sarcasm. It's clear how much he hates it. My cheeks must be on fire they're burning so hot. All I want to do is crawl in a hole and die from embarrassment. But I try to put up a good front.

"What?"

"It sucks is what."

Okay, maybe it's not going to win a Grammy—though who the hell would actually *want* to win a Grammy anyway?—but it doesn't suck. It's a plain-spoken, from-the-heart apology. Screw Chad. I'm proud of it.

Truth is, I don't care if this song winds up on the Unexpected Turbulence set list. I just want it for Ellie, who *finally*, three days ago, after a week of me trying, texted me back.

> **ELIANA**: I'm OK. Don't worry about me. How about we just give each other some space? See you at school.

I was so excited to hear from her I glossed right over her request for "some space" and fired a barrage of texts at her . . . like a madman:

> **ME**: OMG! El, it's soooooo good to hear from you. So. Good!

No response.

> **ME**: Is this about Meg? It was just weird how much she'd changed from the last time I saw her, that was all. Ask Nicky. She looked totally different!

No response.

ME: I don't even like that kind of girl!

No response.

ME: I like YOU! I LOVE you!

Yes. That was how I first told Eliana I loved her. In a frantic, desperate text. True story.

And, of course, no response.

But I didn't stop there.

It went on.

And on.

And on.

For fifteen more texts. Good God, fifteen.

No response to any of them.

"It doesn't suck." Kyle comes to the defense of my song. Sort of. "But these feel more like country lyrics. I don't think it fits our vibe."

I shoot a glance at Drew, who is completely disengaged. He's in his own world, just randomly fingering his bass with the volume down.

"Oh" is the only response I can manage.

Chad clucks like a chicken. Like a freaking chicken. It's supposed to be some kind of victory laugh, I guess. Then he crumples the piece of paper and throws it back at me. He actually does that.

Crumples up the goddam piece of goddam paper and goddam throws it back at me!

It bounces off my mounted tom, rolls off my snare drum, and winds up on the floor next to my bass drum pedal.

"Dick," I mutter. I can't help myself. He *is* a dick. He deserves to be called a dick. But as the syllable is rolling over my lips and out into the world, I know I'm going to regret it.

"What did you say?" Chad's eyes are slits.

I should just grow a pair and repeat it. *Dick*, I should tell him. *You're a dick and everyone in this room, and everyone who has ever spent more than two minutes with you, including both of your parents, knows it. You're a colossal, monstrous, ginormous dick.*

"Nothing" is what I say instead.

"Look, Dmitri." He gives me this look that's all serious, like he's a father talking to his rambunctious son. I hate, hate, HATE it. "You want to be the *third* drummer in this band, or the *former* drummer in this band?"

Chad is making a point that I'm not a founding member of UT and I'm expendable. And he's right, I *am* the third drummer. But the first drummer didn't even have his own kit, so he lasted less than a day; and the second drummer quit after a month because he couldn't stand Chad. I've been the drummer for twenty-four of the twenty-five months of the history of Unexpected Turbulence, and Chad has never let me forget there was one whole month of a Dmitri-free band. God, I hate him. So. Much.

"Back off, Chad."

I also hate that Kyle feels the need to protect me all the time.

And I kind of hate that he thought my song was a country song. How can anyone even tell if it's country or anything else until there's music put to it?

Gah. Let's face it. Right now, I kind of hate everyone and everything.

Eliana

"El?" My mom raps on my door. "It's five o'clock. Time to leave for Aunt Essie's house. Last one there gets the worst white elephant gift."

My mom's younger sister hosts a Hanukkah party every year. It rarely happens during actual Hanukkah because people can't come into town for various reasons. This year we're over two weeks late.

"Isn't that the point of a white elephant? That the gift is going to suck anyway?" I ask through the door.

"Aunt Ricky told me she wrapped up a free makeup kit from the Clinique counter. She used comics from the Sunday paper as wrapping so I can ID it. I want that makeup, El."

My mom is playful, excited to see her family and kibitz with relatives she sees barely once a year. I can't seem to find the energy to peel the covers back from my chin.

"Mom, would it be okay if I stay home this year? I'm really tired, and you know they're going to force me to police the cousins in the basement. Brady always turns on the treadmill . . . I can't stand it."

"Ellie, everyone will wonder where you are." Mom worries about the gossipy aspect of our extended family. She probably worries they'll think I'm crazy again.

She's probably right all around.

"Why don't you tell them I ate at a Chinese buffet on New Year's, and I have diarrhea. They'll totally believe you, and no one wants to say the word 'diarrhea' more than once, anyway. It pains me now to say it twice."

Quiet reflection from the other side of the door.

"I don't want you pouting all night," Mom decides. "So this is your one free pass. Next year you have to go. Or else . . ." I wait for Mom's threat. "Oh, I don't know, Eliana, but this is it. One time. Everyone is waiting downstairs. Call if you need anything."

"Love you, Mommy." I throw out the "Mommy" only at times when I know I've won but probably shouldn't have.

"Love you too, El."

I wait for the numerous creaks and slams of the door leading into our garage, followed by the grind of the garage door opening, then closing.

They're gone.

I'm alone.

Truly, officially alone.

I sigh a grand sigh, a dramatic gesture for the audience that isn't here. With all of the energy I couldn't muster merely seconds ago, I bound out of bed and throw open my room-hole door.

The silence is intoxicating.

Then, like it knows I am by myself, my phone buzzes.

I look at the text.

Dmitri.

Of course.

I close the window, but another text comes through.

I don't care what it says.

I don't want to be contacted.

I don't want to be connected right now.

I want to be completely and utterly alone.

I shut my phone off and toss it onto my bed.

Now I am truly free.

I feel weightless.

Hungry.

Giddy.

Energetic.

I can run around the house however I want, slide across the kitchen floor in my socks and underwear, and suck whipped cream from the can. It is glorious.

There is no one to berate me. No one to ask me to help them. No one to ask if I need help.

If I am okay.

I want to feel like this every day. Every second.

I feel good.

Better, at least.

I feel okay.

Dmitri

"**R**aise," Yia Yia says, looking at Nicky with an honest-to-goodness twinkle in her eye. She pushes two one-hundred-dollar chips into the middle of our kitchen table.

Nicky studies her, looking for some sort of tell. He won't find any.

Two years ago, I got kind of obsessed with poker. This kid at school named Jason Caldwell came in talking about a movie called *Rounders*. Jason was flat-out cool—he wore old eighties concert t-shirts; his hair was unruly and spiky; and he somehow knew how to talk to girls—so his recommendations carried weight. They didn't always work (the film adaptation of *Ender's Game* is a glaring example), but he was spot-on with *Rounders*.

Not only was the film rated R, which when you're thirteen is like the holy grail of movie experiences, but, like Jason, it oozed cool. Matt Damon plays this good guy law student/poker player who gets into trouble with the Russian mob on account of his degenerate friend. The best parts are the poker scenes; they're filled with tension and drama and I defy you to watch them without wanting to learn the game.

The day after I saw the movie—it was on HBO one night after my parents had gone to bed—I got some poker books out of the library and started watching the World Series of Poker on ESPN. (I'm not sure why the tournament is on a sports network, but I guess the Game Show Network would be even worse.)

Anyway, Yia Yia sat down on the couch next to me while I was watching the WSOP. She didn't say a word, but her eyes were glued to the screen. After half an hour, she started to ask questions.

"Why those men put chips out before cards dealed?"

"They're called the blinds," I explained.

"Why that man betting so much money when his card so bad?"

"It's called bluffing."

I went on to explain the game to Yia Yia in as much detail as I could, talking about tournaments, and pot odds, and drawing to an inside straight, all things I'd been learning from those books. Yia Yia's face was inscrutable as she took it all in.

That same night, she made Nicky and me play with her, and I could see she was hooked.

After a few months my interest in poker faded, but not Yia Yia's. She would do whatever she could to get Nicky and me to play with her, sometimes roping our father in.

Dad, who is at the table tonight, has to be the worst poker player ever. He only enters the pot when he has cards, and even when he does, you can bluff him off just about any hand. It's kind of nice (and kind of sad) he thinks the rest of us are so honest that we're never bluffing.

Yia Yia, on the other hand, is a shark.

"Call," Nicky says, sliding his chips forward. The chips and cards we're using are part of a poker set he and I gave Yia Yia for Christmas.

"Call!" my father blusters. He must be sitting on a high pair.

I glance at my cards again—nine, ten suited. I usually like to gamble with this kind of hand. I can make a straight or a flush, and no one will see it coming. But I'm still sour from rehearsal today, and still reeling over Eliana's complete and total dismissal of me.

"Fold," I half mutter, half grunt.

"What the matter, Dimmi-moo?" Yia Yia asks as she scoops the bets and my discarded hand to the center of the table. Yia Yia is *always* the dealer.

"Nothing," I answer, slumping a little more into my seat.

"Not nothing," she says. "Trouble with girlfriend, nai?"

When I don't respond, Nicky answers for me. "Good read, Yia Yia."

"Burn and turn," Yia Yia says with relish, taking the top card from the deck, putting it facedown, and then turning the three community cards faceup in what is known as the flop. There's an ace of clubs, a nine of diamonds, and a six of clubs. I think Yia Yia loves all the trappings of poker as much as she loves the game itself. It makes her feel like a badass. Not that Yia Yia needs any help to be an actual badass. "You should call girl and say you sorry," she says.

"He's tried," Nicky says, "but apparently she's pretty angry."

I give my brother a dirty look and grunt again.

"Then you find other way to tell her sorry."

"He's tried that, too." This time I stare daggers at Nicky, letting him know he's about to cross a line. I showed him the song I wrote for Eliana, and he has to know that's private.

"You should date nice Greek girl anyway," my father chimes in.

"Hush, Basil," my grandmother admonishes.

"It doesn't matter," I say.

"Of course it matter," Yia Yia answers. "Eliana is good girl, and she love you."

"She is good, but she doesn't love me," I answer.

"What you know about girls? *I* know," Yia Yia insists. "She *love* you."

"They too young to be in love," my father interjects.

"No one too young to be in love."

This time my father grunts.

My grandmother looks him in the eye and smiles. "Five hundred," she says, pushing a purple chip in front of her. I'm pretty sure Yia Yia knows my father has a good hand and is trying to scare him off it.

"Fold," Nicky says without hesitation, pushing his cards forward.

"και ποτέ δεν είναι πολύ μεγάλος για να παίξει πόκερ," Dad mutters under his breath. *And never too old to play poker.* This gets a laugh from Yia Yia. She really does love this game.

He looks at his cards no fewer than five times, the sign of a weak poker player. In Texas Hold'em you don't play your hand, you play the other people at the table. When Yia Yia deals, she watches each of us react to our cards before looking at her own. I taught her that.

I think about what Yia Yia said, that Ellie does love me. I think about poker and how you play the person, not the cards. And I think about everything I've done wrong. I now know what I have to do.

"Fold," my father says with disgust, turning over his pair of jacks. I take some small measure of satisfaction knowing I read him correctly.

Yia Yia cackles with delight, scooping up the chips.

"What you have?" my father asks.

"You want to know, next time you pay the five hundred dollar." She looks her son-in-law in the eye and smiles again. "But tonight I feel, what is word . . . filánthropos."

"Charitable," Nicky says.

"Yes, charitable," Yia Yia says, sounding out each syllable. She turns over a five and six of different suits. A garbage hand.

"Σκατά!" my father exclaims. A full-on Greek curse.

For the first time in days, I'm actually smiling.

Eliana

I can't stop thinking, which would be great if it were all good, flowery, happy thoughts. I can't imagine what that must be like. I hate my brain. Why doesn't it have a shutoff valve?

Meg. Ugh. *Dmitri.* Ugh. *Meg and Dmitri.* Ugh and ugh.

But it's more than that. More than them. They're just the obvious choice to avoid the reality of my malfunctioning mind.

Why don't things just feel good like they once did? Because they did once.

Flashback to date number four. Dmitri declared that we needed an "activity date." The choices he offered: skydiving, axe throwing, or bowling. We knocked out choice one because it was too expensive and choice two because we weren't old enough. Which left us with bowling. Except that I sort of have an aversion to bowling because it was my dad's thing. He was even in a league, once upon a time, and had his own monogrammed ball. I have too many memories of being cooped up in the creepy bowling alley childcare room, trying to keep Isaac and Samara safe from the other, less civilized bowling progeny. Maybe my memories are clouded, but I could swear there were kids smoking in that childcare room.

"What about Chuck E. Cheese?" I suggested. As ridiculous as it sounds, I had never been to Chuck E. Cheese, but I had seen so many commercials that, even as a teenager, I was enchanted. Games! Prizes! Pizza! Basically heaven, right? Dmitri wasn't as easily convinced.

"You know, I have been there, and it's not all tickets hanging from trees and hugs from giant mice. I mean, there is a giant mouse. But who knows how many boogers have been rubbed into that fake fur?"

"Boogers and fake fur?" I enthused. I was not to be deterred. "It sounds awesome."

"It really isn't," Dmitri pronounced.

"What do you have against Chuck E. Cheese? Did something traumatic happen to you in a ball pit?" I asked.

"No. And they don't have those anymore. Unsanitary. It's just that . . . never mind. It's stupid. Forget I said anything. Let's go be kids being kids."

"You can't throw a 'never mind' at me and think you'll get away with it. What is it?"

"Promise not to laugh."

"I promise nothing," I said.

"Fine. I always had this vision of what a perfect date was, and I pictured it taking place in a bowling alley," Dmitri admitted.

"That is so cute." I pinched Dmitri's cheek playfully. He pulled away, embarrassed. "Can we compromise? How about we go to Chuck E. Cheese this time, and we go to your fantasy bowling alley the next date? And voilà! We already have two more dates set up. We're practically engaged." I couldn't believe I said that, and quickly backed out of it with a joke. "Chuck E. can be the officiant at our wedding. The theme can be 'booger fur chic.'"

Chuck E. Cheese totally delivered on all of my ridiculous expectations. It was so bright and colorful and loud. The pizza was even good. Dimmi and I played games for over two hours. It was like the montage scene I always dreamed of: Dimmi standing behind me, arms around my middle, as I threw Skee-balls into the gutter. A cheerily competitive Whac-A-Mole game (I won, naturally). Me jumping up and down in excitement as tickets spilled out of a game that Dmitri bested. Brain freeze from drinking slushees too quickly. And, the pièce de résistance, Dmitri combining all his tickets with mine to purchase the large and hideous Mr. Munch stuffed animal.

As we laughed our way to the parking lot, where we waited for his mom to pick us up, Dmitri and I stole kisses and each held one of Mr. Munch's hands. It was, as I predicted, a perfect date.

So what changed? Why is he looking at other girls? Why am I switching classes? Why am I dreading having his locker next to mine? Where did all the happy go?

I look at Mr. Munch, mostly hidden under a pile of laundry in the corner of my room-hole. What if there is some sort of magical power to Mr. Munch, and if I uncover him, the joy and love I felt will instantly return?

I lean off my futon and yank Mr. Munch out of the laundry stank. He looks at me. I look at him. Then I throw him out my closet door.

I feel even worse.

Dmitri

The first day back from winter break, I'm at my new school locker early, waiting for Eliana. I'm wearing black jeans and a Hufflepuff t-shirt. (Ellie made me do the Sorting Hat thing online and my house came out as Hufflepuff. My Patronus was a rabbit. She laughed. At the time I thought it was funny. Now I wonder if it's one more thing she hates about me.)

Both my hands are clutching a laminated sheet of paper. On it, emblazoned in Sharpie, is the song I wrote. I need to corner Ellie, to make her understand how much I love her, how sorry I am.

The hallway starts to fill with other kids, but there's no sign of Ellie.

With only two minutes to the bell, Joe Loskywitz, the kid who sold me the locker, strides up. Joe plays guitar in another band called State of Adventure, and while we're not exactly friends, we're friendly.

"Hey man, wrong locker." I force a smile. "Remember, you sold this one to me?"

"I know, but then the weirdest thing happened over the weekend. You know that tall girl, Janina?"

Oh. Shit. "Yeah?"

"She texted me that the weird girl who used to have this locker wanted to trade with me. I made another fifty bucks. I don't know what's going on, but I totally need the cash, so cool." I kind of want to punch him for calling Eliana a weird girl.

Joe takes a book out of his backpack, tosses the bag into what is now *his* locker, and shuts it. "Oh, and hey, great show at the Entry." He spins the lock and disappears down the hall.

I feel like I've been hit by a Mack Truck.

No.

I wish I *had* been hit by a Mack Truck.

Eliana

$\mathcal{I}$ can't do it. I can't get out of bed. My covers will not move from off my chest. The time on my phone reads 7:30, and I know I need to leave for school in fifteen minutes in order to be on time. It's the first day back after winter break. It's six degrees outside. The start of a new semester.

None of these are reasons why I can't get out of bed.

I don't want to see him. I don't want to see anybody today. I don't want to shower and get dressed and put two shoes on in order to get somewhere where I will have to interact with other humans.

Why would anyone want to talk to me anyway, especially Dmitri? Obviously, I am a pathetic, jealous loser who isn't "that kind of girl." What exactly does that mean? It seems so trite. So cliché. I thought Dmitri was better than that. I thought I was better than this.

Janina finally came back from the ends of the earth, bronzed beyond her already perpetually bronzed state. She visited me in my room-hole yesterday, and although I was able to extract myself from the covers, I wasn't really up for leaving my space.

Janina knocked on my closet door around noon. I wanted her over earlier, because early mornings can be my worst time of day.

Who am I kidding? Every time of day feels like the worst lately.

"I can't get used to this time difference." Janina yawned and stretched. She had on one of my favorite tops, a fuzzy cream-colored sweater with a rainbow running over her chest.

"Yes, it must be so difficult to adjust after days in paradise, away from the person who constantly harasses you for help because she has no idea how to handle anything by herself."

"Uh . . ."

"Sorry," I offered weakly. "I have no idea what I'm doing, and this is all too familiar. I feel like I'm an alien on the wrong planet."

"What planet are you on? And also, what planet are you from?"

"Shitty metaphor. Forgive me. I mean that this planet, Earth, is filled with beautiful people and not beautiful people, and that's all that seems to matter. Like, it doesn't matter how smart you are or how capable you are of walking long distances or how commit-ted you are to watching and reading a series for the rest of your life. Nooooooo. All that matters is that you giggle and pander and blink your eyes seductively. It's such bullshit." It was then that I began to burrow my way back under my blankets.

"El. You have to get out of that mindset. People do not think as black and white as that. Or if they do, they probably live in their parents' basement and the only actual human contact they make is with their own hand."

"Ew." I pulled the blankets up to my chin.

"Yes. Ew. And you don't want those guys. You want the nice ones. Dmitri seems like he's pretty nice."

"Janina, you didn't see him. He was ogling this girl. *Ogling.* He didn't even care that I had to go to the bathroom by myself."

"Does he usually help you with that?"

"Well, no. But there was much ogling. Did I mention the ogling?"

"A bit." Janina nodded. "Are you sure he was ogling and not just making eye contact with the wrong pair of eyes?"

"Did you just refer to boobs as 'the wrong pair of eyes'? There is nothing right about that."

"I'm just trying to give him the benefit of the doubt before things happen that you might regret. I'm guessing you've been avoiding him."

"How did you know?"

"Because that is your go-to deal. I'll also guess that he's sending you texts trying to get you to talk to him?"

"Only about seven hundred thousand."

"That's good! He's groveling. That's better than ogling, right?"

"He's groveling because of the ogling, Nina. Look at this one text:

DMITRI: Is this about Meg? It was just weird how much she'd changed from the last time I saw her, that was all. Ask Nicky. She looked totally different!

"And then this one:

DMITRI: I don't even like that kind of girl!"

Janina finally got it. She shook her head and said, "'That kind of girl'? How about the kind of guy who talks to his girlfriend about the development of another girl's body?"

Then she looked at the ceiling. "Dmitri, you dumbass. Why are guys so stupid? Seriously. They could stop being this way. If girls didn't keep going out with them, evolution wouldn't keep perpetuating this complete idiocy. Okay, here's what we're going to do . . ."

That's when Janina came up with the brilliant idea to switch my locker away from Dmitri's newly acquired locker. This way I can at least avoid the inevitable awkwardness for a tiny bit longer. Also, less human interaction is really my preferable state right now.

If I ever leave my room.

Because not having a locker next to Dmitri doesn't mean that I'm not going to have to see him at some point. It doesn't mean that I'm not going to have to face the fact that I am not "that kind of girl." And he obviously wants that kind of girl. And he, unfortunately, must be that type of guy. Am I overthinking it? Am I focusing too much on Meg in order to cover up the reality of my returning depression? What are we paying a therapist for anyway?

Nope. I can't get out of bed today.

Dmitri

*B*OOM!

I'm body slammed against a row of lockers, my arm wrenched behind me in what I imagine martial artists call the Killing Twist, or the Spiral Grip of Death, or something like that.

Like most institutions of higher learning, Walter Mondale Preparatory High School has an obligatory alpha-male bully; ours is named Ignatius Blatt, better known as Iggy Blatt. (Kind of easy to understand how a person named Iggy Blatt winds up as the school bully. I mean, what were his parents thinking?) He's a big kid, maybe six foot two, and while he'd be a shoo-in for the football team, he doesn't play any school sports. I think he models himself after the Judd Nelson character in that movie *The Breakfast Club*, which, if you've never seen it, is one of the many reasons I'm glad I'm not in tenth grade in the 1980s. Most of my friends' parents love that movie. All of my friends hate it. (*My* parents love *Zorba the Greek* with Anthony Quinn. Yay, me.)

Anyway, I'm expecting Iggy Blatt to lean in and tell me which heinous crime against humanity (and bullies) I've committed, but instead, it's a girl's voice in my ear, and it sounds pissed.

"You are a complete jerk, you know that?"

Janina.

Damn, she's strong. I'm trying to move my arm, to turn around, but I'm completely immobilized. And it hurts.

"I told you. I made it very, very clear. You were not to hurt Eliana. But what did you do?" She's on a roll so I don't answer. "That's not a rhetorical question, dipshit. What did you do?"

"Iin nah reawy shaw." With my face eating the metal of some random kid's locker, my words come out funny, so Janina loosens her grip. I stretch my jaw to make sure it still works. "I'm not really sure."

"Who's Meg?"

Crap. "Janina, it was a total misunderstanding."

"Were you ogling? I've been told there was ogling."

"Only because she looked so different from the last time I saw her!" I protest. "I mean, her underwear was blue!" Yep. I say that. Out loud. To Eliana's best friend. The same friend who's pinning me to a locker like she's John Cena. I am exactly this stupid.

Janina relaxes her grip for a second and I think she's going to let me go. Instead, she slams my face against the locker again, harder this time.

In the background I hear someone say, "Hey, Dmitri's getting beat up by a girl!"

"Janina," I stammer, a line of drool snaking its way from my lower lip down toward the combination lock. "Can you just turn me around so we can actually talk?"

There's one of those pauses where time seems to stop; Janina must be weighing her options. Not wanting to actually kill me, she lets go. My first instinct is to run, but I don't. When I turn around, Janina is standing there, arms crossed tight over her chest, her eyes red. She cranes her neck around to look at the crowd of kids gathered behind her, spits "Piss off" through gritted teeth, and waits a second while the assembled mass disperses. Now it's just the two of us.

"What," she says, turning back to me, her voice both restrained and dripping with venom, "were you doing looking at another girl's underwear?"

"I wasn't. I mean, I couldn't help but notice it because her skirt was so short. Honest. It was like a car wreck. I couldn't look away."

Janina bites a fingernail while she processes this information. "You really hurt her feelings, you know."

"I do know. I've tried to apologize like a million times." I sound like I'm whining, but I can't help it.

"Yeah, she told me."

"I even wrote her a song." I reach into my backpack and pull out the laminated piece of paper. For a second, just the briefest second, Janina's eyes soften. Then they turn back to stone.

"Give me that."

I do as I'm commanded.

"Will you give it to Ellie?" I ask as Janina reads the lyrics. "Is she even here today? I didn't see her in film class."

This makes Janina's head jerk up. "She didn't tell you?"

"Tell me what?"

"She dropped film class, Dmitri."

"Because I looked at another girl?"

"No, just before winter break. And Ellie's not here today. She wasn't feeling well." Janina gives me a long hard look before asking, "You know why Ellie missed some school last year, right?" There is caution in the question.

"I didn't know she *had* missed school last year." This conversation is confusing the crap out of me. Wait. Ellie dropped film class . . . *before* winter break?

"Look," Janina says, "I'll make sure she gets this." She waves my lyrics at me. "Just don't do anything else stupid."

"Like what?"

"I don't know. Just don't do *anything*."

Janina spins on her heel and walks away, rereading my song as she goes.

"Don't do anything stupid," I say to myself as the bell rings. I'm not sure that's possible.

Eliana

"Eliana?" My mom raps gently on my closet door. She gave me a pass yesterday from going to school since it was the first day after vacation, and I basically took advantage of how busy she was going to be getting herself and the other kids ready. "One day. That is all you get. We can't start this again, Eliana. You beat this, and you move on." She dictates this speech, abbreviated from one I'd heard dozens of times last year before my hospitalization. I hear both the hope, that I *will* beat this, and the fear, that it's all happening again. I feel exactly as she does except a million times worse because I do not want to be the old me again. I don't want to be crazy, depressed, hospitalized Eliana. I don't want to have to give up my clothes and my shoes and my laptop in order to talk about myself in a sterile room on therapeutic couches for weeks until I'm "better." Because what would be the point? I'm obviously not better. I'm obviously never going to be better.

"El?" It's 7:12 A.M. Day two of the week after winter break. My clothes haven't been changed in three days, and I've now watched all eight Harry Potter movies two times each and reread books four and six. My high octagonal window twinkles with frost crystals. It is too cold to get out of bed, even if I wanted to. Which I do not.

"El." Mom is more insistent now, stating instead of questioning. Soon it will turn to demanding. I have been here before. I will be here again.

"Tomorrow, Mom. I promise I'll go tomorrow," I groan from under my protective layer.

"Tomorrow is not good enough, Eliana. Because we both know that if you don't go back today, you will be saying the exact same thing tomorrow. And tomorrow will turn into a week, and then two weeks, and then we're back in that whole stream of shit again."

My mom is swearing. That is a rare occurrence and one that doesn't bode well for me. When she swears, she means business. Usually it takes several hours of me pleading not to go to school to crack her calm and collected facade. She has lost all patience for me, for this, having been through it before. She is tough-loving me, something we both learned during hours of family therapy last year. I don't like how it sounds coming out of her. I don't like that she's talking to me this way. I don't like that I drove her to it.

"Eliana!" Mom pounds on the door once, hard, with the palm of her hand. I assume it's the palm. I hope I haven't driven Mom to punching my closet door.

"What?" I yell back. I try to feel angry at her, mad that my mom won't let me do what I want to do. Mad that she won't leave me alone. But I know she wants me to be normal again. Because I want it, too. I'm failing both of us.

"Get out of your closet, take a shower, put on some fresh clothes, and I will drive you to school." Mom breathes out as calmly as she can, speaking through gritted teeth.

"Do I have to?" I ask, pretending like I have a choice. Pretending

I'm some regular teenager trying to convince her mom that she doesn't really need to go to school and deserves a second day of hooky.

"Yes," Mom argues, and I hear a *click* as the locked door to my room opens. "Thank you, Samara." Mom looks back at my sister, who escapes with her bent hanger/lock opener.

Mom is dressed for work in a pair of black pants and a striped long-sleeved t-shirt. Her closet is filled with slight variations on this look. In fact, she owns six pairs of the same exact pants because, as she puts it, "Who's going to notice that their high school science teacher wears the same pants every day?" I choose not to tell her about the student teacher I had freshman year who ran out of the class crying after a group of students made fun of her, to her face might I add, about the few outfits she alternated between each day she attempted to teach us. I can still picture her sad little ballet flats.

God, everything is so sad.

"Up!" Mom shoots out her arm at me, a direct order to get out of the blankets and into the world. I look at her with pleading eyes, but she is stoic. She must have practiced long and hard because my pathetic puppy face used to make her crumble.

"I don't know if I can, Mom." I really don't. What if I get to school and I can't sit through my classes or I freak out and run through the halls like a total lunatic? What if I need to see Mr. Person, but he has someone else in his office or worse—he turns me away because he doesn't want to see me anymore? Because we've already done all of this?

"Eliana, you can do this. You have been doing it. You are a

strong, brave girl who has been through some stuff and made it to the other side. Not every day is going to feel wonderful. But that doesn't mean that you are going to completely shut down again. I know you aren't. Really." Mom pulls the covers down so she can take hold of my hand. I don't know if she truly believes what she is saying. I certainly don't. But I don't want her to be disappointed in me. Not for one day, anyway.

I let her pull me out of bed.

"That's my girl. Now get in the shower. You stink." Mom pushes me along with a smack on my tush. "You have ten minutes, and then we have to go. I only got a sub for my first-period class."

I slog my way through a shower, letting the water fill my open mouth. I gurgle, and the water bubbles over my tongue.

School won't be that bad. Janina's locker is next to my new one. I can skip lunch and hide out in a corner of the library to read book number seven. I can sneak into a girls' bathroom if I see Dmitri in the halls. Not that that stopped him before.

Why can't everything be the way it was the night of the Greek festival? Full of hope and promise and excited touches?

I miss those things. I knew they had to end sometime, though. Keinehora and yin and yang and all that.

I bet he's already written a song for her.

Dmitri

When I rewind the VHS of our relationship—okay, stupid analogy, but Ellie and I have this film thing between us, and her dad has all those old videotapes, and, well, you know—anyway, when I *look back*, I think it all started to go south on date number five. Two weeks before Christmas break. At the bowling alley.

Before I explain, I know what you're thinking. Things went south when I ogled Meg's royal blue underwear. And they did. They totally did. I suck. I know that.

But really, if I replay everything that happened between me and Ellie, Christmas was the first reel, not the last. And it started with the bowling date.

Eliana and her father had picked me up at home, and from the moment I got in the car, I could tell something was wrong.

"Hey!" I said to Ellie, likely with an idiotic grin on my face because I was so happy to see her. "Hi, Mr. Hoffman."

"How goes it, Dimmi?" Ellie hated when her dad tried to sound young or cool. And apparently, she really hated it that he called me Dimmi.

"Dad, his name is Dmitri." The acid in her voice could've eaten through bars on a prison window. Truth is, I kind of liked her dad being familiar. It was a refreshing change from Basil and Aphrodite

Digrindakis, the official poster children (poster parents?) for the Twin Cities Hellenic Society. Okay, my parents are not actually on a poster, but they probably should be.

"That's all right," I cut in. "I don't mind." I didn't want her dad to feel bad, and I didn't want him to think I was fussy about my name. (*It is not Charlie or Chuck or Chad. Please call me Charles.* Who wants to be *that* guy?)

Eliana rolled her eyes, clenched her jaw, and let out a long, low breath from her nose, all of which made my Spidey-sense tingle. There was danger nearby. I'd learned enough about Ellie's moods to know not to approach this particular flavor of emotion head on.

"So," I offered, trying to change the subject, "ready to bowl a turkey?"

Eliana turned to me, one eyebrow cocked.

"It's three strikes in a row," her father chimed in, his voice animated. "Are you a bowler, Dim—Dmitri?"

"I've bowled some," I answered.

"What's your best score?"

"One seventy-six."

"Say, that's not too shabby."

"Daaaaaaaaaaaaad," Eliana reprimanded with a disgusted whine in her voice. Her dad shrugged, embarrassed. I squirmed in my seat and looked out the window.

We rode the rest of the way in silence.

"Really, is there anything more repulsive than rented bowling shoes?" Ellie held her white-brown-and-red shoes away from her body, like she was holding a snake. After her father dropped us off, I got us a lane and we turned in our sneakers, consenting that they be held hostage until the rented bowling alley footwear was safely returned.

Sometimes this is just Eliana's sense of humor. She's snarky in a really funny way, and I love it. Other times, though, that kind of biting comment can be a sign she's in a bad mood. I wanted to believe it was the former, but given the car ride, I worried it was the latter.

She must have seen the look on my face, the "uh-oh" look, because her free hand hooked itself through my arm and she pulled me toward our lane. "C'mon, you turkey. Let's go bowl a turkey."

And then for a while, everything was fine. Not great, but fine. We bowled, we ate nachos and drank Cokes, we laughed, and we talked about nothing and talked about everything. Then I said this:

"Maybe Chuck E. can officiate our wedding here." I meant this as the second half of a joke Ellie had started during our prior date, at Chuck E. Cheese.

"What?" Eliana went from relaxed to rigid faster than the speed of sound. Her "what" even made a kind of sonic boom. "God, Dmitri," she huffed under her breath.

I didn't dare remind her of her proclamation at Chuck E. Cheese, that the stupid mouse from that house of horrors would be the one to unite us in wedded bliss. She'd said that, not me.

I wasn't sure what to do, so I sat back down while she bowled a frame.

Sometimes Ellie and I communicate better remotely than in person, so I took my phone out and texted her. I figured it would be cute. A story we could tell our kids someday.

ME: Hey, you okay? I'm worried about you.

I peeked over my shoulder before throwing my next ball, watching as Ellie took her phone out, glanced at it, and sighed heavily. She put the phone away without responding.

Not sure what else to do, I took the three steps to the line and threw my next ball. A strike. My third in a row.

A turkey.

Neither one of us commented on it.

Yeah, that date was definitely when things started to come undone.

Eliana

I don't know why I do the things I do. It's like I have no control over my stupid brain. That's why I like the quiet. Like to
stay quiet. In silence, I can't make any mistakes.

To be clear: Dmitri was not a mistake. At least on my end. He's
a great guy. A great boyfriend (much of the time, at least). A great
drummer. He even has great hair. But what is wrong with him that
he chose me for a girlfriend? I made the mistake of letting him
think I'm normal. That I'm capable of having a hand-holding,
romantic-texting, family-meeting relationship.

I even said that ridiculous thing about getting married at Chuck
E. Cheese. And then he remembered it and had to bring it up
again just to prove what a loser dork I am. Mortified. It makes my
stomach wring itself into a knot just thinking about it.

If I hadn't gotten involved with Dmitri, then I wouldn't have
someone always here trying to see if I'm okay. He asks me that at
least twenty times a day. Texts. Messages. Meaningful looks. He.
Won't. Stop.

I. Am. Not. Okay.

And he has no idea that the more he asks, the worse I feel about
not being okay.

What must it be like to be normal?

Dmitri

I tried texting Ellie last night to see if she was feeling okay (I knew she wasn't sick; she was just avoiding me), but she never answered. I also wanted to find out what Janina was talking about with Ellie having been out of school last year. How come I didn't know this? Did Ellie have scarlet fever? Bubonic plague? Was she in juvie? I thought about texting my go-to guy—well, gal—for information, but things are weird with Reggie right now so I nixed that idea.

Having hardly slept, I'm up early. Yia Yia is the only person in the kitchen when I come down. She's hunched over a cup of her steaming-hot, mud-thick coffee. "The only thing Turks ever get right," she once told me about coffee.

"Tikanes, Yia Yia," I mumble as I cross the room. It's a casual greeting shared among Greeks. It takes me a beat to realize she hasn't answered. "Yia Yia?" I ask as I turn to look at her. She's asleep in her seat, snoring so faintly as to be inaudible unless you're listening for it.

She looks frail. All skin and bones under her gray dress, her cheeks sallow, her skin almost colorless. I forget sometimes just how old Yia Yia is.

I decide not to wake her and slip out of the house before anyone else gets up. The first bell rings at 8:05, and after a brisk bike ride, I'm in the halls of Walter Mondale a full hour early. Other than the Math Club kids, I'm the only student in the building. I camp out by my old locker, hoping to catch Ellie when she arrives.

It's weird to watch the school come to life. Students, teachers, and administrators filter in a few at a time, the low thrum of humanity mushrooming toward a kind of crescendo. And then, at seven fifty-five, boom! Everyone, all at once.

Everyone except for Eliana.

I wait a full two minutes after the late bell rings before dragging myself to homeroom, where I'm admonished by the teacher and a permanent mark is made on my permanent record for being tardy.

Whatever.

I trudge through periods one and two before getting to the Art and Craft of Cinema. It was hard to sit through class without Ellie yesterday; it will be even harder today. Only, the desk next to me is now occupied. A girl from my geometry class, Daisy Something-or-Other, smiles at me as I take my seat, while Mr. Tannis takes attendance.

It's weird the way Ellie's desk just got filled. That's how the world works, I guess. The little holes—or, in this case, the big holes—left behind by absences or partings just get filled in, like water finding every crack in a sidewalk; life washing over everything, partly cleansing and partly drowning it.

"Hey," Daisy whispers at me. Can't she sit somewhere else? I mean, her normal seat is like five desks away, and kids don't usually move seats. I'm just not in the mood.

But me being me, I don't want to be impolite. "Hey," I say back.

"You're Eliana's boyfriend, right?"

"Yeah." I already don't like where this is going. "I think so." I wish I hadn't said that, but she glosses over it.

"And you're in Unexpected Turbulence?"

"Um, yeah." Okay, I like that question better. "How come?"

Mr. Tannis clears his throat and stares the two of us down. Daisy, who I'm pretty sure is some sort of Queen Bee in the school, stares back at him. I don't have that kind of moxie, so I duck my head and examine the top of my desk. It's the oldest, worst, and least believable ruse there is. The "if I don't make eye contact with you I can't get in trouble" ruse.

"Dmitri? Something you want to share with the class?" And that has to be the oldest, worst, and least believable ruse used by teachers. I mean, does anyone ever say, "Yes, in fact I do have something I'd like to share with the class. Thanks for asking!" Again, whatever.

Anyway, Daisy stops talking after that, but she does toss a note on my desk:

Wait for me after class.

Freaked out, weirded out, nervous, and a little bit intrigued, I don't hear another word Mr. Tannis says for the rest of class, which is a bummer. He's starting a unit on film adaptations and is talking about *High Fidelity*, a movie I love. (I didn't even know it was a book.)

When the bell rings, Daisy is waiting for me in the hall.

"Hey!" She's a little too bubbly. Not just her greeting, but her whole persona. Her brass-colored hair has too much—what do barbers call it? Product? Yeah, it has too much product. And she wears too much makeup. And her clothes are just a little too perfect. Daisy is pretty in an airbrushed sort of way. If someone were to hose her down, she'd be pretty ordinary. Which would make her prettier.

"Hey," I say back. "What's up?"

"I'm a big fan of your band." Okay, I'll admit, this is the easiest and smartest way to get me to let my guard down, and it almost works. *Almost.*

"Thanks. Have you seen us play?"

"Not yet. But I'm definitely coming to your next show." Inexplicably, she reaches out and squeezes my bicep. I'm not ripped like an athlete, but drumming does give my arms a decent muscle tone. She giggles. Giggles?

"So listen, I just want to make sure Eliana is okay."

Wait. What?

"Why wouldn't she be?"

"Well, you know, because of everything that happened last year."

There it is again. *Last year.* I'm about to blurt out, "What the hell happened last year?" but something tells me that would be a bad idea. I don't trust this girl, and I don't want to tip my hand that I'm in the dark. Plus, I don't think Daisy's motives are all that honorable here.

"Yeah, but that was last year. Everything is okay now." I lie. Or at least I think I'm lying. I have no idea.

"Okay, good." She smiles. It's the fakest smile I've ever seen, like her face is broken. "Mental illness can be so hard to cope with. We've all been so worried about Eliana, the poor thing. When I saw she was out of school the last two days, well . . ." Her voice trails off.

Three things occur to me all at once.

THING THAT OCCURS TO ME #1: Eliana suffers from some sort of mental illness. What is it? Schizophrenia? That's the one I hear about the most. Does she have multiple personalities? Why didn't she tell me? I can help her. I have to help her. I will help her.

THING THAT OCCURS TO ME #2: It's very, very obvious Daisy is telling me this to throw Ellie under a bus. To drive a wedge between us. To make me not like Ellie, to look at her differently. And I don't think Daisy is doing this because she likes me. I think she's doing it because she's a bitch.

THING THAT OCCURS TO ME #3: Daisy said "we." Who's "we"? Is Janina part of this? That's what I need to do. Right now. I need to talk to Janina.

"Right," I say, coming over the top of her fake smile with an even faker smile—seriously, I think it might be causing damage to my lips and cheeks. "Thanks for your concern. I'll be sure to share it with Ellie."

Daisy's smile fades a bit; she's probably wondering if I'm screwing with her.

"Oh, and hey, I'll put your name on the guest list for the next Unexpected Turbulence show."

She lights up again. "Really?"

"Really."

"Can you put my three friends, too?"

"Sure, I'll put Daisy plus three."

"Thanks!"

No way am I putting her on a guest list. I'll have to remember to tell the person at the door, whenever and wherever our next gig is, not to admit someone named Daisy trying to scam her way in.

But that's for later.

Right now I need to find Janina and get some information.

Right.

Now.

Eliana

My mom pulls up in front of the school. I feel like we're in the opening scene of *The Breakfast Club*. Who does that make me? The princess? Hardly. The jock? Not so much. The basket case? Great.

"Remember what Sheila told you to say to yourself: 'I may not like it, but I can get through it.'" My mom loves to quote my therapist. I guess she figures if she pays her a ton of money to "help" me, it might as well come with some handy-dandy pocket quotes.

"That worked fine when it was getting a shot at the doctor's office, Mom, but I don't really see how it applies to school." Actually, it's pretty glaringly obvious how it applies to pretty much everything I may or may not want to do, but I feel like being contrary. My mom did manage to get me out of my room, into the shower, dressed, and in the car. How did she do that? My mom should be a hostage negotiator.

"Eliana, you've got this." Mom bores into my eyes with a look that reads, "You better got this, or we are going to have to do something drastic and I don't know what that looks like anymore."

My stomach lurches. I don't know if I do got this. Or if I do have this. Or if I want this at all. Why couldn't teleportation exist?

Or Floo Powder? Why isn't there someone inventing something useful out there that can just get me the hell out of here?

I close my eyes and practice some deep, circular breathing. I envision my inhale creating the right curve of a circle, my exhale the left side. Two more times, and I secretly pray that my mom thinks I'm asleep and takes me home. I wink open my left eye. Mom watches me with impatience.

"Eliana, I have to get to work. I don't want to sound insensitive, and you know I support your emotional needs. I just think your emotional needs are to go to school like any normal day."

"'Normal,' Mom!" This word is off-limits when I'm dealing with my shit. She knows that.

"You know I didn't mean 'normal.' I meant, 'regularly scheduled.' This isn't about semantics, Eliana. Get out of the car, and go to school. The end. Period."

Mom is resolute, and I am too nervous and tired to try and argue. I flap open the door handle and slug my backpack over my right shoulder. I am angry at my mom, but I'm also right there with her: If only I could be normal. If only she could have a normal daughter. If only my mom didn't have to ask me to try to be normal. What must it be like to actually be normal?

Now "normal" doesn't even sound like a normal word.

"Please don't be mad at me, Eliana. Or if you are mad, at least try and go to school the whole day. Use that anger, right? Constructively!"

Mom has run out of useful things to say. I've already missed most of first period, another tardy to add to my tarnished record. Do colleges look at numbers of tardies?

How can I even think of college when I can barely make it to high school?

Mom is still talking to me as I attempt to put one foot in front of the other. "You can do it, Eliana. I love you."

I do my best peeved-teen face and slam the car door. That even feels like I'm pretending. Mom drives off without a care and leaves me alone at the gates of Hell.

I laugh to myself, at myself, for being so dramatic.

Now to go hide in Mr. Person's office.

The front office knows me well. Not in the way they know class presidents or the kid who lit off a bunch of fireworks in his locker. They know me because of all of my late/tardy/absent/messed-up-schedule situations. They know my face and my name, and they don't ask questions. I guess it's cool and kind of respectful in one regard, like they're trying to give me privacy. But on the other hand, it would be kind of nice if they asked me how I was doing or why I'm late or if I'd like to lie down with a bag of powdered Donettes and a coffee in the nurse's office and just forget the rest of the school day altogether.

I sign in, and the secretary, Mrs. Blair, acknowledges me without a word but with a late pass thrust upon the counter.

I'm fine. Really. I'm only late because I couldn't get myself out of bed. Thanks for asking.

"I need to see Mr. Person," I tell her.

Mrs. Blair can't be bothered to look up from her extremely important paper shuffling when she replies, "Is he expecting you?"

"Probably," I say. I mean, he knows at some point I'll be in to see him again.

"Go ahead." Mrs. Blair gestures down the hall that leads to the guidance counselors and goes back to ignoring me, the one thing she seems overly qualified to do.

The door to Mr. Person's office is closed, a rare occurrence, and I hear voices inside. How dare he meet with a student other than me!

I pass the time playing a Harry Potter game on my phone. Phones aren't technically allowed out during school hours unless it's an emergency, but since it's keeping me from having a panic attack and running out of the school and into oncoming traffic, I think they'd let me slide. Not like anyone would notice anyway. The guidance counselor hall is a relatively deserted wasteland at high school. The only time it's ever busy, at least as far as I can tell, is the first day of first semester when everyone thinks they were placed in the wrong classes. I do see a few random regulars: the kid who keeps getting kicked out of classes because he's an asshole and the kid who insists he should be in more challenging classes because he's an asshole. As I begin to contemplate whether or not I happen to be a guidance counselor asshole, Mr. Person's door opens up. I don't recognize the boy who walks out, but he is most definitely a freshman who has not had the good fortune of a growth spurt. His eyes are red, and he sniffs in that "post-crying" way. I should say something because it feels so negligent when no one says anything to me. But what would I say? "I get it, dude. Life sucks. School sucks. Let's get out of here and binge-watch the last sixty years of *Dr. Who* without taking a breath. No one will notice we're gone." The only thing I manage to do is avoid making eye contact, and I weasel my way into Mr. Person's office.

Without being invited, I sit in the only spare chair. The chair should have my name stenciled across the back, like I'm starring in this show. Or at least I'm the special guest star.

"Eliana." Mr. Person leans back in his springy old chair, his favorite posture for me. The "what can I do for you *this* time?" posture. "Didn't you start a new class yesterday? Don't tell me you already don't like it? Although, I wouldn't be surprised."

"Less sarcasm, more support, please, Mr. Person. I am in a vulnerable place today." I was trying to sound snarky, but it was a completely truthful statement. Which now makes me feel truly vulnerable. Dammit. I choke on my next words, holding in what I can of my newly quavering voice. "I missed school yesterday. The only reason I'm here today is to appease my mom, and I don't know if I can do it. Yes, I want to switch out of yearbook because there is no way in hell that I am going to be able to feign mirth and revelry about a school that I can hardly get myself into."

Mr. Person is less fumbly than usual. Maybe he can see I'm telling the truth. Or worse, maybe he sees the beginning of another fall.

"Sure, sure, we can get you out of yearbook. What did I say your other options were?" Mr. Person starts clicking around on his computer, but I already know my choices.

"It's either shop or study hall," I remind him.

"So what are you thinking?" He leans back again in his chair, this time less annoyed and more concerned.

"I like the idea of shop," I say. "But I had an incident with a planer in middle school. A huge wedge of wood jammed underneath my fingernail when I was attempting to build a napkin holder, and I had to go to the doctor to get it removed. I fainted. There was blood. It was not a good scene. I hate to say it, but I think I'm going to have to choose study hall."

I actively wince the moment the words escape my lips. Study hall is such a waste of time. I could be at home watching movies or devising schemes on how to not leave my house, instead of sitting at a tiny desk listening to people breathe and flirt and fart all around me. No one ever accomplishes anything in study hall. It's a fact, and Mr. Person knows that.

"You could . . ." Whatever Mr. Person is about to say is obviously something he knows I do not want to hear. ". . . go back to film studies?"

Gah! I twist and turn in my seat as though the room is suddenly filled with my kryptonite. It's like my fear of relationships and my fear of failing as a student are waging an invisible war inside my gut. "Or not?" Mr. Person recognizes my, shall we say, reluctance. "Here. Why don't we make a pros and cons list? You always like those." He doesn't wait for my answer and grabs a sheet of paper, jotting down "Pros" and "Cons" at the top.

After a solid twenty minutes, we come up with:

Pros
I will get an A in film class
I like movies
Film class is more interesting than study hall

Cons
I will have to see Dmitri
I will have to talk to Dmitri
I will have to continue avoiding Dmitri

"I don't know how comfortable I am with this conversation, Eliana. Are you sure you don't want to set up a meeting with one of the social workers? We have some nice girls' groups in the school, too."

"Do you know who is in those girl groups, Mr. Person? All of my old friends who ditched me after I was hospitalized last year, thanks to said school social workers who convinced my parents I *should* be hospitalized. No, thank you."

"Is this Dmitri fella really all that bad?"

The biggest problem is that he's not bad at all. He's sweet. And he writes me songs. And I think he loves me. But it's not enough to change who I really am, which is this insecure weirdo who would rather pretend to be in a relationship with magical guys than in a real one with a guy who is kind of magical.

"Fine. Put me in study hall. But I can't promise I won't be back in your office."

"I would never assume that," Mr. Person concurs.

"And I'm staying in here the rest of the day."

"Um."

"Or else no deal, Mr. Person!"

I realize I should have no upper hand in this matter, but Mr. Person doesn't argue. I spend the rest of the day in his office, an excused non-absence, doing my schoolwork and helping Mr. Person with his daily Jumble. When the final bell rings, I am proud to say I've made it through a day of school. If only tomorrow could be this easy.

Dmitri

*J*anina tells me everything.

I corner her at her locker after fourth period and ask what the hell happened *last year*. At first she tries to fend me off.

"You're going to have to get Ellie to tell you about it, Dmitri." Janina won't make eye contact, which isn't like her. Then I say what must be the magic word, or rather, name.

"Who is Daisy and why is *she* asking me about last year?"

Her head jerks up. "Shit."

And the floodgates open.

Janina tells me about depression and anxiety and hospital stays and time missed from school. She tells me about Daisy and the other members of the Bitch Patrol—that's what she calls them— and how they totally dissed Ellie. She uses words like "lost," "adrift," "stuck," and "gone" to describe what Ellie went through.

Gone.

A thought pops into my head. "Did she try to . . . hurt herself?"

"She fought her way back is what she did. Eliana Hoffman is the bravest person I know, and so much tougher than she realizes." Janina's voice catches. I can't help but notice she didn't answer my question, but I don't push it.

"And she's . . ." I don't have the vocabulary to even talk about this so I just end with, "Again?"

"Yeah."

"Is it my fault?"

Janina breaks eye contact, which feels like an answer. "I don't think anyone, even Ellie, knows what makes her feel this way."

"So what do we do?"

Then this tall, beautiful, superconfident girl says, "I have no idea. Love her, I guess."

That fills me with both terror and hope. Terror, because if Janina doesn't know what to do, I feel sunk. Hope, because loving Ellie is something I can do. And I can do well.

I notice a flyer on the wall over Janina's shoulder and it gives me an idea. I reach forward, causing her to flinch—which, after she brutalized and humiliated me at my locker yesterday, makes me a tiny bit happy—and take the flyer down. "I'm going to fix this," I say, and I start to head for my next class.

"Dmitri," she calls, and I turn around. "This isn't something you can fix. You have to let El tell you what she needs, and be there when she needs it."

Bullshit, I think to myself. What she needs is to know how much I love her. Because love is everything.

The bike ride to Ellie's house after rehearsal takes only twenty minutes. When I ring the doorbell, her mother is so happy to see me her eyes well up. She pulls me inside and wraps me in an embrace.

"Thank you for coming, Dmitri." It's almost like she called and asked me to be here. I wonder if I missed a message from Mrs. Hoffman and make a mental note to check my iPhone later.

I've been to Ellie's house a few times before and have met her whole family. It's weird for me to see a house with so many kids. It makes me realize there's an energy missing from Chez Digrindaki. Or maybe it's just different. The energy here teems with life and possibility. At my house it's . . . I don't know . . . Greek.

"Dmitri! Dmitri!" Ellie's youngest sister, Ava—complete with pigtails and a doll in her hand—dances circles around me.

"Ava," Mrs. Hoffman says, "can you take Dmitri up to Eliana's room?"

I've never been up to Ellie's room. I've had dinner with the family in the dining room, watched TV in the living room, and hung out with Ellie in the basement and on the patio in the backyard. But never upstairs. I've wanted to go, but have never been invited.

Given the reason I'm here, the idea of going to Ellie's bedroom now feels like I'm entering the final level of a dungeon on a D&D campaign, and the Dungeon Master has saved his best tricks for last. In other words, I'm shitting a brick.

Ava chatters all the way up the stairs, but I'm so nervous I don't hear a word of what she says. We enter a bedroom with bunk beds and posters of princesses and unicorns, but Ellie's not here. I worry Ava has diverted me away for a tea party or something—I don't have a sister, so I'm not really sure what little girls do; I fig-ure it's got to be tea parties—but then she crosses the room and bangs on the closet door. Ellie told me her room was a closet; I figured she was just being dramatic.

Huh. I guess not.

"Go away!" comes a shout from the other side. I know it's Ellie, but it doesn't sound like Ellie. It kind of freaks me out.

"You have a visitor!" Ava shouts, carefully pronouncing each syllable in "visitor," making sure her own voice permeates the wood. For such a little kid, she's loud.

The door opens and there's Ellie.

After everything Janina told me, and after not having talked to Ellie—other than the text about needing space—I don't realize I'm holding my breath until I exhale. I see Eliana. Sad, beautiful Eliana. I want to wrap her in a hug and never let her go.

I don't.

The look on Ellie's face tells me she was expecting someone else.

"What are you doing here?"

"Hey."

"Look, Dmitri, I don't care that you looked at another—"

"Janina told me everything," I interrupt. This stops Ellie in her tracks.

"Everything about what?" But I can see on her face she already knows the answer to her own question.

"Why didn't you tell me?"

Ava is still standing there, listening to us go back and forth, like she's watching a teen drama on television she doesn't really under-stand. "Ava," Ellie says, "privacy, please." Ava shrugs her shoulders and skips out of the bedroom, closing the door behind her.

"Ellie," I say, "I love you." A long, low breath escapes through her lips, and her shoulders drop.

"Sit down." She flops down and nods to the mattress for me to join her. It's covered in dirty clothes; Ellie doesn't bother to move them, which I take as a bad sign. Her computer is open and frozen on a scene of Daniel Radcliffe in the owlery at Hogwarts. "Look. This isn't about you. I don't mean that to sound mean, but it's the truth. Yes, I'm hurt you think that Meg girl is prettier than me—"

"I don't."

"But this has nothing to do with you or her or anyone else. This is just who I am. It's pathetic. It's sad. It's ridiculous. And I never wanted you to see it."

"Ellie," I say again, this time taking her hand. She bristles when I do, but doesn't let go right away. "I *love* you." I put emphasis on the "love." "Let me help you."

"It doesn't work like that, Dmitri."

"Work like what?"

"Love doesn't figure into this equation. And you can't help me. Only I can help me, and I don't know how." Her voice chokes.

"Then let me help you help yourself."

I can actually feel Ellie shrivel in front of me. I want so badly to reach forward and hug her, but she pulls her hand back and now it's like she's surrounded by a force field.

"Did Janina give you the song I wrote?" I'm not sure what else to say and this just sort of pops out. It makes Ellie groan; she flops back on her bed.

"I'm the one who's sorry." I don't understand her answer until I realize she's talking about my lyrics. So she did read it. That, at least, gives me some hope.

"You're sorry? About what?"

"About not telling you. About being this way. About not being good enough."

"Ellie, you're more than good en—"

"That's not what I mean."

"Then what do you mean? Tell me. I want to help."

Ellie puts her forearm over her eyes. I think she might be crying, but I can't be sure. I don't know what to say or do next, and I'm thinking of going to get her mom, when I remember the flyer in my back pocket.

"Hey!" I blurt out. It must startle Ellie, because she moves her arm and props herself up on her elbow.

"What?"

"This!" I thrust the flyer at her. She reads it and looks at me.

"Winter carnival?" she asks.

"Yeah! They even have something called the Frozen Ferris Wheel!" I try to give her my best smile. "We should go."

Ellie lies back down and is still for a very long moment. For a second I worry she's passed out, or gone catatonic, and I start to think again about getting her mom. "If I promise to go," she finally says, "will you give me some space?" Her eyes stay closed while she's talking. "Like starting now?"

On some deep level I feel like it's a bad idea for me to leave, but I've secured a future date and figure I should take what I can get.

"Deal," I say, and get up to go. "And El," I add, "just know that I'm here, always. Okay?"

She opens her eyes, looks at me, nods, and pulls the closet door closed.

Eliana

Mom was so thrilled I made it through my day back at school that she didn't mind at all when I locked myself in my room-hole the instant I arrived home. I failed to mention that I pretty much spent the entire day hiding out with a balding, middle-aged man. I know exactly what my therapist would tell me: This was your first step, and tomorrow you will make an even bigger stride when you go to your classes. Easy for her to say. Not only do I not want to go to my classes, I don't want the stress of running into Dmitri in the halls. Why doesn't his family just move to a faraway city and make things easier on me? We could have long-distance conversations that slowly dwindle when we realize that we're too young for this level of commitment, and he should move on without me and allow me to wither away under my blanket for my remaining days.

I'm all cozy-wozy on my futon, having finished all my school-work and homework in Mr. Person's office (really, can't I just go straight there from now on? I'm so much more productive when I'm not distracted by other people). My laptop, my friend, plays *Goblet of Fire*, and I slowly relax from having to leave my sanctuary for a whole day. Then my phone buzzes. Of course. I'm hopeful it's Janina, so I can quickly tell her I'm watching GOF (she knows this is a sign that I am trying to get out of my head for a while) but it's someone unexpected. It's Nicky. He texts me occasionally, usually looking for Dmitri.

NICKY: Hey, El. Checking in.

ME: Dimmi's not here.

NICKY: No. Checking to see how you are.

ME: Why? What did D say?

NICKY: Nothing. Just haven't seen you at our house since Xmas. Hope the aunts didn't scare you off.

ME: Nah. Your aunts are great. I'm just a little low.

NICKY: Want to talk about it?

ME: Thanks, but not really.

NICKY: Well if you ever need to, I'm here.

ME: Cool.

NICKY: No problem.

ME: I'm going to go now.

I throw the phone to the corner of my room, as though that will stop it from receiving texts. It buzzes again, probably with some kind of sign-off from Nicky. It was nice of him to check in, but it also feels like now I have another person to answer to for feeling shitty. Which just adds another layer of shitty.

Goblet of Fire, take me away. I need the break after the home invasion from Dmitri.

I know he was here to apologize, again, about Meg, but I didn't want him to think that she has so much power over me. It's not Meg that drove me to this state; it's my messed-up brain. I stopped him, but then he stopped me. He found out about last year, and then went all sappy on me. I think he told me he loves me more times than both of my parents combined. And now he wants to save me, as though just his presence and his professions of love are enough to lift whatever plague I have. Doesn't he realize that's like believing that merely telling someone with diabetes "I love you" will cure them, instead of having them take insulin and manage their foods? Depression is not a choice. It's not something I can drop like, say, a film class. It comes. It goes. Sometimes talking helps, sometimes drugs do, too, but sometimes it hangs around even when I should be happy. Even when I should be living my stupid teenage life like all of the other stupid teenagers around me.

It makes me hate everyone. But no one more than myself.

And then Dmitri handed me this flyer. He wants to take me to a carnival. Because nothing cures depression like a winter carnival. I guess it's sweet. I can't even tell anymore. To appease him, to get him out of here, I told him I'd go. Really, though, I can't imagine standing outside in ten-degree weather, watching artists hack away at ice sculptures as smiling children fly down hills of snow on cafeteria trays. I used to love the winter carnival. My parents took us because it was free and got us out of the house during the winter.

Who knows? It could be fun.

Fun.

Fun.

Fun.

Say it enough times and it doesn't sound fun at all. Or even like a real word. Maybe if I go and pretend I'm not a real person, it will be fun. Maybe if I pretend I am going to Hogwarts instead of Walter Mondale Preparatory High School, tomorrow won't be so bad. I can pretend that math class is transfiguration, and that after school I have Quidditch practice. Sometimes I replace one of the Weasley twins as beater when they're having an off day.

Yeah. That doesn't sound crazy at all.

Dmitri

The feel of a drumstick hitting a snare drum is hard to put into words. The skin on the snare is stretched so tight the little plastic tip at the end of the stick literally *bounces* off it. It's how you do a drumroll; you force each stick into a controlled and repeated bounce in successive hits. In isolation, that little bounce is like a hop in your step, an encouraging punch on the shoulder; it's filled with promise and opportunity.

I'm completely losing myself in rehearsal today, letting my arms and legs carry me to a place that's safe and apart from everything else.

We finish the song with a crisp, sudden stop; Kyle and Drew deadening the strings of their instruments, and me hitting and then immediately catching and holding the crash cymbal while kicking the bass drum at the same time. Ending songs like this is a great way to showcase how tight Unexpected Turbulence really is.

"Fucking A!" Chad shouts.

"Fucking A?" Kyle looks both confused and amused.

Chad stares at the rest of us and shakes his head, overemphasizing his disbelief at how stupid the three of us must be. "It's from the eighties, dumbasses." The eighties. Ugh. Nostalgia should be a thing of the past. "Anyway," Chad continues, "I got us another gig." He pulls the mic out of its stand and flings it right at my face before pulling it back by the microphone cord at the last second. It's a trick he likes to do—sometimes aiming at Drew, sometimes at the audience, sometimes at me—and why he insists on never using a wireless mic. It makes me flinch every single time, including today. He lets loose a throaty laugh at seeing me twitch. What a dick.

"Fucking A," Kyle says. It's dripping with sarcasm, but he laughs to break the tension and says, "No, seriously, that's great. Where and when?"

"Friday night. Battle of the bands at a high school out in St. Louis Park. They're expecting a couple of hundred people, and top prize is five hundred dollars."

Even though Chad is a douche, he does do a good job of lining up shows for us. The idea of a gig, especially one with a prize and a nice-sized crowd, brings a smile to my face. Same for Kyle and Drew. Feeding on the energy, Kyle plays a riff to start another song. I'm playing the drum fill that pulls the rest of the band into the groove when it hits me.

Friday night.

The winter carnival.

Shit.

Eliana was back at school today but didn't say two words to me. I tried to catch her in the hall, but she bolted every time she saw me, and she wasn't in PE. And, of course, my texts—sixteen of them—went unanswered. It left me with a sense of being in deep water, and being too tired to swim to shore.

Playing the drums at rehearsal today has been a kind of cleanser, washing all those feelings away.

Until now.

My sticks slide right off the mounted toms and fall to the floor. Everyone stops playing and stares at me.

"Really?" Chad barks. Like I said, dick.

"Did you say Friday?" I ask.

"Yeah. Why?"

"I can't make it."

"Why not?" Chad actually smiles when he asks this, like no matter what excuse I offer, he's going to give me shit.

I think about lying. I mean, if I tell them I have a date, they're all going to laugh at me. But what would my lie be? That I have some family thing? Some church thing? I'm going out of town? Besides, I learned a long time ago that lying almost always backfires.

In the third grade, the vice principal of our elementary school caught me peeing on the side of an equipment shed by the playground. Other boys were doing it, so I joined in, wanting them to think I was cool. The school sent an email home and my father sat me down and grilled me about it.

"It wasn't me," I told him. "I wasn't one of the kids who peed. I was just in the wrong place at the wrong time."

"Demetrios." My dad only used my full name when I was in trouble. "I not care so much about peeing. But if you lying at me, we have bigger problem."

Stick with the lie, I told myself. "I swear, Dad, it wasn't me."

"Dimmi." He hung his head in disgust, or shame, or frustration, or something. "Did school not tell you they have security camera all over playground?"

There was a long pause during which neither one of us moved. Someone watching the scene from outside might have thought time had stopped. I was busted; there was nothing left to do but own up and apologize. Which I did. My father sent me to bed without any supper and I cried myself to sleep.

The next day I looked all around the equipment shed for cameras and couldn't find a single one. I'd been played. My dad's little traps stopped working after that, mostly because I just took the easy route and told the truth. Which I guess was his point. Score one for Papa Smurf.

"I have a date," I tell the band.

"A date?" Chad laughs. "Are you fucking kidding?"

I don't know why that question gets under my skin, but it does. "No, Chad, I'm not fucking kidding. I have a date." My answer is laced with venom.

"Can't you postpone it?" Kyle asks. "I'm sure Eliana will understand." And now I'm trapped. I can't tell them about Ellie and depression and missing school and *last year* and our relationship being on the brink of annihilation. As far as they know, it's just like any other Friday night date, and that's all they need to know.

"Not this one," I say, and leave it at that.

"Well, Demetrios," Chad begins, knowing how much I hate it when anyone uses my full name, "seems like you have a choice to make." He leans forward and points the microphone right at my face. "This band or that girl. It's up to you."

I glance at Kyle and Drew, but each is looking at his shoes.

This band or that girl.

Shit.

Eliana

I never know how to feel on one of these days. I mean, it's the feeling piece that's all messed up. When I wake up and *don't* hate the world. When I look in the mirror and things aren't that bad. When I eat breakfast without the cereal boring an uncomfortable hole into my stomach. Is the fog lifting? Is my depression on its way out again? Or is it just a short reprieve? Sometimes it tricks me. Sometimes I can feel almost normal, and I laugh along with a joke, and I listen in class like a good student, and I live as though the moment is all there is. I stop thinking about how much I hate life, how much I wish I were anywhere but here, how much I hate me.

Aside from being confusing to myself, it seems to really freak other people out. My mom looks at me with great suspicion, as though my good mood is all a fake-out in order to steer her away from the fact that I plan to do something really horrible later in the day. She told me this once, which adds an extra layer of weird to an already out-of-the-ordinary good mood. Just another way depression screws with you. I can't just live my life and feel the way I feel, like a normal person who may be having a good day or a bad day. All of my days are defined to the extreme. My emotions are examined tenfold with a gigantic microscope and an expectation that whatever mood I'm in could come or go at the slightest trigger.

Fun times.

"You sure you don't need a ride to school?" Mom stalks around the kitchen, eyeing me but trying to look like she's not eyeing me.

"I want to walk. I like walking." I dip my spoon into my cereal bowl and retrieve the last softened piece of Alpha-Bits.

I watch as Mom argues with herself, nodding her head, opening her mouth to say something, then holding it in. She can't deny that I enjoy walking, that I've been a walker since before, during, and after depression.

"Walking is good for me, Mom. It's exercise. It's endorphins," I remind her.

"It's fifteen degrees out."

"I'll bundle up. School is less than a mile away. Please?" Mom considers. "What happened to parents spinning yarns about back in their day having to walk to school in zero degrees uphill both ways? I am practically begging you to let me walk to school. There is something wrong with this picture." I'm jokey, but it sucks. I have to convince my mom to let me walk to school. What other kid has to do this? Why can't I just be normal for a day at least?

"Okay. But you're wearing that scarf-hat thing your grandma bought you." She refers to a faux-fur leopard-print hat, connected to a scarf, complete with tiny leopard ears. It's not exactly my style, but it is warm. And I look kind of cute in it for sure.

"Okay." I act like this puts me out, but it's a small victory toward normalcy.

Bundled up so my eyes peek above the fluff of the scarf, I trek to school. By the time I arrive, my eyelashes are frozen and my nose has leaked all over the fur. My lungs burn, but in a good way, a way that tells me I did something productive. I don't feel bad, even if I look it.

Of course the moment I walk into school, I spy Dmitri down the hall. I don't need him to see any more of my bodily fluid (which sounds really wonky, but I'm referring to tears and snot). I quickly duck into the bathroom and unwrap myself from the moist animal covering. My cheeks are pleasantly pink. I have always loved how I look after being outside in extremes, from cold or heat or sun. I grab a hunk of toilet paper from a stall and proceed to blow my nose until clear. With my hat-scarf, I dab my eyes, sticky from the cold, and look myself over. Crisp and wintry with a dash of static cling. Not a bad look for me.

Three minutes until first bell, I strut out of the bathroom feeling pretty proud of myself. I'm semi-chipper. I've got pep in my step. And my step leads me directly into Dmitri.

"You do love a girls' bathroom, don't you?" I smile at him. He looks really freaked out. Crap. Am I supposed to not smile at him? Am I supposed to be the constantly depressed angry girl? Is that what he expects? Or worse, is that what he wants? Is he my Edward Cullen?

Did I just make a Twilight reference?

"Hey," I say to Dmitri, not too happy but with sincerity. If one can say "hey" with sincerity. God, I am really overthinking this moment. And all prior and subsequent moments as well.

"Hi." Dmitri looks excited. Like, maybe too excited. Like maybe he wants to pull me back into the bathroom and have his way with me. Oh my god. That was very "Twilight" as well. I haven't read that series in like seven hundred years, and all of a sudden I'm living it? I thought I was supposed to be playing Hogwarts today. No matter. Fiction feels good.

I act on this fictiony, foxy version of me and offer myself up to Dmitri for a hug. Still not big on PDAs, I allow Dimmi to kiss me on the forehead but try to avoid any actual lip-locking while we're surrounded by a viewing public.

"You look beautiful today," Dmitri coos in my ear. My chilled cheeks burn.

"Must be the fresh air. I walked to school."

"You seem different. Good."

"Good is different?"

"No. Different is good. I mean, you seem different than you have lately. Like, you're talking to me. And smiling at me."

Dmitri pulls back and cups my chin. His expression is almost desperate, and I feel this wicked sense of power. This boy loves me, and my good mood makes him feel better. It's crazy that I could affect a person that much.

I kiss him. Hard. At first I feel his hesitation, or maybe it's confusion, and then he is into it. Really into it. To the point where when the bell rings, I wonder if he'll be able to walk to class comfortably.

I peel myself away, breathing heavily, and tell him, "We have to get to class."

"Right." He nods at my lips.

"I'm looking forward to the carnival Friday," I say, gathering my bag and my being.

"Right," he says again, this time with a concerned squint in his eyes.

"We are going, right?" I ask. My eyes are wide and pleading. I am a character in a novel.

"Yes. Yes, of course." He nods violently, then kisses my cheek. "I should go," he acknowledges.

"Me too. See you later?" I ask.

"Yeah." His eyebrows are fully crinkled and thinking. I don't know what I said or did to make him so confused.

My mood begins to immediately slip a couple of notches. I knew it was too good to last.

Dmitri

My teeth are chattering like one of those sets of toy teeth that bounce across the table when you wind them up. The temperature, *without* the wind chill, is two degrees Fahrenheit.

And it's windy.

Eliana and I are among the few brave souls dumb enough to attend the Excelsior Winter Carnival in these conditions. Her face is covered by a spotted-fur hat and scarf, making her look like a half-human, half-leopard-cheetah thing. She loops her arm through mine, pulling us close for warmth, but it isn't like the public display of affection at school this week; this is about survival.

I wasn't sure which Ellie I would see tonight. Would it be the cagey girl with soft eyes and sharp edges, so shrouded in mystery she made me fall in love with her? The sad girl, so off balance as to be falling over all on her own (in a metaphorical kind of way)? Or the perky, almost bouncy girl I found in the halls of Walter Mondale Preparatory High School two days ago, so unexpected she confused the ever-loving crap out of me. (I wonder where that expression comes from—what exactly *is* "ever-loving crap"?)

When my dad and I pulled up to Ellie's house in the Digrindakis Boat—aka the Cadillac—Ellie yanked the door open, said a muffled "Hello, Mr. Digrindakis" through the spotted fur across her face, and slid close to me. The only noises she made on the drive to Excelsior were occasional grunts I took to be a "yes," a "no," or a chuckle in response to my inane banter. It's not easy to carry on a conversation by yourself, but apparently I was determined to try. Sometimes I just can't help myself.

"Where to first?" I ask once we're through the front gate, my dad's taillights retreating in the distance.

The carnival features a midway with games; a row of vendors selling mostly German food, including funnel cakes; and a few of those portable, suspicious-looking rides that travel from state fair to town carnival to god knows where else. But none of those are the *real* attractions. People from all over the Twin Cities come to the Excelsior Winter Carnival for two reasons (or so said the website): the ice sculptures and the Frozen Ferris Wheel.

"Sculptures," Ellie spits out as she ducks her head into my shoulder to avoid a microburst of wind, the moisture in the air stinging my cheeks like little darts. I wonder if this is what acupuncture feels like.

We follow signs to the "Sculpture Garden," and when we get there, the world falls away.

There are no fewer than fifty ice sculptures—from small, delicate depictions of winter wildlife (deer, foxes, squirrels), to a flawless recreation of the *David* (something we were forced to learn about in art appreciation class, and thanks to this ice sculpture, something I can now finally appreciate), to a life-sized replica of the DeLorean from *Back to the Future* (my all-time favorite old movie). The display of raw artistic talent is breathtaking. Ellie and I both stand up straighter and unconsciously let go of each other as we are rendered mute by what we see.

"Holy . . ." She doesn't finish her thought.

"Yeah," I answer in a breath.

There are so few people at the carnival, we're alone as we wander through the statues. It's otherworldly, like we've landed on some remote ice planet; like we've stumbled on an important archaeological find on Hoth.

Ellie points out a few a sculptures she likes and I do the same, and for a couple of minutes at least, the stress we've been feeling in our relationship evaporates. I'm with the first Ellie, the mystery girl who lets her guard down just for me, or that's how it feels anyway. And I realize that's why I love Ellie so much; she makes me feel special, privileged that she lets me in when she keeps everyone else out, that she allows me to know *her*. It confirms in my mind I made the right choice in coming here tonight.

Chad had texted me yesterday to find out whether or not I was in for the gig. When I told him no, he told me rehearsal was canceled. That was it; nothing more. I tried texting Kyle to see how much damage I'd done with my decision, but he never responded. (There wasn't any reason—there's never any reason—to reach out to Drew.) I didn't tell Ellie anything about the band and the canceled gig. I didn't want her to feel bad or give her an excuse to break the date.

The sound of our boots crunching on the frost replaces our conversation as we approach the final sculpture at the back of the garden, the curator of this little museum having saved the best piece for last: a ten-foot-tall copy of the Frozen Ferris Wheel. It's situated in a way that if you approach it dead on and squat down a bit, you can use the trick of perspective (something Mr. Tannis talked a lot about when we watched *Vertigo*) to make the ice sculpture line up perfectly with the actual Ferris wheel in the background. And most amazing of all, the ice sculpture Ferris wheel turns on its axis, just like the real thing.

It's incredible.

"Whaddya say?" I ask, jutting my chin at the twin wheels. "You game?" Ferris wheels are an important part of our shared mythology, our origin story if you will, and I really want us to ride that frozen beast together. It feels like it will be magical.

Ellie's eyes dart from the Ferris wheels to me and back again. With her face still covered by fur, her eyes are the only thing I can see.

"Sure," she says.

I buy us two tickets from a dimly lit wooden shack, the attendant inside kept warm by a space heater, and we get in line. There is only one other couple in front of us; I'm just wondering who else is idiotic enough to be out here in these temperatures, when the guy turns around.

"Dmitri?"

It takes a minute for me to recognize Dan. He works the sound board at an all-ages club called Minor's, a semi-regular haunt for Unexpected Turbulence. He's a nice guy we've gotten to know a bit, and always does a good job with our mix.

"Oh, hey, man," I answer. "Crazy weather, huh?" Only Dan doesn't answer. Instead, he looks at me like I've got two heads. "What?" I ask after a long and uncomfortable minute.

The Frozen Ferris Wheel comes to a stop, and the really unhappy hipster staffing the ride holds the door open for Dan and his date.

"What are you doing here?" Dan asks, as his girlfriend slides into the waiting compartment.

"What do you mean? Same as you. Enjoying the Minnesota winter." I try to smile but the cold makes my face hurt.

"No. I mean what are you doing *here*? A friend just posted an Instagram pic of Unexpected Turbulence taking the stage at a high school in St. Louis Park. A battle of the bands, I think." Dan is half in the Ferris wheel compartment when he adds over his shoulder, "You quit the band or something?"

I don't have time, or the presence of mind, to answer before Dan follows his date into the Ferris wheel and they're whisked away.

Two things happen next:

First, I experience the same thing Jimmy Stewart's character did in *Vertigo*, where Hitchcock zooms the camera in while physically moving it backward on a track. It gives the feeling of the world contracting and expanding at the same time; a literal and visual sense of vertigo.

The second thing is that Ellie pulls away from me, looking like I just slapped her in the face.

I switch to some kind of autopilot, as if I've been drugged, and allow myself to be ushered into the confines of my own cage on the Frozen Ferris Wheel. For a minute, I don't even realize Ellie is right beside me. Before I know what's happening, the two of us are catapulted into the frigid night sky.

Eliana

The air is excruciating. I know we're Midwesterners and we're supposedly built for this, but I don't know if any human is designed for the impact of a moving Ferris wheel against the frigid wind. My boogers are freezing fast. My eyelashes are stiff. And my mind is numb at the prospect of Dmitri being here with me instead of his band. Did he quit? Did they fire him? Is he on a break? What do me and this torture wheel have to do with it?

I peel my frozen lips apart and blink my eyes rapidly until they can move again. This really is a stupid idea for a carnival. I guess that makes us even stupider for partaking. As best I can in the current conditions, I turn to Dmitri. "Why aren't you at the Unexpected Turbulence show?"

Dmitri's eyes widen like he wasn't expecting me to ask that question. As if we could go about this evening as though such a critical fact hadn't just been lobbed at us by the fates. It's almost like he's forgotten I was sitting next to him. "Um. Yeah. I really don't know," he says, scratching his head through his knitted beanie. "I told them I couldn't play the gig. I thought there wouldn't *be* a gig."

Our gloved hands grip the safety bar in front of us. If this ride is supposed to be romantic, the weather and the news certainly have removed any of that sentiment.

"Why did you tell them you couldn't play?"

Below us, the light bounces off the ice sculptures spectacularly. I consider what would happen if someone dropped a match from the Ferris wheel. Not that I'd do it. But what if.

"I . . ." Dmitri hesitates. "I wanted to bring you to this carnival?"

It is not a solid fact. It is a question. It makes him pause. He regrets it. He regrets bringing me to a carnival because it means that he is not playing with his band. He should be with his band. He belongs with his band. He doesn't belong on this rolling monstrosity next to a girl with frozen snot who is not holding his hand or even smiling at what should be something fun. Because I am not fun. I am trapped inside my brain, thinking thinking thinking, and he has chosen my mess over his happiness. It's too much.

"You should've gone to the show. You should've played. You didn't need to bring me here." I speak through gritted teeth, out of anger and because it's too damn cold to open my mouth all the way.

"But I wanted to be with you. I want to show you how important you are to me."

"I don't feel important. I feel like some pawn in your songwriting arsenal. I feel like you need me to feel important, not because you make me feel important."

Dmitri fumbles. "Wait. What?"

"I'm not your damsel in distress, Dmitri. Sure, I'm in distress, but there's nothing you can do about it. And as much work as you think I am to 'save,' you're just as much work. I'm tired of having to answer texts and tell you I'm okay or not okay or what you can do to help me. Because there's nothing you can do."

"That's not true! I can help you! I can be there for you and show you how much I love you and protect you and take your mind away from things!" Dmitri practically shouts this down to the only other fools who are out in this weather. It doesn't feel reassuring. It's embarrassing. It's embarrassing to be in a state where someone wants to help me. And what makes Dmitri think he's the hero who's going to do that? I tripped *him*, does he remember? I don't want to need help. I just want to be alone.

"I can't do this anymore, Dmitri. I need to go home. Now."

I say this and realize we are at the very top of the Ferris wheel. Stopped to let on a couple with dazzling love in their eyes. Assholes.

"We can figure it out, Ellie. I love you. I can help—"

Before he can finish that ridiculous, repetitive sentiment, I stop him. "No, you can't! Stop saying that! Help yourself. Get out."

"But, we're like fifty feet off the ground."

"You know what I mean, Dmitri. Get out of this relationship. Think of the songs you can write about your crazy ex-girlfriend and how she broke up with you on the Ferris wheel. You can thank me later." I have so much bile in my voice, but inside I'm crumbling so much I fear I may rain down from the top of the Ferris wheel.

We finally begin moving again, and I'm surprised when I peek over at Dmitri and he looks incredulous. At me. I've done it. I've made him turn on me. Just like I did to all my friends. My siblings.

Now he won't want to help me. He probably won't ever want to see me again.

"But I love you, Ellie." He is broken. I broke him.

The Ferris wheel cascades downward, and the carny stops us abruptly at the bottom. He unlatches the safety bar, and the instant I'm free I start to run. It's not easy to run when it's this cold. Within the first fifty yards my lungs burn and my throat crackles. I hold the scarf over my mouth as best I can and keep running. I run even though I hear Dmitri yelling something after me. At me. But I am gone. And he doesn't follow. I knew he wouldn't.

I am alone. Just like I should be. For better or for worse. And it will always get worse.

Dmitri

*A*fter texting Ellie an untold number of times to see if she was okay—even though she told me how much my texts annoy her—this is the only one that got a response:

> **ME**: My father's really worried. He says he was responsible for you and needs to know you got home safely. Can you at least tell me that? That you got home safely? If not, he and I are going to have to go out in the boat and look for you.

My phone chimed two seconds later.

> **ELIANA**: Yes. I got home safe.

I send one final text.

> **ME**: Ellie, I get that you're mad at me, though I'm not really sure why. But are you mad enough to end this? Is it really over?

My answer comes in the form of deafening silence.

After we stepped off the Ferris wheel and Ellie ran, it took two whole minutes for my brain to catch up with what was happening. By the time I went after her, it was too late. She was gone. I guess she left the fairgrounds, found a spot I wouldn't think to look for her, and called her parents to pick her up. Or maybe she just took a Lyft home.

When my dad came to get me and my date was gone, I had to tell him everything. It was embarrassing, like a colossal admission of failure. What's weird is that I found myself telling him more than he really needed to know to understand the situation. I more or less vomited the entire history of my and Ellie's relationship on the car ride home, starting with my tripping in gym class and ending with the Frozen Ferris Wheel.

Dad was quiet for a long moment, his eyes fixed on the road in front of him.

"I proud of you, Demetrios."

Not what I expected. Dad and I don't talk about things like feelings and relationships. "Proud?"

"You choose love over music. This a very Greek thing to do."

I had no freaking idea what that was supposed to mean and told him so.

"We are people who give the world music, and . . ." He fumbled for words and slipped to Greek. "και λογοτεχνία, και δράμα και χορός." (*And literature, and drama, and dance.*) He said this with force. "But all this," he said, back to English, "what is word, culture? Yes, culture. All this culture, it exist because of love."

I wanted to tell him it wasn't just the Greeks, but the Chinese, and the Babylonians, and half a dozen other cultures from across the globe that invented music and drama and dance, that art in any of its many forms is probably native to humans, regardless of where or when we're from. But I was too tired and too shell-shocked to pick a fight.

"You understand?" he asked with utmost gravity.

"Yes. Love is everything," I answered without emotion. I wanted to say love is everything that hurts, but I didn't. I was starting to feel numb.

That was all hours ago, anyway.

When I think of it now, I probably should have paid more atten-tion, because maybe Dad was onto something. I'm just not sure what.

It's past midnight, and I can't fall asleep. I keep playing the scene from the Ferris wheel over and over in my head, and each time I do, my emotions morph ever so slightly from sad to angry until I'm one hundred percent pissed off.

I probably should have realized I was smothering Ellie, that all my texting was too much. But really, what the hell was I supposed to do when she wouldn't even talk to me? Just pretend everything was okay?

She's being selfish. (As mad as I am, I still feel really guilty for even thinking that, but my train of thought is out of control and if I try to stop it, it's going right off the tracks.) Ellie didn't even care that my band did a gig without me. She should have been consol-ing *me*; instead, she made it about her.

"You know what?" I say to Joey, Johnny, Dee Dee, and Marky, all clad in leather on the poster on my wall. "I deserve better than this." I pause for a second before adding a dramatic "Fuck it."

I pick up my phone and compose a text.

ME: Hey Meg . . . Just thought I'd say hi and see if you want to hang out soon.

There's a long pause as I watch the three little dots letting me know she's typing a text. Something about the way they look makes me nauseous, like the motion of a rolling ship at sea, like I'm going to hurl.

MEG: Hi, Dmitri! What happened to you tonight? I was at the UT show, but you weren't there. Anyway, I got to meet Chad. We've been hanging out for hours. He's so cool!

Meg was at the show? She hung out with Chad? Wait. She's *still* hanging out with Chad? She thinks *Chad* is cool?

MEG: He says you quit the band . . . why? Anyway, gotta go. I'll talk to you soon.

I don't answer. There's too much to unpack in that text to even think about answering. My mind is swirling with images of the band playing, and Chad and Meg kissing, and Ellie's gritted teeth and fire-tinged eyes hating my freaking guts. So I start crying—not a loud wailing cry, more of a strangling muffled sob—and keep crying until I fall asleep.

Eliana

Six days. That's how long I was under my blankets. My mom was too busy dealing with Asher's and Ava's strep throat/ear infection combo to argue with me about school. But her patience waned. I had an appointment with Sheila Grossman. Instead of an expensive inpatient program, she laid out a plan to put me on homebound. That means I'm home (duh), but I pick up and send in my schoolwork. I'll have regular Sheila Grossman appointments (yay) and try to work through things without the added stress of social interactions. At least for a month or two. And while this feels good, like a tangible plan, it doesn't feel like a solution. It won't change the fact that I have a giant "Depressed" stamp marring my school files.

Dmitri

I try to text Eliana a few more times the day after the Frozen Ferris Wheel, but she doesn't answer. She isn't in school on Monday. Or Tuesday. Or any day after that. By the end of the week, I can't take it anymore, so I corner Janina.

"Let it go, Dmitri." There is a real sadness in Janina's eyes, like someone she knows has died; I don't know if that person is me or Eliana. I try to press Janina, to find out if Ellie is okay, to find out if I still have a chance, but she doesn't give me a thing.

I text Ellie again that night, the anger I was feeling a week ago having evaporated and leaving a residue of desperate sadness in its place. Only the text fails because the number—Ellie's number—no longer exists.

Well, okay then.

A normal person would probably take this as a sign it's time to move on. Turns out I'm not normal. Inspired by something I saw in a movie, I send a large pizza to Ellie's house, with "I Love You" spelled out in pepperonis. Who wouldn't fall for that?

The pizzeria calls me back and tells me an older woman (Ellie's mom, I guess) refused delivery, and they want to know what I want them to do with the pie. I tell them to just give it to the staff.

Strike one.

I also work up the nerve to text Chad that night, to begin the process of working my way back into the band. I swallow my pride and apologize for missing the gig. This is what I get back:

CHAD: You blew it, Demetrios. But don't worry, I'll be sure to mention you in my autobiography someday.

Eliana

Homebound is glorious, even if it does sound like I should have an ankle bracelet. I get to leave the house. I'm *supposed* to leave the house, as part of my agreement with the parents and Sheila Grossman. Schoolwork is sent home, schoolwork is returned online, I get to spend all of the rest of my delightful alone time doing whatever I want. (If by "alone" I mean with a middle-aged man in the basement. At least he does get take-out sandwiches for me every once in a while. And we have made it a point to watch one classic movie together every Friday at lunchtime, which isn't as bad as expected.) Doing "whatever" includes, but is not limited to, reading, walking, puzzling, and watching heaps of movies. Nowhere in that list do I have to talk to anyone but my family and Janina. It might help that I changed my phone number.

Dmitri

The day after the pizza debacle, I begin a program of writing Eliana three letters a day, on actual stationery and mailed with actual stamps. I figure there is no way she can ignore that.

Five days later—by then I figure that at least my first six letters (two days' worth) have arrived—Janina finds me in school and tells me to cut it out.

"You just need to give her space. Leave her alone. Let her figure things out."

Knowing that my letters are getting through gives me a rare moment of hope. Then Janina hands me six postmarked, unopened envelopes.

Strike two.

If this isn't bad enough, I reach out to Kyle, but he's not answering my texts.

It's feeling like the universe is conspiring against me.

Eliana

I'm on the couch, trying to watch *The Dark Crystal* on Netflix, when Dad plops himself next to me. He's not overly close, which I appreciate, and he's not talking to me, which I also like. In fact, I kind of don't mind that he's here. It's lonely being home all the time with just my head to keep me company.

Dad manages to keep silent for all of three minutes, when he weighs in on the show. "They've kept the feeling of the original movie while coming up with an entire new world of Gelfling. I'm impressed." I nod, because if I engage too much, that'll encourage him to talk more. Three more minutes and another comment, this time about the legacy of the Jim Henson Company. I'm not completely listening. It's a comforting din my dad brings with him. For about ten minutes. Then it's overkill, and I wish he would stop trying to be my friend and just be my dad.

"Dad, can we maybe just watch in silence for a few hours?" I ask. That was one of the things I liked about Dmitri. He knew when to let the power of the screen take over. Or at least when quiet felt right. Maybe it was the musician in him.

I can see how painful even five minutes of quietude is for my dad, maybe because his daughter told him to shut up or maybe because it is that hard for him to be quiet, but he opens his mouth, holds up a finger, and announces, "I'm going to get a paper and pen. That way I can take notes on all of the talking points for a later discussion."

"You do what you gotta do, Dad," I say.

Dad stands up, walks away, and doesn't come back. I'm both happy and sad. That's what I get for leaving my room-hole.

Dmitri

*J*anina isn't the only one to warn me off my current path.

"You need to move on."

Nicky and Yia Yia are waiting for me in the kitchen after school. I told Nicky about my failure at sending the letters. I guess he ratted me out.

"Dimmi-moo," Yia Yia begins, "she good girl, but maybe you need give her space." Why does everyone in the world care about Eliana getting space? What about my need for a *lack* of space?

"You're freaking her out." Nicky's voice is definitive, like he knows something.

"Did you talk to her?" I hold my breath while I wait for him to answer.

"No. I tried to text to see if she was okay, but she didn't respond to me, either." Part of me is happy he didn't get an answer, and part of me wants to punch him in the face for trying.

The two of them, my brother and grandmother, prattle on a bit longer about how I'm pushing Eliana further away, and how girls like boys with some semblance of dignity. I ignore the obvious dig about my own lack of dignity and try to hear what they're telling me.

But really, what do Nicky and Yia Yia know about girls? Nicky's never had a girlfriend, and Yia Yia is like a hundred years old. (It's weird to think of Yia Yia as a teenager at all.)

I promise to think about what they're telling me, knowing full well I'm going to ignore every last bit of their advice before any of us ever leave the room. Time for a new plan.

Eliana

"*Y*ou are not to tell me anything. Like, *anything*, that Dmitri says, does, touches, smells—"

"Smells?" Janina interrupts.

"Yes, Janina. I do not want to know what he smells. I want to know not a thing about Dmitri while I am on homebound. That is your job as my best friend. If I catch a whiff—"

"What's up with you and smells, El?"

"Just promise me I can work through what I need to at home without worrying if he is sad or happy or with someone else. You are my only lifeline to Walter Mondale High School. Keep it under lock, okay?"

"You can count on me, sir."

Dmitri

With pizza and letters having failed, I turn to the canon on how to win the love of a reluctant girl (see *Cyrano de Bergerac* and *Say Anything*). I stand outside Ellie's house at ten thirty P.M., singing "Girl on the Ferris Wheel."

Loudly.

Very loudly.

All the lights in Ellie's house are off and stay off. The only lights I do see are the flashing red-and-blue strobes of a police cruiser rounding the corner after my third encore. I'm through the hedges before the cops spot me.

Prickly things stab my neck as I hide in shrubbery and cry myself to sleep. I wake up shivering and cold an hour later and know that it's really and truly over.

Strike three. I'm out.

Eliana

Even with Janina banned from discussing anything Dmitri, I still had to deal with the (super embarrassing, and did I mention mortifying) moment when Dmitri stood outside my window, à la Lloyd Dobler in *Say Anything*, and blasted "Girl on the Ferris Wheel" at me. I peeked through the tiny window in my room-hole, but refused to step out the door. My mom must have called the police, because I watched him zoom off, followed by a police car.

I almost called him. Or texted him after that. It was kind of sweet, in a dumb eighties-movie kind of way. But then he'd know my new number. And then I'd be right back where we started. Can't go back to the carnival.

Dmitri

Reeling from getting dumped by Ellie, and looking for something good to latch onto, I throw a Hail Mary and track Kyle down at a local coffee shop he likes to frequent. He's sitting by himself writing in what I know to be his lyrics notebook. He squirms when he sees me coming, but at least he doesn't get up and leave.

"I'm sorry, Dmitri," he starts before I can say a word. "I tried to talk Chad into giving you another chance, but he won't listen."

Kyle wraps both his hands around a chipped mug of something frothy, like he needs something to hold on to while he's talking to me.

"At the end of the day," Kyle adds, "this band doesn't really exist without Chad."

I think about pleading with Kyle, maybe even suggesting he leave UT and that he and I start a new band, but the words die in my throat before they ever reach my mouth. I know he's right; Chad is more important to UT than I could ever be. And for reasons I've never understood, Chad has wanted me gone from the band for a long time.

This is it. It's over. I am firmly, completely, and forever out of the band. Unexpected Turbulence has been the defining and central core of my life for two years, and it's over.

No band.

No Ellie.

No life.

Hello, rock bottom, my name is Dmitri. Nice to meet you.

Spring

Eliana

"You should really put in a request for a new office next year, Mr. Person. One with a window." Mr. Person shrugs noncommittally. I imagine he has put in that request numerous times in a passive, nice-dude sort of way, which is why he has the dank dungeon office and all of the newer, shinier guidance counselors have the rooms with views. It's a shame because today is one of those late March days, the ones that come out like a lamb. It's fifty-five degrees outside, and here in Minnesota that means much of the population is breaking out the shorts. It will probably snow again next week, but as long as it's here people take full advantage. It's a perfect day for a run.

While Mr. Person clicks and clacks, I shuffle through the mountain of papers required by the school to cover the two months I went on homebound.

"Looks like you did very well while home," Mr. Person tells me as he looks over my exams. "And, might I add, you look very well." I suppose I could be grossed out that my guidance counselor complimented my appearance, but the dude is right. After my meds were tweaked a few times, we found the right concoction for both my depression and anxiety. Instead of staying in my room-hole all day, I did my schoolwork at the puzzle table.

And funny enough, that night at the winter carnival taught me something: I love to run. I have been walking long distances for years, but it never occurred to me to pick up the pace. The cold in my throat, the sticky sweat in my eyes, and the burn in my chest felt amazing. And distracting. So I kept running. Every day I was home, I ran. Sometimes for twenty minutes, if it was insanely cold or snowy and slippery, and sometimes for an hour or two. I convinced Janina to join me on some days, and in turn she convinced some of her beauty-school friends. On occasion we had ten girls running together. My mom even took me out to buy proper running shoes and some good sports bras.

If this keeps up, maybe I'll join cross-country in the fall. Maybe.

"As requested by Sheila Grossman," Mr. Person gives a shout-out to my therapist, "you will have a lighter than usual schedule for the rest of the year until you're back in the swing. Two study halls, an independent study for English, and a free pass on PE. Don't go selling it on the black market." A free pass in PE means I don't have to take gym for the rest of the year. Ironic, in my newer fitness stage. Not like what we do in high school gym class could ever really be equated with fitness, but I wouldn't mind a run in the middle of the day.

Which reminds me of Dmitri and that day where he tripped. If I had been a runner back then, I would have been in a different lane. The PE tumble would never have happened. Would we still have connected? Would it have gotten so complicated? Would I have gone over the edge?

Who can say?

I haven't talked to Dmitri since the Frozen Ferris Wheel. It helped that I changed my phone number. Really, the only people who ever used my phone were my parents, Janina, and Dmitri anyway. It was easy enough to tell Janina and my parents the new number. And that was it. Janina was given the direct order not to tell me anything about Dmitri. I was instructed by Sheila Grossman to delete any and all social media accounts, so I could just focus on myself and getting better and feeling good and returning to normal-ish.

That doesn't mean I'm not nervous about seeing Dmitri now that I'm back at school.

Mr. Person hands me a pass to my next class, history, and declares, "You are released back into the wild." He is trying to be funny. Not a bad attempt.

"You're a peach, Mr. Person," I say, not exactly sure what the phrase means. I hope it's not some sort of sexual innuendo.

I really need to get out of this office.

"Remember what I said about the room with a window, Mr. Person. You deserve it."

Mr. Person nods humbly, with a dash of sarcasm.

And I'm out. Into the wild. The hallways of Walter Mondale High School.

I round the corner and walk right into Dmitri.

Dmitri

I kind of hate spring. Yeah, it's full of hope and promise and blah blah blah, but in Minnesota, it really just means more mud. I am so tired of mud. Plus, everyone's so cheerful that the deep freeze is finally lifting, it's like they've all forgotten how crappy their lives are. Whatever.

Last week I removed all the photos and magazine clippings taped to the inside of my school locker. First were the ones related to Unexpected Turbulence; there was a really good review from a weekly arts paper, a photo of the four of us onstage at the Entry, and a copy of the lyrics to "Girl on the Ferris Wheel." I tore them down and tore them up. The other pictures I pulled off my locker were, of course, of Ellie. There was a picture of the two of us at that Harry Potter restaurant; a strip of four pictures from a photo booth, both of us making silly faces; and a stunningly beautiful photo of Ellie from two years ago. She told me it was the only picture she'd ever liked of herself, which was such an Ellie sort of thing to say.

It wasn't until I took those pictures down from my locker that I finally acknowledged and accepted it was over. Despite what people tell you, closure doesn't feel good.

I'm not sure what I'm projecting to the outside world, but after

Nicky and Yia Yia had their intervention weeks ago to get me not to contact Ellie, they've been watching me closely, likely waiting for me to explode, or fall over, or melt in a puddle of something they can't repair. I love them, but I'm finding it hard to take, like the signal-to-noise ratio in my life is a lot more noise these days.

The second bell is about to ring, and I need to get to my science class. I take one more look at my naked locker interior, heave an involuntary sigh, close the door, and turn to go.

And I walk right into Eliana.

Eliana

D mitri looks ... okay. I remember his hair being messy, but more of a deliberate messy than its current state. He hasn't shaved in at least two days, which in Dmitri terms means almost a beard. He wears his favorite t-shirt, a Titus Andronicus concert shirt from two years ago, but it looks like he's been wearing it for four days straight.

My heart feels concern for him, as a friend who cares, but no more. I don't want to hug him or kiss him or jump into his arms. Which I guess is the normal reaction to seeing a person in the hallway. Should I feel more for him?

Let's start with something easier. "Hi," I say. I smile, a non-toothy-but-with-eye-crinkles smile. A smile that says, "It's nice to see you." Sheila Grossman said it was important for me not to lead him on if I am certain I don't want us to be together. And I am certain. Not because of anything Dmitri did but because I'm not in a place to be in a relationship with anyone other than myself.

That sounds so cheesy.

But if I want to keep moving up and out of my dark days, I need to do it without any baggage weighing me down.

Which makes Dmitri sound like baggage.

Thank god he can't hear the conversation going on in my head. I wish he would say something.

"It's nice to see you," I say. Shit. Is that leading him on? Or was that too generic? I wish I had practiced this with Sheila Grossman.

One of the things Sheila Grossman and I did that I found really helpful was to have complete conversations with each other as though I were talking to other people. For example, I felt really stressed about the fact I had to break up not only with Dmitri but with his entire family. I wasn't only disappointing him, but like seventy more people. I wasn't as concerned with his sixth cousins or whoever, but Nicky and his Yia Yia were pretty great. Sheila Grossman and I had several conversations as though I were talking to Nicky and Yia Yia, and they were very accepting of my decision to end our relationship.

Although, now that I think about it, that's really stupid. Because how does Sheila Grossman know what Yia Yia is thinking? Maybe Yia Yia set up some sort of Greek voodoo doll of me and intends to use it on what would be Dmitri's and my first anniversary. Maybe Nicky was the one who sent that pizza, but instead of a loving gesture it was actually poisoned and I'm supposed to be dead right now.

Or maybe I'm overthinking things.

Say something, Dmitri.

"Are you going to say anything?" I ask, smile fading, eyes growing colder.

Sheila Grossman believes I am too quick to judge and may put people off with my facial expressions. I attempt to relax my face into neutral territory. I don't know if it works. Should I stop refer-encing Sheila Grossman?

"Sorry," Dmitri says, and looks down, scuffing his tennis shoes against the linoleum.

He doesn't say anything else. Is this a "sorry for not talking"? A generalized "sorry for how things ended up"? A sorry because he hates me and feels bad about it? I wish I could read his eyes, but I can't see them under his mop of dangling bangs.

Am I supposed to say "sorry" in return? I've never really done this—a breakup or the aftermath. It was a lot easier to be broken up with a person when I was completely removed from the world in which we were together. Now I have no idea what to do. He's still not talking.

"How's Yia Yia?" I ask. I figure that's a kind question, one that doesn't have anything to do with his band or other girls or our relationship. Plus, I want to know.

It hits some sort of speaking button because Dmitri looks up at me. Those big, dark eyes. So much sadness.

"She's dealing with some health issues," he says.

"What kind of health issues? Is she okay?" I ask with genuine concern.

He flips his hand side-to-side to indicate "so-so."

I want to hear more, to talk about Yia Yia and ask what I can do to help. To see how Nicky is doing and where Dmitri is with his band.

But the bell rings.

"I want to talk more. Really, I do. But it's my first day back, and I have to get to class for a 'healthy start.'" I air quote, using Sheila

Grossman's term. I cringe that I both used therapy lingo out loud and air quoted. But I don't have to time to explain. "Catch you later?" I ask with hope.

He nods nearly imperceptibly.

I run off to my first class and pretend I am a normal sophomore. At first, I'm overwhelmed by the quick and vague run-in with Dmitri. I try not to dwell on the bigness of it: *He was my first boyfriend. We broke up. I haven't seen or talked to him in months.*

He's just a friend you haven't seen in a while. Everything is okay. You are okay, Eliana. I breathe in slowly for six seconds, pause at the bottom of the circle, then breathe out through my nose for the second half of the circle. After three repetitions, I am ready to be present.

I am a student at Walter Mondale Preparatory High School.

I am in class.

I am listening.

I am not a crazy person who can't handle this.

Dmitri

E liana looks good.

Really good.

Her skin seems less pale; her teeth are whiter—or maybe I only notice because she's actually *smiling*; and her hair is clean and bouncy, like a commercial for Pantene or something.

And it isn't just how she looks. It's how she *is*. Ellie isn't awkward or closed or any of the things I remember. Did I imagine them?

No. Something has changed.

My brain does all sorts of mental gymnastics to avoid the truth: *Maybe*, it thinks, *she's on better meds. Or maybe she's seeing a new shrink. Or I'll bet she found a hobby. That has to be it. A hobby.*

But I know better. The thing that's changed is us . . . me. I'm gone, and she's a new person. It was me causing her to be depressed and anxious and everything else. I'm a disease, a cancer. I am blight.

Feelings of guilt over having caused her so much pain and distress flutter around my consciousness, but they don't take root. They're overwhelmed by something else:

It's.

Not.

Fair.

She shouldn't get to feel so good while I feel so bad!

Yeah, I'm not proud of it, but that's exactly what I think.

I don't hear or recall a single thing Eliana says before the bell rings and she practically skips off to her next class. Just like her younger sister skipped the day I was in her bedroom. Maybe the whole Hoffman family is high on skipping. I try to replay the scene of running into Ellie in my mind later, but find only a vague, amorphous image of a glowing, radiant girl swishing her hair in slow motion to the sound of "Moving in Stereo" by the Cars.

Maybe I watch too many movies.

I don't have time to process any of this, because when Ellie moves out of my field of vision, Reggie is standing there, as if having appeared by magic. She looks me up and down—her mouth scrunched up, her eyes narrowed to slits—like she's trying to see inside my head.

"You're coming to my house after school," she says, leaning forward and poking me in the chest.

"What?"

"My house. After school. You. Me."

"Look, Reg, I—"

"'Look, Reg' nothing. You've been avoiding me and everyone else like the plague. Time's up, Digrindakis. You're reentering the world. Today. After school. At my house."

Reggie, I notice, is wearing her Titus Andronicus shirt, too. We went to that concert together, before I'd ever heard of Eliana Hoffman. Is that a coincidence? I shake my head. Of course it's a coincidence. How could Reggie know which dirty shirt I was going to scoop off my bedroom floor this morning?

She reaches forward and takes my hands in hers. "Just say yes, Dmitri."

Her palms and fingers are rough and calloused from gymnastics, but her grip is gentle and warm. Her gaze locks with mine and before I know what I'm doing, I lean in to kiss her.

"What the hell?" Reggie pulls back, her face a mask of shock or amusement or anger. I don't know.

"What? I thought . . ."

"I'm gay, you dumbass!"

Again, the only thing I can manage to say is "What?"

"Just come to my house after school, okay? But maybe leave your libido in your locker, you perv." She rolls her eyes and bumps my shoulder as she walks past me to her next class.

I almost don't go.

I made such an ass of myself in the hall, trying to kiss Reggie, I don't know how I'm ever going to look her in the eyes again. But fear of having to face Reggie is outweighed by fear of pissing Reggie off.

It starts to drizzle by the time I reach her front stoop. It's a cold drizzle that I just know will turn to flurries. The weather, as it so often does in Minnesota, matches my mood. I'm still trying to process the rare Eliana-sighting, my mind tumbling through what feels like an infinite array of scenarios on what it all means, that I don't even notice Reggie opening the front door.

"Snap out of it, Digrindakis," she says to get my attention. She leaves the door open and retreats inside; I follow.

I've been to Reggie's house a million times. We would play here when we were little kids, making up all sorts of adventures: Star Wars, army, Avengers. Her imagination was so vivid, always adding little details to our scene—describing the bad guys' clothes, talking about the frozen landscape, imagining pretend weather anomalies that would jeopardize our pretend mission. I just wanted to get to the part where we saved the universe, but always went along with Reggie's detours, because really, they were what made the game fun.

All that ended around the third grade, when it stopped being okay for boys to hang out with girls. The world is so stupid. Right now I just want to tear apart her couch—the same off-white couch with the same plastic covers—and make a pillow fort. (Her mother always yelled at us when we did that.)

Reggie walks past the living room and turns down the stairs to the basement.

"Where are we going?"

"I have to show you something." She emphasizes the word "something," and I pause.

"I thought you said you were gay?"

I worry for a second Reggie won't hear this as a joke—and it is a joke, a nervous and stupid joke—but she does.

"Ha, ha, Digrindakis. Ha. Ha."

We get to the bottom of the stairs and the basement looks like it always did, just without the mess of toys. When we were little, the floor was covered with so many action figures, Matchbox cars, and little green army men (I guess you could say Reg was a tom-boy), it was hard to walk. Today it's just the taupe-colored carpet. Though there is one noticeable new addition to the room: There, in the corner, is a maroon Gibson SG guitar on a stand, plugged into a Peavey amp.

What the . . . ?

I look at Reggie.

"I've been taking lessons."

"Really?" I can't help but smile. I think it's the first genuine smile to cross my face since looking at those ice sculptures in January.

"Yep."

"Are you any good?"

Reggie picks up the guitar, straps it on her small frame, and flicks the power on the amp. There's a staticky click and hum; god, I love that sound.

Reg takes a deep breath and starts to play.

Right away I recognize the song as "Pulling Teeth" by Green Day. I'm even more surprised when Reggie starts to sing.

"I'm all busted up . . ."

Before I know it, I'm singing with her. The two of us bop and croon off-key until she strums the last chord, letting it ring.

"Holy crap! That's awesome, Reg!" And it is. She's good. She's really good!

"Yeah?"

"Yeah!" I tell her. "You should totally get in a band."

Her eyes bore a hole through my face when I say this. For a split second I'm confused, and then I get it.

"Wait. Really?"

"Yeah, dumbass. Me and you. We're starting a band." It's not a question; it's a statement of fact. That is so Reggie.

And I am so in.

Eliana

I have been back at school now for over two weeks. And I'm still going. One day at a time. One foot in front of the other. All we are is dust in the wind, dude.

Today is Saturday, and I can't wait to head out for a run. I used to have a love/hate relationship with the weekends. I guess I also had a love/hate relationship with school. For a time, weekends meant going out to see Dmitri's band and trying not to have a panic attack at how much I did not fit in. Then weekends became the relief days of the week, where I didn't have to pretend I could handle going to school. School once was a place where I was in my element: sitting quietly, answering questions correctly, reading books and trying not to get caught. Then the whole experience became so fraught with stress. Would I be able to sit through my classes without getting a stomachache? Would I have to give Dmitri a public display of affection when I wasn't in the mood? Would I run into one of my old "friends" who made me feel like more of an outcast than ever?

But now . . . I don't care. Maybe it's the drugs. Maybe it's the endorphins from running. Maybe it's the lighter class schedule and the lack of boyfriend to answer to.

Does it matter?

I tie on my running shoes and adjust my extra-supportive sports bra. It doesn't even faze me that it looks like I have one wide boob. I step out of my room-hole, and there is my sister Samara tying *her* running shoes and putting on *her* sports bra. My sister has actually started running with me. Sometimes when we run, we talk. Shocker.

"You ready?" I ask Sam. She nods, and we scuttle our way down the stairs and out the front door. It's nice out for April: sunny and low sixties. Sam's in shorts, but I prefer a solid pair of full-length leggings so I don't have to start shaving again until really necessary. Actually, I'm considering not shaving at all this year. Because is it ever really necessary? What benefit does it have, except for the razor and shaving-cream industry? Not like anyone will be looking at my legs anyway.

Samara and I jog lightly for five minutes until we reach Janina's house. Janina agreed to run with me, but reluctantly, because as she says, "It's not a sport if you can't win." I told her that it is a sport because we need special shoes and there is sweat involved, but she is ultracompetitive. I let her race me to the stoop at the end of our runs. Maybe in the fall I'll convince her to join cross-country with me. If I actually decide to join.

Janina, Samara, and I run for the next forty-five minutes. Samara taps out to leave for a protest sign–painting party at her best friend Keely's house. I wasn't aware of a protest, but according to Keely's mom, "There is always something somewhere to protest."

Janina and I continue on until we hit a 7 Eleven. "Want a Slurpee?" she asks.

"They always give me stomachaches," I answer.

"Me too," she concurs. "Want one?"

"Sure." I shrug.

We decide to buy small Slurpees because maybe that will prevent the weird stomach/gas situation that inevitably flares up after the frozen, frothy drink. I attempt a side-by-side concoction of half cherry cola and half piña colada, both beverages I do not ever consume in their traditional format but enjoy immensely when spewed forth from a nozzle at 7-Eleven. Janina goes straight-up wild blueberry, which sounds both boring and repulsive to me, but when she pulls a five-dollar bill out of her bra and declares, "I'm paying," I decide to keep my mouth shut about her flavor choice.

We pop a squat on the curb outside, making sure to steer clear of any parking spaces. I have read far too many stories of people failing to brake for one reason or another (Texting! Senile! Forgetting which pedal was the brake!) to trust the small, concrete lump between us and several tons of steel.

"I've been meaning to ask you, and I didn't know when it would finally be copacetic to bring it up," Janina says.

"Wait!" I interrupt. "Head banger!"

"You mean brain freeze?"

"You call it what you want, I'll call it what I want. Is it really necessary to correct me while I'm dying here?"

"I'm sorry you are dying. Along those lines—have you talked with Dmitri yet?"

"How is 'I'm sorry you are dying' along the same lines as talking to Dmitri?" I cough out the cold in my chest.

"I just meant that the relationship is kind of dead. Right? I was looking for a hook. It's been so long since I was even allowed to utter his name, but it's not like we don't share a massive cinder-blocked building with him every weekday."

"It's weird," I say, sipping slowly so as not to reignite the pain in my head. "I sometimes see him in the hallway, and I'll throw him a smile. The look on his face is a cross between joy at the sight of me and disgust. Inevitably he turns and darts in the other direction."

"Makes you feel powerful, doesn't it?" Janina nods knowingly.

"What? I don't want to feel powerful. It makes me feel sad, really. I kind of miss the guy."

"The guy or the smoochies?"

"The smoochies were nice, for sure, but too many other things come along with smoochies. When I think about him in that way, I remember weird things. Like this nose hair that would some-times appear, and I was always too afraid to say anything because I didn't want him to feel self-conscious."

"So you just stared at it for hours hoping to disintegrate it with your mind."

"Exactly. And the deodorant he used. Initially I really liked the smell, but then it made my stomach turn. There was something tangy about it."

"Please don't start telling underwear stories. I feel like that might be where you're headed."

"Ha and no. It's just . . . those are the kind of thoughts I don't want to have again."

"What kind of thoughts *do* you want to have again?"

"Dmitri and I used to do this thing where we'd flip through old yearbooks in the library at school. People looked so dated and embarrassing. We would be laughing so hard we could barely stand up. I miss that. And when he'd play new music for me and look at my face for a reaction. I liked the way he seemed like a little kid in those moments. And I know this is stupid because it got to a point where it set off all kinds of panic attacks, but I sort of miss his texts."

"You're kidding. You used to text me all the time about his texts, and then it would become some bizarre meta-texting bitch session."

"But it would be different if we were just friends, wouldn't it? Like me and you, except with different smells and less jogging."

"I would not mind passing the jogging baton to Dmitri, truth be told."

"I'm keeping you in shape! You love jogging with me!"

"I love drinking Slurpees and doing something that makes you feel good," Janina admits.

"Wow. You really *are* a good friend."

"I don't sweat like this for just anyone."

I lean over to hug Janina. "Have some of my sweat, too."

"Ewwww," she complains, but hugs me back. "I think you should text him."

"Really?" I ask, my face muffled in her sticky shoulder.

"Sure. What could go wrong?"

"You had to say that, didn't you?"

"I did," she laughs.

When I get home, hair damp and clothes ripe, I close myself

into my room-hole. My phone, replete with shiny new phone number, beckons me. I consider showering first, but it's not like Dmitri can smell my texts.

I decide not to overthink it. I'm just an old friend, reaching out and saying hi. Ain't no thang.

> **ME**: Hey, Dmitri. It's Eliana. New number.
> Thought I'd check in and say hello. Hit me
> back if you want.
>
> **[SEND]**

Dmitri

*O*ur new band is called the Frozen Weirdos, because, well, we're kind of weird and we live in Minnesota. And if Minnesota is nothing else, it's frozen.

We tried lots of different names before settling on FW. The list of finalists included Husker Don't (for obvious reasons); Spitter (it was meant to poke fun at Twitter but was too obtuse— Reggie's word, not mine); and Duh (because really, duh). The instant reject list included American Standard (like the name printed on toilets); the Noyarc (crayon spelled backward); and Woofing Cookies (really?).

The day after Reggie and I met in her basement, she introduced me to the rest of our band: First was this half-Persian, half-Greek eleventh grader named Davoud (everyone just calls him Dave) who plays bass. He's way more Persian than Greek, so while he and I don't bond over a shared heritage, we do bond over being something other than Americans of northern European ancestry. Seriously, there has to be more blond hair and blue eyes in the Twin Cities than in Stockholm.

Second was a freshman girl named Missy who plays keyboard and sings. When Reggie introduced us—in the halls between periods three and four at school—I asked Missy if her name was short for something. She stared at me for a minute and then just walked away. I didn't ask again. Missy is all attitude, but she can play, and she can sing, and she's way better to look at than Chad. She has this kind of in-your-face sexuality that scares the crap out of me, but I guess that's the point.

Reggie, Missy, and Dave are familiar with each other in a way that makes me wonder if Reggie had the band members already lined up and was just waiting for me to come around. I decide not to ask about it. Either way, Reggie really is a good friend.

We practice in Reg's basement, which saves money on a rehearsal space, and feels more relaxed. Her mother hates it— "Will you kids please keep that racket down!"—but then Mrs. Reynolds hates everything. Her default facial expression is a snarl. The apple, it seems, didn't fall far from the tree. God, I hope that doesn't mean I'm like my father.

In the three weeks the Weirdos have been playing, our set list has expanded to seven songs (including two written by me). My favorite is a kick-ass, punked-up cover of this old Patsy Cline song called "Walkin' After Midnight." Missy half sings, half screeches it, à la Kate Nash. It kills.

Since I'm the only one in the band with experience gigging, Reggie, Dave, and Missy look at me as a kind of leader, which is pretty funny when you think about it. Unexpected Turbulence is still playing out a lot, and is still getting a ton of attention. I do miss it sometimes, but really, I'm way happier as a Frozen Weirdo.

I like my bandmates, and I like our music. That's all that really matters.

We're on a water break during one of our practices—we jam almost every day—when I see I have a text. I don't recognize the number.

> **ELIANA**: Hey, Dmitri. It's Eliana. New number. Thought I'd check in and say hello. Hit me back if you want.

Wait.

What?

I look again to make sure it's real.

It is.

Then I look again.

Other than awkward and painful encounters in the hall at school—I'm counting down the days to summer break so I won't have to endure those encounters for at least a couple of months— Ellie and I haven't talked in forever. And we definitely haven't texted. Texting was one of her chief complaints against me. Hell, she even changed her phone number to get away from me.

What.

The.

Fuck?

After my stomach is done doing somersaults, I look at the message again. (Full disclosure: My stomach is *not* done doing somersaults and isn't going to be anytime soon.)

Check in?

Say hello?

Hit me back?

If you want?

Okay, yeah, I'm freaking out. I must be hyperventilating or something because Reggie is staring at me.

"You okay, Digrindakis?"

"Uh-huh," I say, "it's nothing." But Reggie keeps staring at me. She knows me too well.

The time stamp on the text is from ten minutes ago. It must've come through while we were playing "Girl on the Ferris Wheel." Does that mean something? It has to mean something. Doesn't it? Am I supposed to answer this? Do I answer now? Later? Tomorrow? Do I even *want* to answer this?

"Let's play another song," Reggie says, still staring at me. I nod and grab my sticks in one hand, still clutching my phone in the other.

I take my seat behind the drums, eager to get into a new groove, when the phone buzzes. At first I think it's another text and every muscle in my body clenches. But the buzzing continues. It's not a text; it's a phone call.

Holy shit! Is Eliana calling me??

I look at the phone and see it's not Ellie; it's Nicky.

Nicky never calls me. *Never.* He texts sometimes, but not that often. He's just not a guy who likes his phone.

Completely freaked out and off-balance, I push the accept icon and hold the phone to my ear.

"Hello?"

There's heavy breathing like Nicky is in some kind of trouble, and all thoughts of Eliana—well, most thoughts of Eliana—go right out of my mind.

"Nick?"

He clears his throat before he speaks. "It's Yia Yia."

Eliana

"Does this look okay?" I straighten the black skirt I borrowed from Samara. It's actually from a production of *Oliver!* where she played a street kid, but it was the only black skirt I could find in our room. She said it would be fine if I snipped open the elastic at the waist to make it fit, and it's undetectable as long as my black t-shirt doesn't ride up. The cardigan, borrowed from my mom, is also black, with scalloped edges and floral buttons. "I feel like I'm going to a job interview," I admit.

My mom adjusts the shoulders on the cardigan and tucks my hair behind my ear. "You look nice. Don't worry. No one is going to be thinking about your clothes."

"That makes it sound like I don't look nice." I slouch.

"No no. I only meant that when you go to a wake, people aren't thinking about those things. They will be happy you are paying your respects."

"But what if they're not happy? What if Dmitri's family yells at me to get out because they think I'm some kind of traitorous skag? What if Dmitri won't even talk to me?"

"You're sure you don't want any of us to come, honey?" Mom asks.

"No. That seems weird. You didn't really know them, and I kind of just want to deliver this card, show my face, and go."

"That's very nice of you, El. Whatever went on between you and Dmitri, I'm sure he will appreciate this."

"I really liked Yia Yia. I feel like she was the only one in his family who really *got* me. Maybe even more than Dmitri."

"Women are pretty insightful. Men . . . not always so much. Don't tell Isaac and Asher I said that," she asides.

"Too late. I'm inscribing it on your tombstone."

"Eliana!" my mom scolds.

"I'm just kidding. Sorry. I'm nervous."

"Well, take these, and offer our condolences as well." Mom hands me a tray of puffy peanut butter cookies with Hershey's Kisses in the center. "Don't worry about getting the tray back."

"I wasn't worried about that." I half smile.

Mom and I load ourselves and the cookies into the car. I click from radio station to radio station, but there is nothing on. I'm too anxious to fumble with the aux cord to my phone. I settle on a benign oldies channel. Cars line the street two blocks out from Dmitri's house. I imagine hundreds of people filling every crevice of every room, weeping loudly and exclaiming sadness in Greek. "Drop me off on the corner, please. And then don't leave?" I request.

"You're sure you don't want me to come in?" Mom asks again.

"I'm sure, but stay close. Park on a side street and be ready to burn rubber to the house if I need a quick escape."

"Do people really still say 'burn rubber'?"

"I just did. You're welcome. And thank you."

Deep breath, cookies grabbed, and I'm out the door and walking down the street toward the Digrindakises' house.

I'm so nervous about ringing the doorbell, scared at who might answer. But the door is already wide open, people walking in and out. A few faces look vaguely familiar from the big Digrindakis Christmas extravaganza, but I was too nervous then to commit their names to memory. They don't seem to notice me anyway. I have to remind myself that no one is focused on my presence here. This day is about Yia Yia, and I want to be here to pay my respects. But where do I put the cookies?

From across the room I see Nicky. He's in a black suit, and I've never seen his hair so combed. A smile of relief melts onto my face, but I rein it in quickly for fear of looking too happy at a wake. Nicky walks toward me, a welcoming smile on his face, and I relax my shoulders, which, I now realize, were practically hitting my earlobes.

"Hey," he says. "It's good to see you." Nicky attempts to lean in for a hug, but the cookie tray blocks him.

"I brought cookies. My mom made them." I present the tray to Nicky and feel like I should curtsy.

"Awesome. Peanut butter? Dmitri loves these." I suppose in the back of my mind I knew that when I told my mom these were the best cookies to make.

"Is he around?" I ask. "Of course he is. Stupid question." I roll my eyes, super self-conscious that I'm here, that I haven't been here in so long, and I have no idea how to act.

"Yeah, he's just upstairs. Want me to get him, or you could just go up there?"

"Is he alone?" I ask, because I don't want to interrupt anything. I ask because it is possible Meg is here consoling him. And that would be okay. I just don't need to walk in on it.

"I think so. He said he wanted some air but knew going outside would mean running into more people," Nicky says.

"Do you think he would mind if I went up there? I don't know if he'd want to see me."

"I don't think he'd ever not want to see you, Ellie."

I hope my cheeks are smart enough not to show how warm they feel at this moment.

I wiggle my way through the crowd of mourners, many of them speaking Greek, most of them holding plates heaped with food. I hope my mom's peanut butter Kisses cookies aren't silly-looking.

Too late to worry about that now. Instead, I worry about knocking on Dmitri's closed bedroom door.

First I listen. I consider putting my ear directly on the door, or finding a glass to hold up like in a wacky sitcom, but both options seem weird. I opt for the straight knock. *Rap rap.*

"Yeah?" Dmitri calls from inside. His voice sounds weak.

"Dmitri? It's me. Eliana."

I hope there's not a secret trapdoor hidden under my feet and that Dmitri isn't about to pull the lever to send me to a watery pit filled with alligators.

Shockingly, there is not, and Dmitri opens the door.

He is also in a suit, black like his brother's but with a light striped pattern. Underneath is a white shirt and purple checkered tie, hanging around his neck. His dark eyes feel darker, the circles exaggerated. When he looks at me, his eyes well up. "Hey, El," he says.

Then he hugs me. A deep, tight, sad hug. I feel his body jerk from crying. I've never seen Dmitri cry. I don't know that we've ever been in a situation together that would have warranted crying from him. Maybe he's not much of a crier, except when necessary. Like now.

"I'm so sorry," I say as I pat his back. He eases his hold on me and quickly turns away to wipe his eyes on a balled-up tissue in his fist. He then uses the same tissue to blow his nose in that honking fashion I've never been able to achieve.

Cleaned up, Dmitri plunks down on his bed and asks, "Want to sit?"

I could take the chair in the corner out from under the desk and sit there, but it feels rude. Distant. I sit next to him on the bed.

"How'd you know about Yia Yia?" he asks. He looks at me so intensely, I remember what I didn't like about that feeling. And what I did.

"My mom read about her in the newspaper obituaries. She reads them every week. Was Yia Yia sick long?"

"She was sick, but it wasn't like she was *dying* sick. It wasn't expected when it happened."

"That's hard," I acknowledge.

"You will like this: She died while watching a Harry Potter marathon on TV."

I chuckle and then gasp, "Am I allowed to like that? Am I allowed to laugh?"

"Of course. Yia Yia loved to laugh. And she loved Harry Potter, too, you know. When you and me broke up she told me it was probably because we were from different houses."

"You're kidding," I say.

Dmitri pauses. "Yeah. I am."

I smack him on the arm. "You're not supposed to joke about Yia Yia! We're supposed to be somber."

"I've had days' worth of somber. I was hoping you came by to cheer me up?"

I worry there's a tinge of innuendo in that hope.

"I didn't know I could still do that for you," I admit. "I came by because I liked your Yia Yia, and I hadn't seen you in a while and I wanted you to know I was thinking about you."

"You were?" More hope.

"Yes. I miss my friend, Dmitri. You know, the idiot who jokes about his recently deceased Yia Yia?"

"Yeah. That guy's a tool."

"Sometimes," I agree. "But sometimes he's pretty cool, too."

"You look good," he says.

"Thanks," I say.

For the next hour and a half we sit on his bed and talk. About Yia Yia. About his new band. About running. Eventually I text my mom and tell her she can drive home. She answers back that she left right after she dropped me off.

Dmitri

As Greek Orthodox people go—or maybe I should say as Greek Orthodoxy goes—Yia Yia was kind of a rebel, the original punk rock grandmother.

"I no want wake. Burn body to ash, simple church service, you have party at house." My mom told this to me, Nicky, and Dad the night Yia Yia died, as we sat around the kitchen table and told stories about the woman we all loved so much.

With an almost spooky kind of prescience, Yia Yia had given detailed instructions on how to treat her passing only a week ago, in private, to my mother. When my mom asked Yia Yia why she was talking about it, Yia Yia didn't answer; she just smiled that *Mona Lisa* smile of hers. Mom didn't think anything about it, so hadn't mentioned it to the rest of us until it was too late.

"Όχι," my father said. "No. It not right. Body moost be buried. Body moost be anointed."

My father was right; Greek Orthodox tradition was pretty clear on this point. When you die, you have a wake in a funeral home, your body is anointed by the priest while your family watches, you're buried in the ground, and then everyone has lunch. Cremation wasn't even legal in Greece until a couple of years ago.

But the way my mother told it, Yia Yia had fallen in love with the idea of having her body cremated and the ashes spread in the vegetable garden she cultivated in our backyard. She wanted her remains to mix with the soil, the carbon nurturing the tomatoes, carrots, bell peppers, and cucumbers she grew. Even without Yia Yia's ashes, those cucumbers were the largest anyone had ever seen. I could only imagine what they would be like when infused with Yia Yia's essence.

The thought of that garden, and how it would wither and die without my grandmother to love it—the way she loved all of us—made me well up. It made me wonder how we would survive. The hole left in the world by Yia Yia was a palpable thing. Especially at that kitchen table.

"See?" my father blustered at seeing me start to cry. "This make Dmitri sad! We moost honor tradition." He practically harrumphed. If he'd been wearing suspenders, which he sometimes does, he'd have hooked his thumbs through them in triumph.

"No, Dad," I answered, composing myself. "Just the opposite. That Yia Yia marched to the beat of her own drum is why I—it's why we all—love her"—I choked up and corrected myself—"*loved* her so much."

"But no wake? People come here with food? It so, so ... Jewish."

I rolled my eyes. Nicky patted Dad on the arm and offered, "It's fine, Dad. It's what Yia Yia wanted and her wishes should supersede tradition." Sometimes I think my brother is the Buddha.

The church service, two days later, was surreal.

I've gone to Sunday school and church every weekend as long as I've been alive. Rain, shine, healthy, sick, the Digrindakis family is like the postal service; we always make our rounds. I've stood, knelt, prayed, accepted communion, and studied (the Greek Orthodox interpretation of) the Bible with diligence, and here's the thing: None of it has ever felt right to me.

I believe in God, or at least I think I do, but not *their* version of God. When I pray, my prayers are full of hope and promise. When the church has me pray, it's full of fear and intimidation. Case in point, a few small snippets from the Greek Orthodox funeral service:

> *O God, you who of old created me out of nothing in*
> *your divine image, and returned me back to dust, from*
> *which I had been made, for my disobedience; to your*
> *own likeness again restore, and the ancient beauty,*
> *I pray return to me.*

And . . .

> *I am an icon of your ineffable glory, even though the*
> *marks of sin are on me; take pity, Lord, on your own*
> *creation, and cleanse me in your compassion . . .*

And . . .

> *For you are the resurrection, the life and the repose of*
> *your servant* (Name) *who has fallen asleep . . .*

I've heard the term "fat-shaming," about how skinny people make heavy people feel bad about their bodies. This is a kind of *life*-shaming. Like the dead are making the living feel bad for all the fun we're having. I call bullshit.

And yes, in the little funeral service booklet they hand out so you can follow along, as if it were a program handed out to theatergoers at a play, it does actually say "your servant *(Name)*" throughout, like a form you have to fill out at the department of motor vehicles.

By the time we get back to our house and the "party" Yia Yia had wanted, I'm too lost in my own head for company. I kiss my aunts, uncles, and cousins, say a weak hello to Meg and Alex, and slink off to my room alone. I put Roxy Music's *Avalon* on the turntable and keep the volume low so no one will hear. I love the dreamy, romantic feel of this record. The sounds of the assembled family downstairs—Greeks are loud, like the Who loud—mixes with the music, making a rolling wave of white noise. I'm just starting to drift off when there's a knock on the door. Before I can even think about who it might be, a familiar voice says, "Dmitri? It's me. Eliana."

I didn't expect Ellie to come today, but at the same time, I'm not surprised she's here. And I'm glad. I open the door, and the next thing I know, I'm crying in her arms. It's the only time I've really cried since that first night after Yia Yia died; it doesn't last long.

Ellie and I talk about Yia Yia for a bit before our conversation drifts to everything else that's been going on in our lives. El and I sat in this very spot so many times and made out that I'm afraid reflex will take over and make me try to lean in, but I don't. It's not that I don't want to kiss Eliana *ever* again, I just don't want to right now.

We wind up talking and listening to music for hours, only getting interrupted by relatives a few times. It's nice.

When the party starts to break up and it's time for Ellie to leave, she and I hug again, and make a promise to stay in touch and see each other soon; to be friends. But even as the words are spoken, I recognize them as the empty kind of promise people make when things are ending. It's a load of bull crap people invent to protect each other from future hurt.

But who knows, maybe this will be different.

Maybe.

When I wake up the next morning, I throw on my dirtiest pair of jeans and rattiest t-shirt, and go out back to till the soil in Yia Yia's garden. I let the sun bake the back of my neck as the dirt gets lodged under my fingernails. The only other time I feel this good is playing the drums. I stay in the garden for hours.

Summer

Eliana

I can't stop staring at Mr. Person's legs. It's not often one gets a view of the pasty white stems of a guidance counselor. I must look away. I can't look away. So much hair.

Mr. Person looks up from his computer, where he has been clicking to finalize my files for the year. My eyes dart from his legs to a snow globe above his desk. Funny to think that the ground was covered with the stuff just a few months ago. Now it's eighty degrees outside, and I'm planning on attempting a seven-mile run when the final school bell rings.

"A few hiccups, but it looks like you've had a pretty good year," Mr. Person declares.

"A few hiccups?" I ask.

"Doesn't matter how many hiccups you had as long as someone shouts 'Boo!' and scares them out of you, right?"

"That's kind of a terrible analogy, Mr. Person."

"Give me a break. The bell is going to ring in a minute. Pretend like I said something meaningful."

"No, you did, Mr. Person. I appreciate your help. Or at least the solace of your cave-like office."

"Get excited for my window next year. You'll hardly recognize me."

"Yes. You in natural lighting may scare me off."

"Then I should have moved to a room with a window months ago."

"Ha ha, Mr. Person."

The bell rings, and the voice of the principal vibrates over the PA. "School's out for summer! Be safe out there!" Alice Cooper's "School's Out" blares metallically over the speakers, unpleasant enough that anyone with solid hearing will want to leave the building in a hasty fashion. A clever way to clear out the school so the custodians can start their massive end-of-the-year cleanup.

"That's my cue," I shout over the music. Mr. Person grabs a set of headphones and, unplugged, slings them over his head to block out the sound.

"See you at the end of the summer for cross-country practice!" he yells.

"Probably!" I yell back.

The administration seems to have forgotten that they work in a high school filled with teenagers who listen to music louder than this plugged directly into their ears on a regular basis, so when I head to my locker to clear out the remnants of the last year, the halls are still filled with students oblivious to the soundtrack of seventies youth.

Most of the crap in my locker is just that, crap, but there are a few things worth saving. I find a note from Dmitri:

Can't wait to hang out after school

It's not dated, but I know it's from early in the school year. A freakin' lifetime ago.

There's a stack of hall passes from Mr. Person after he became tired of me coming to his office so frequently, needing space from whatever class I was in. I should bequeath these to my brothers and sisters if I have any left after I graduate.

And I discover the culprit of the foul stench emanating from my locker for the past several weeks: a shriveled-up apple core underneath a pair of gym shorts. A lethal combo.

My phone buzzes with a text from Janina.

JANINA: You still at school? Want to meet at the 7?

Ever since Janina and I ran to the Slurpees, she has been semi-addicted. My stomach can't handle it, but I keep her company and dine on Red Vines instead.

ELIANA: Want to run first? Seven miles to the 7-Eleven?

The mountain of recyclables piles up on the hallway floor. Students kick their way through the deluge, without care that someone has to clean it up if they don't. That always bothers me, and I complain loudly, "Where do you think this stuff goes if you don't put it in the recycling bin? Heathens!" I grab a handful of papers and stuff them down into the nearest green container, a lone activist on a mission to give the custodians and the earth a break.

My phone buzzes again, a presumed RSVP for the run from Janina. However, the text is not from Janina but from Dmitri.

DMITRI: You're coming to the show tomorrow, right?

ME: What do you think?

DMITRI: I think you better be there or I'm playing a special sequel I wrote called "The Girl Who Dumped Me on the Ferris Wheel."

ME: I kind of want to hear that song.

DMITRI: You. Are. Coming.

ME: You. Are. Correct.

DMITRI: Good. And I'll see you in the morning at your house.

Dmitri is helping me clean up the basement. Together we have already cataloged 112 of my dad's movies in order to sell them online. My mom suggested that if Dad could make some money and clear some space from the movies, he could go back to school for the degree he has always wanted: high school teaching. I'm really hoping he doesn't finish the degree before I finish high school, but I'm also pretty excited. Dad will finally get out of the basement, and I may finally have a bedroom to share with Samara that's the not the size—and shape—of a closet. And Mom will once again have a partner in parenting instead of a basement-dwelling, film-obsessed weirdo. Or at least she can have a film-obsessed weirdo who actually brings money into the house.

And it gives me lots of extra time with Dmitri.

Sometimes Dimmi and I take breaks from the cataloging to watch an old movie. Most recently we stumbled upon *Rabid Grannies*, a foreign, dubbed horror movie about, well, a group of old people who kind of eat each other. We laughed through the entire film.

We do that a lot together now, laugh. It's pretty great. Mostly pressure-free. But when there is pressure, it's the good kind. Because even though it's in my gut, it's not that icky, barfy feeling. It's the pleasant twitter of butterflies, flitting around with anticipation. Because I don't know what is going to happen next. And for once in my life, finally, I like how that feels.

Dmitri

*B*AM!
    THWAP!
BAM!
THWAP!

The first song at the first-ever gig of the Frozen Weirdos—the day after the last day of school—starts with a Queen-like "We Will Rock You" beat. It leads us into Reg's screeching guitar, a superfast groove with thumping bass, and riffing (almost rapping) vocals. The lyrics are mine.

> *Roots deep*
> *A towering, flowering leap*
> *Watching me scramble up the heap*
> *Of this twisted, knotty day*
> *Soil thick*
> *The air and my hair slick*
> *Feeling like a sunburned hick*
> *Thanking you for showing me the way*

I wrote those words working in Yia Yia's garden the day after her funeral. I spent hours there. I didn't really know anything about gardening, so I just went on intuition. I pulled weeds, pruned plants that looked unruly, harvested vegetables that seemed ripe for picking, and sometimes just sat and breathed in the air. It sounds corny, but I had the feeling Yia Yia was with me, guiding my hands.

At one point my father came out and stood over me, watching. I looked up at him, using the back of my hand to wipe the sweat from my forehead, and waited for him to say something like "This not for you; this woman work." But he was silent. He turned on his heel and went back in the house. He came out twenty minutes later in a t-shirt, tan shorts, black socks, and work boots, and got down next to me. We didn't talk, we just pulled weeds together. It was, and I think will always be, one of the happiest moments of my life.

I was surprised when Ellie texted me that same night asking how I was doing. I figured she was being polite—Ellie is big on manners, the kind of girl who can actually stand on ceremony—so I responded, politely, that I was *doing fine,* and *thanks for asking.*

Then she texted me the next day. And the day after. And three times the day after that. *Good God,* I thought, *is this what I did to her?* But I knew my barrage of communication had been so much worse. Not that this was bad. Just the opposite; it was welcome.

At the height of our relationship, Ellie and I texted a lot, talking about everything and nothing—movies, music, school. That's when we were at our best. It started to go south when our conversations droned on and on—pretty much entirely my fault—about the state of us.

Now that we've reestablished our texting rhythm, Eliana

invited me over to help sort through her father's movies so he could list them for sale online. I didn't know what to make of the invitation, or if I should even go. I asked Reg.

"Of course you shouldn't go. But you're going to anyway, so why are you asking me? Dumbass."

I love Reggie.

Any hesitation I had evaporated the moment Ellie led me to her basement. I had seen Mr. Hoffman's DVD/VHS collection before, or thought I had. There were three bookcases on one wall with DVDs and cassettes shelved spine out. I figured that was it. Eliana had hauled the *rest* of his stuff—seventeen boxes (seventeen!)—out of storage, and stacked them in the middle of the floor.

"I think your father might need an intervention," was all I could I think to say.

"Duh."

We got to work.

There were some real gems in the collection, and some truly weird stuff, too. I was worried one film, *Bikini Bloodbath Carwash*, was actually porn. I showed it to Ellie, and she freaked me out by shoving it in the DVD player. Turns out it was just a dumb horror-slasher flick with a lot of sudsed-up college girls. We laughed a lot at that one and many of the others. We laughed so much—enjoyed each other's company so much—that progress cataloging the DVDs was slow.

We didn't kiss, we didn't hold hands, but we did sit with our shoulders and knees touching. I tried to pretend I didn't notice. I think Ellie did the same thing.

I scan the crowd for Eliana now, my gaze moving over so many familiar faces. Nicky is here, and, somehow, he's managed to drag my parents. My mother is swaying to the beat; my father looks like Frankenstein, stiff and unmoving. I'm surprised he doesn't hold his arms straight out. But he's here.

Kyle and Drew from Unexpected Turbulence turned up, and I can tell by the look on Kyle's face he approves of the Weirdos. For some reason that matters to me. Chad isn't with them, not that I would expect him to be.

I spot Janina towering up from the back of the crowd, with Ellie's sister Sam at her side. I don't see Eliana at first, but then some dancing people shift and she comes into view. Her hair catches the light and kind of glows. She's wearing a white t-shirt, black skirt, and black sneakers. Simple, understated, and so freaking beautiful.

She catches me gawking at her and waves, her mouth betraying her normal stoic demeanor and turning into a pretty wide grin. Both pretty, and pretty wide.

I smile back and strike the crash cymbal, ending "Towering Flower," my song about Yia Yia. I twirl my sticks in the air, kick the bass drum in a steady beat, starting another song.

I've never been more ready for the music and whatever else— for everything else—that comes next.

ACKNOWLEDGMENTS

Julie

This book was so much fun to write. Writing novels can be very solitary, and I am grateful for the camaraderie, communication, and connection this book brought to my life. Len, thank you for being a great partner. You listened, you shared, and damn if we didn't work well together.

Thank you to my book family at Feiwel and Friends: Jean Feiwel, Liz Szabla, Anna Roberto, and Rich Deas, and my amazing agent, Rosemary Stimola, for bringing me this collaborative opportunity. You knew it was what I needed to keep writing, and I am so thankful for the experience.

Thank you to my family and friends for listening to me talk about this book for several years because being a parent, librarian, and writer are not the easiest concoction for writing a book.

Thank you to the teachers, grocery store clerks, delivery drivers, postal workers, restaurant workers, and all the other people who keep this world running. Thank you, thank you, thank you.

Len

While publishing is a collaborative effort, writing is not. You lock yourself in a room (or sit anonymously in a coffee shop) and put pixel to screen. (Sorry, luddites … I haven't put pen to paper in years.) So, what is the writing process like when you *coauthor* a book?

Good question. And it's where these acknowledgments must begin.

Julie Halpern and I have never met in person. Let me say that again. Julie Halpern, the person with whom I cowrote the book you've just finished and (I hope) have enjoyed, and I have never met. Julie's editor at Feiwel and Friends thought we would make an interesting writing duo. So they introduced us, sat back, and let the magic happen.

And magic it was.

I offer my *enormous* thanks to Julie for being such a wonderful writing partner. As our characters blossomed so too did our writing relationship. And while the journey was filled with roller coasters, "bumpy" cars, and the occasional Tilt-a-Whirl, it really was most like a Ferris wheel, the two of us getting to know each other and seeing more of the landscape with each trip around. Thank you, Julie!

I met Liz Szabla—the aforementioned editor who thought it would be a good idea to put me and Julie together—thirty years ago, and I have admired her from day one. A huge thanks to Liz and her editing partner-in-crime, Anna Roberto. Together, they made this a better book. Thanks also to copy editor Nancee Adams, proofreader Valerie Shea, production editor Lelia Mander, art director Mallory Grigg, and everyone else at Feiwel and Friends, including and especially Jean Feiwel. And thanks, as always, to my agent, Sandra Bond.

Thank you to Ellie Digrindakis Koulos and her mom, Athena Digrindakis, for not only helping me get the Greek translations correct, but having such a perfect name for me to borrow for Dmitri. Ευχαριστώ!!

As always, the biggest thanks go to Kristen, Charlie, and Luke for allowing me the time and space to live out my dream of being a writer. I love you more than words can ever express.